PRAISE FOR *THE DEAD MAN*

The Dead Man is a wonderfully affecting, memorable, and original tale. Nora Gold is a natural storyteller, and her ability to make us understand the shimmering and complex landscape of love has its haunting echoes in the Israeli landscape. This is an ingeniously and gorgeously crafted story, radiantly musical in its rich textures.

—JAY NEUGEBOREN, author of *Imagining Robert, Max Baer and the Star of David,* etc.

The Dead Man is terrific. Eve, a composer obsessed with a former lover, pulls us deep into her evolution, thanks to astute, compassionate novelist Nora Gold. This compelling story is a must-read for anyone fascinated by the complexity of male-female relationships and the mysterious radioactivity of love.

—SUSAN WEIDMAN SCHNEIDER, Editor-in-Chief, *Lilith Magazine*

Nora Gold's *The Dead Man* is a powerful story about a woman's struggle with love and loss, and how her art—her music—becomes both the expression of, and antidote to, the darkness she has felt. This is a wonderful story about resilience, about the ability of the human spirit not only to repair and redeem itself, but—even more—to triumph over darkness and adversity.

—JOSEPH KERTES, author of *Gratitude* and *The Afterlife of Stars*

Nora Gold writes with consummate skill. She's the real thing.
—GEORGE JONAS, author, poet, journalist

Nora Gold's writing is beautiful, nuanced, and honest. *The Dead Man* is an intelligent novel about love and art, and the passions that fuel them. Set against the backdrop of contemporary Israel, *The Dead Man* portrays a talented, obsessed composer, and offers a rare glimpse into the fascinating world of sacred Jewish music.

—AYELET TSABARI, author of *The Best Place on Earth*

Nora Gold has an eye and ear for colourful detail in this novel about the creative process, lifting the veil on unknown corners of the world of Jewish music.

—CHARLES HELLER, author of *What To Listen For in Jewish Music*

THE
DEAD
MAN

Canada Council for the Arts **Conseil des Arts du Canada**

We gratefully acknowledge the support of the Canada Council for the Arts and the Ontario Arts Council for our publishing program. We also acknowledge the financial support of the Government of Canada through the Canada Book Fund.

Cover design and illustration: Val Fullard

The Dead Man is a work of fiction. All the characters and situations portrayed in this book are fictitious and any resemblance to persons living or dead is purely coincidental.

Library and Archives Canada Cataloguing in Publication

Gold, Nora, author
    The dead man : a novel / by Nora Gold.

(Inanna poetry and fiction series)
Issued in print and electronic formats.
ISBN 978-1-77133-261-3 (paperback). -- ISBN 978-1-77133-262-0 (epub). -- ISBN 978-1-77133-264-4 (pdf)

    I. Title. II. Series: Inanna poetry and fiction series

PS8563 O524 D42 2016   C813'.54   C2016-900298-5
                                                 C2016-900299-3

MIX
Paper from
responsible sources
FSC www.fsc.org **FSC® C004071**

THE
DEAD
MAN

a NOVEL

NORA GOLD

inanna poetry & fiction series

INANNA PUBLICATIONS AND EDUCATION INC.
TORONTO, CANADA

TABLE OF CONTENTS

PART I
EXPOSITION

1. OVERTURE

SHE'S NEVER BEEN OBSESSED BEFORE. This is her first time and it's kind of interesting. It's like watching some psychopath in a movie, stalking someone, plotting to kill them, except that the psychopath is her. In Canada it's not so bad — she can't call Jake from Toronto because he'd see the area code and guess it was her. So it's only in his country, in Israel (where she'll be in ninety minutes) that it happens. There she won't be able to walk by a pay phone without having to wrestle down the desire to do again what she has already done numerous times: Dial his number and then keep silent on the end of the line — an ominous, threatening silence. And then hear the anger mount in his voice as he says, "Hello? Hello? *Hello?*" And then, when he gets no answer, he'll slam down the phone with a bang so loud that it hurts her ear. When Jake's wife answers the phone, though, it's not anger; it's fear. Instead of her voice getting stronger and more violent like Jake's, Fran's gets smaller and thinner ("Hello? Hello? Hello?") till at the end there's almost nothing left of it. It's a high and squeaky-scared voice, like a mouse or a little girl. On one of the last times, though, instead of going squeaky-scared on her third hello, Fran gathered all her remaining strength and called out "Jake!" in a loud, frightened voice — calling him, Eve knew, from the phone on the kitchen counter to Jake's study upstairs. Then Eve hung up fast before Jake could come on the line, and stood in front of the orange pay phone on a Tel Aviv street corner, her knees trembling and her hands sweaty.

Eve looks out of the airplane window. It didn't start out like this — as a form of stalking, or harassment, or whatever this would be considered under Canadian law. It started out just as a phone call because she missed him. She loved him and wanted to hear his voice again. But he told her not to call or write him anymore. He said this had to end once and for all — this relationship of theirs, their love, was destroying his marriage. So Eve wasn't allowed to call him after that. But she needed him still. She needed to hear his voice just one more time. His beautiful, deep voice. Even anonymously, if that was the only way. So she started phoning him and hanging up, each time thinking this time would be the last.

Eve looks out the window at the clouds below. In the beginning dusk, they look like furry, pale grey animals. The backs and sides of hippos, or rhinos. Flying animals floating in the sky. Sleeping in the sky. Jake never sleeps in in the mornings. The first time she called and then hung up on him, it was only six o'clock in Israel, but he was already wide awake. He always woke up before six, and his wife never did before seven, so as Eve had predicted, Jake picked up the phone. He answered the way he always did, with a musical wave in his voice, "Hel-lo-o," with the middle note higher than the others: C, G, E, Eve registered automatically. At that point, Jake's voice still sounded quite normal, if a little surprised at a six a.m. call. But after his first hello, when Eve didn't say anything back, it quickly got more insistent: "Hello? **Hello?**" and then turned frustrated-enraged, "Who *is* this?" and Eve hung up swiftly in fear. He was yelling at her. One and a half years after sending her away, after surgically removing her from his life, here he was, yelling at her. But a couple of hours later Eve, though blushing at the memory of this phone call, was also grinning broadly. There was a funny side to it. And it was validating, too. It reminded her of something that deep-down she knew but kept on choosing to forget: that Jake was not the gentle, sensitive man he'd become in her fantasies (or anyway not only this); he was also someone with profound anger and a very short fuse. Laughing, Eve felt powerful. She had played a trick on Jake, but there was no way for him to know it was her, so he couldn't retaliate. However powerless she had felt over the previous year and a half (powerless to regain his love, or even to make herself visible to him), she realized now that she wasn't actually all that powerless. She could call him. She could torment him. So over the next three years, Eve phoned Jake's house five or six times on each of her visits to Israel (which, between seminars, board meetings, and holidays, turned out to be seven different trips). Seven trips at five or six calls each trip — she quickly does the math — that's altogether thirty-five or forty calls. This may sound like a lot, but really it's not all that much. Anyway, she had no alternative. She had to keep calling back because she kept missing Jake and getting Fran instead.

The first time this happened, Eve was taken aback by how nice she sounded. Jake's wife had a sweet voice. She was a therapist, Jake had told her once. Not a music therapist, like Eve, or any other real type of therapist — Fran hadn't studied any mental health profession in university; she just did some sort of New Age bodywork. But still, on the phone, Eve could hear some of that in her voice: the therapeutic tone, the desire to proffer help. In this first "conversation" with Fran (which came after Eve had already called and hung up on Jake several times), she could tell that he and Fran had discussed these calls, because Fran reacted now without surprise. She seemed to have decided that the silence on the other end of the line wasn't coming from anybody dangerous. Just a shy first-time client (or maybe a troubled old one) who had dialled her number but then couldn't screw up the courage to ask for an appointment.

"Hello?" said Fran in a normal voice on that first phone call. Then, after Eve said nothing, Fran said "Hello?" again, but this time encouragingly, with a sort of professional kindness. When Eve still didn't answer, Fran asked in a warm, empathic way, "Is there something I can do for you?"

Yes, thought Eve: You can let me be friends with your husband. (Friends — just friends. I would settle now even just for that.) And Fran sounded so nice that Eve, always drawn to, and eager for, kindness and human warmth (and in this case to the therapist-empathy that dripped like milk and honey from Fran's voice), nearly said this out loud. But then she remembered that as sweet as Fran sounded on the phone, she was the one who had told Jake that he and Eve couldn't stay friends. Friends — just regular friends — that's all Eve was asking for by then. But even this regular non-physical friendship with Jake meant the world to her. She would never have allowed herself to become intimately involved with him if he hadn't promised her, repeatedly and unequivocally, that for sure — a hundred percent for sure — they would remain friends afterwards, no matter what happened. Staying friends meant to her that she hadn't been cheap. That *it* hadn't been cheap. That apart from the sex, there had been a real relationship between them. Which there had.

But Fran would not agree. She would not allow Eve and Jake to be even the most casual, innocuous of friends. They couldn't even meet in a public place for a coffee (in Aroma or Caffit), surrounded by dozens of other people (mostly English-speakers like them, and at least a few of whom knew either Jake or Eve) once or twice a year when she came to Israel. So now Eve didn't let herself fall for the sweetness in Fran's voice. Fran was her sworn, life-long enemy. Eve wouldn't say a word to her, not a single word. She just hung up the phone that day. After that, in the subsequent calls, Fran started sounding afraid.

Then about a year ago, making these phone calls stopped being fun. They even started becoming onerous: a chore, a responsibility, something Eve had to cross off her list of things to do while in Israel. She had no choice but to call Jake at home because he worked primarily at home and was rarely at the institute he'd founded. And she had to call the family phone number because Jake didn't believe in cellphones. And she had to call from a street pay phone, otherwise he or Fran could trace the call to her cellphone or hotel. And it had to be early in the morning before Fran woke up so that she'd get Jake on the phone, not his wife. And it began feeling like a huge pain, having to wake up early on a holiday in order to rush to the nearest pay phone a block and a half away before seven a.m.

But even more than all that, it started to get creepy. Creepy hearing Jake's rage and Fran's fear. Instead of feeling powerful and in control, Eve began feeling powerless and out of control. She wasn't doing this anymore out of her own free will; it had turned into an obsession. A compulsion. An obsessive-compulsive disorder. By this time a year ago, the third week in December, she couldn't walk past any pay phone in Israel without wanting — without needing — to stop and call Jake. This offended her self-respect. What was she? A slave to this thing? Plus, one day she told an Israeli friend she had known for many years about these phone calls — told her about them, laughing, like it was a joke she was playing on Jake, just something slightly bizarre. But instead of laughing along with her, her friend blanched and looked at her strangely. Eve realized then that what she was doing was crazy, truly crazy, and maybe she, too, was crazy, tottering somewhere very close to the edge. So she forced herself to stop making these calls.

Still, even though a year has passed since she last phoned Jake (and it's five and a half years since she and Jake parted ways), Eve knows that when she lands in Israel one and a quarter hours from now, and passes her first pay phone in the airport, it will take an enormous effort on her part to just keep on walking. To not stop in front of the pay phone, slide in her phone card, and dial Jake's number, to hear his voice one more time. She turns now toward her window. Outside, darkness is gathering at the edges of the sky and sea. I can do this, she thinks. I'll just do what I did the last time I was here. After they land, after she has collected her bags from the carousel and is heading for the exit, as she approaches the first set of pay phones in the airport, she'll tell herself to keep on going, keep on marching. And, at the same time, she'll reach deep into the concealed pocket inside her purse and touch the Israeli phone card she always keeps there, the one with the picture of a tiger on it — this "transitional object" of hers, as she knows it's called in psychology. She'll touch it and she'll stroke it over and over again, the way she once stroked Jake, and the way she used to stroke her favourite doll when she was little and afraid. Her tiger card, smooth and sleek between her fingers, will comfort her and give her strength.

*

Eve's eyes are shut, and she is lying with her seat pushed back as far as it goes and a blanket over her head. At the beginning of this flight the blanket stank of some industrial cleaning chemical and felt coarse and scratchy against her face. But now she doesn't notice. She's listening to the "Largo al Factotum" from *The Barber of Seville*. She doesn't just hear this music; she feels it in her body. Its notes dance like tiny leprechauns on the skin of her arms and up and down the length of her muscles. She can sing this music, dance it, and play it on several instruments. As far back as she can remember, her father walked around the house singing opera, and this aria was one of his favourites. He sang it in the shower, of course, but not only in the shower. Also while making her breakfast. And dressing. Knotting his red bowtie in front of the mirror. Running the comb back through his increasingly thinning hair while he admired his reflection. And then, feeling satisfied with his appearance — and more than that: proud as a peacock — he'd sing to the mirror, "Figaro Figaro Fiiigaro!" with the same joyful, shamelessly bragging self-worship as Figaro himself. Now, listening to this music, she is once again three years old, hearing her father's voice singing "Fffiiiiiiigaro!" Or else, she's three years old and cuddled up with him on his lap, listening to music together as they did every Saturday afternoon, just the two of them, before Daddy got married again, to Julia. First Eve and Daddy would hear an opera on the radio broadcast "Live From the Met." Then they listened to records: mainly Schubert, Mozart, and Brahms. Now, listening to *The Barber of Seville*, she is back in that world.

"Crapper omlep?" someone says right in her ear.

"What?" Confused, groggy, she drags the blanket from her face, causing her earpiece to fall out, putting an end to Rossini. A flight attendant, perky in a navy blue uniform and bright crimson lipstick, is leaning toward her with a smile. "Crepe or omelette?"

Crepe or omelette. "Omelette." But she's sorry as soon as she unwraps the tin foil and is hit by the rotten, institutional smell. She tentatively tries the yogurt — it's sour. The roll, even after she has slathered it with butter and strawberry jam, is so stale when she bites into it that it's inedible. She pushes away her tray.

The pudgy man on her right, however, is digging in with gusto. She watches him for a couple of seconds in amazement: *How can he eat that shit?* The man turns and smiles at her. Eight hours ago they chatted for a few minutes before they both went to sleep. He's part of a church group visiting Israel for the first time, which she found interesting until he began talking about the importance of settling every inch of the Holy Land before The Day of Reckoning comes. Now she gives him a vague half-smile, turns away, and again gazes out the window. It's darkening quickly. The sea, the sky, and all the clouds in between are melding together into one big indigo-charcoal-coloured mass. If my clients knew how fucked-up I am, she thinks, they'd never come to me for music therapy.

They think I'm so sane and "healthy." When for the past five years, I've been more fucked-up than all of them rolled together.

It's not just the pay phone business, she knows. It's the thousands of letters, maybe the tens of thousands, that she has written to Jake since they broke up. For the first few months, she wrote them down on paper or on the computer. Then after a while it felt like too much work — there were too many words, too many pages — so she just spoke them aloud to him in her head. She was already in the habit of sharing everything with Jake. They'd emailed each other at least four times a day every day of their five-month relationship because he was in Israel and she in Canada (other than the seventeen days she spent in Jerusalem). These letters became the emotional focal point of her life, so that even after they broke up, she kept on composing letters to him. Letters full of rage and raging desire, as well as all the other things she felt and thought that she used to discuss with Jake, but now had no one to discuss with. For instance, music. She would be sitting in a concert composing a letter to him, telling him that she found the flautist too "technical" and cold, yet the violinist accompanying her was too romantic and emotional. What do you think? she would ask Jake in the concert hall.

She also shared with him all sorts of little incidents that occurred in her day-to-day life. The people around her were sometimes strange or hurtful, and imagining Jake's response helped her put into perspective the things they'd said or done. He had an ironic, wry way of seeing things, and he'd look down from above on human folly and stupidity with a sardonic twist of his thin lips. That twist she loved. Those lips she loved. She had never before been with a man with the same sense of humour as her (not even Brian), and it was both a relief and a joy. It was a joy, too, being on the top of Mount Olympus with Jake, standing there side by side with the great man, looking down with him on everyone and everything in the little world below. Jacob Gladstone was a world-renowned music critic, music theorist, and ethno-musicologist who was universally acknowledged as the greatest living authority on Jewish music. He was also credited with the recent renaissance in Jewish sacred music because of the Jewish Institute of Sacred Music (JISM!) that he'd founded fifteen years before. Eve, listening to him talk about his work, felt that through him she had entered the inner circle of the international Jewish music scene. This was confirmed for her when Jake told her what he thought of the latest CD by Nathan Singelman. (*The* Nathan Singelman: the founder and editor-in-chief of *Niggun*, the pre-eminent journal of Jewish music.)

"It's second-rate," Jake confided to her on what turned out to be the last of their phone calls. (They spoke on the phone only infrequently because of the risk of Fran overhearing; there were just four calls, one hour each, over the whole five months.) Nathan was twenty years younger than Jake, looked up to him as some sort of father figure/mentor, and paid him handsomely to contribute quasi-regularly to *Niggun,* playing the role of its in-house public intellectual. Nathan, with an obsequious note attached, had recently sent Jake a copy of his CD to get his opinion of it, and Jake had written him back something complimentary. But to Eve he told the truth.

"It's utterly mediocre," he told her bluntly on the phone. "The first part isn't bad, but then at the end he wimps out. He obviously didn't know how to finish his composition, so he just tied it up with a big phony bow. One of those pat, conventional endings. Shows a total lack of courage and character. You'd never do something like that, Eve — just wimp out. You've got backbone. You're brave."

Of course she loved hearing that at the time. But not long afterwards he left her, and along with the many other things she didn't understand was why he'd said that to her. Why compliment someone you're about to dump? Her friend Bonnie thought this was Jake's way of telling her (and even more so, himself) that she would be okay. She was brave and strong, so he didn't have to worry about her, or feel guilty for what he'd done. Who knows? Eve thinks now. But no, I'm not brave. I'm not brave at all. I wanted to die when you left me. When I got that email from you, it was like someone had blown a hole the size of a cannonball right through my stomach, and I was slowly bleeding to death, though no one seemed to notice. I went on with my daily routine — I had to take care of my boys, I had to earn a living. But all I really did was wait for you to come back.

She sips some water from the plastic bottle on her tray. Her lips were getting dry; the water helps. "*Mayim Hayim*," says the label, and under it, in letters formed out of different-coloured flowers: "Live Your Life." She pulls the blanket over her head.

There is only one letter to Jake left in Eve now. All those hundreds of thousands of words, all those tens (or hundreds) of thousands of sentences, have now boiled down into one: the one-line letter she has been writing and re-writing for the past two and a half years. From all its long simmering and bubbling, this letter has, like any well-cooked sauce, become concentrated down to its essentials:

Dear Jake,
Thank you for your invitation to meet next time I'm in Israel, but I am going to decline.

She'll be cool but not cold, she decides for the hundredth time. She also won't be snarky or hostile, much as that's how she feels. Because at this point Jake is the most powerful man in the world in her field. With a single review, he can make or break someone's reputation — he does it every day — so she can't afford to make an enemy out of him. She is just starting out as a composer — she began composing late in life — and she hopes that maybe he'll even help her at some point (back then he intimated once that he would). So she has written this letter very carefully. Two or three hundred times. Two or three hundred drafts didn't seem to her excessive last week when she thought about it, given what's at stake. It's not that many drafts, she told herself; it's not even one a day for a year. But now as she pulls off the smelly blanket with a sigh and looks out the window, it seems quite mad. And anyway how stupid could she have been to imagine that Jake would ever write to her again? How could she ever have believed something so ridiculous?

But she had. She had because Jake had promised he'd contact her again. And also because she had taken him for what he presented himself as: an honest man, a man of integrity. (He used these words — *honesty, integrity* — more often than anyone else she had ever met.) So it took her a while to realize that he was a liar. She had laughed with him like a co-conspirator, an insider, when he lied to Nathan Singelman or to Fran. Yet for some reason (naïveté? wishful thinking?) it never occurred to her that sooner or later it would be her turn. In his final email to her, the follow-up to his break-up email, he wrote,

We'll meet again, Eve, I'm sure of it. In three to five years, when things have cooled down. Even Fran agreed that in three to five years we could be friends. You and I have lots to talk about, and when the time is right, we'll do it.

He said three to five years. He said so. She had it in writing. So for the next three years, she counted every day she didn't hear from him, and every week, every month, and every year. Counting down to the three-year mark, the earliest possible point of re-connection, according to his promise. When he didn't contact her then, she was astonished and deeply wounded. At the four-year mark, as well, Jake didn't contact her. But both these times she assured herself that he would be in touch with her before the five years were up. She was sure of this, because he'd said "in three to five years." Five years was the outer limit. So even though by the last year leading up to the five-year mark, she was functioning fairly well externally — building her music therapy practice, seeing friends, keeping in touch with her two boys, both now away at college, and even doing some composing — in fact all she was doing was waiting to hear from Jake.

But not anymore. The five-year mark came and went six months ago, and now she is starting to really grasp that Jake isn't ever going to contact her again. It's hard to take in emotionally, but intellectually at least, she knows it's true. For Jake, the whole thing's probably in the past, and has been ever since they broke up. Most likely he hasn't thought of her even once in the past five and a half years. Plus even if he did, she is a sore point with his wife, so why would he jeopardize the peace he has re-established with Fran for someone he no longer even cares about?

Of course he'll never write to her again. Why would he?

But still. That letter — the one she keeps re-working in response to the one he'll never send — lives on in her with a life of its own.

Thank you for your invitation to meet next time I'm in Israel, but I am going to decline. At this late date, I don't think we have anything to say to each other...
(No, don't write that.)

This letter pops into her head unbidden, whenever it wants, as do a few other specific phrases:

Do you love me?
Hold me. Hold me tighter.
I've never loved anyone more in my life.
You don't love me anymore, do you?
No. You don't care if I'm alive or dead.
I don't love you either.

I haven't loved you for a long time now.
Please don't love me anymore.

These phrases, like the letter, don't have meaning the way such phrases or sentences usually do. They don't mean what they appear to mean. They're old, dead words — words that have lost their meaning — but somehow keep popping up, and ejaculating themselves, inside of her. They're like a computer glitch, some weird default computer program that keeps appearing on your screen. They're a stupid, meaningless recurring tic.

Not surprising, though. None of this is uncommon in people who have been traumatized, thinks Eve, as the lights in the cabin turn a shade brighter. I have a broken mind. I've never had a broken mind before. A broken heart, yes. Other men have broken my heart. But only Jake has broken my mind.

She begins to laugh. Crazy. *Crazy.* Waiting all this time. Wasting all this time. Crazy. And sad.

As she laughs, she hears a baby cry on the other side of the cabin. It cries in just two tones — going from a high A to a high B-flat — over and over again. How do babies know how to cry in musical intervals? she wonders. She straightens out her messed-up blankets and retrieves her earpiece from the tangle. Well, one thing that's not sad is music. All those letters she wrote to Jake, and all those letters she read of his, were not (as her father used to say) a total loss. She got a beautiful song cycle out of them. About a year ago, on a long, boring, rainy day, she started setting some of their letters to music, and in a way used these to tell the story of their whole relationship, and she likes how it came out. She patterned this composition on the love songs Schumann wrote for Clara and presented to her on the night before their long-awaited wedding. Originally Eve called her song cycle "The Life Cycle of Love," but by the time it was finished, she was juggling titles like "The Death Cycle of Love," "The Bi-Cycle of Love," and "Cycles of Love and Hate." She still hasn't settled on a title and she also doesn't yet have an ending. But now she begins to hum one of the letter-songs from this cycle under her breath, softly, so Born Again won't hear. This one is a medley of some of the things that Jake said or wrote to her five and a half years ago: "For a single hour with you, I would burn every music score in the world."

"I've never loved anyone in my life more than I love you now."

"You're the best friend I've ever had. I've never before had a friend like you."

"Look at me, I'm crying I'm so happy. I haven't cried since I was seven years old."

"I'm a new man. I'm not the same person who walked into this hotel room four days ago. You've given me a new life."

"I can't imagine living my life ever again without you in it. We'll always be together, Eve, one way or another. At the very least as friends. That much I can promise you for sure."

The letter-song that she is humming is set to flute, harp, and strings, one of her favourite combinations because of Mozart's concerto for these instruments. Her letter-song has various complex strands, and multiple voices interweaving with each other, but at the same time it has a simple, beautifully haunting, singable theme. As she quietly hums it now, she can feel herself lying in Jake's arms. She is safe and secure, knowing how much he loves her.

The flight attendant with the bright crimson lipstick reaches over Eve's pudgy neighbour to collect her tray. "It's almost untouched," Eve tells her. *Almost untouched* is another way of saying *almost virginal,* but you can't be "almost" a virgin; either you're a virgin or you're not. The flight attendant removes Born Again's tray. Born Again is bug-eyed now, watching the beginning of an episode of *Curb Your Enthusiasm.* Eve's amazed. What kind of an idiot starts watching a thirty-minute TV show twenty-five minutes before landing? Doesn't he realize they're going to turn it off in the middle? Pull the plug on Larry David? He'll be right in the middle of a sentence, and the screen will go dark.

On her neighbour's screen Larry David looks sort of like Jake. He has much less hair, and straighter hair, than Jake. But still there is something similar about the two of them. They're both white-haired, lanky, sixty-five or seventy-year-old Jewish males. They're both impatient men who don't suffer fools gladly. And they're both brilliant, charismatic, socially awkward, neurotic, tender-hearted, cruel, narcissistic, endearing, and fucked-up. Of course, to be fair, there are differences between them, too. Jake is an intellectual, a thinker, and "L.D." just a comedian. Jake is a serious person; L.D. is funny. Very, very funny. Or as L.D. would say, "Pretty, pretty..."

Suddenly there's no more Larry David: the screen's gone black. The pilot's voice booms over the loudspeaker: "This is your captain speaking. We are now beginning our descent into Israel."

Eve, even though she anticipated Larry David's disappearance, is annoyed by it. Descent? she thinks contemptuously. One doesn't descend to Israel; one ascends. Arrival in Israel is a spiritual ascension. Don't Canadian pilots know anything?

"Please place all your hand luggage below the seat in front of you, switch off all electronic devices, and fasten your seat belts."

She obeys. But as she is shoving her carry-on under the seat in front of her, some of those phrases return.

I don't love you anymore. I don't. I haven't loved you for years.

Then: *Do you love me?*

There's a pause.

No. Of course you don't. You don't care if I'm alive or dead.

She straightens up in her seat and looks out the window: blackness dotted with yellow lights.

Not *You don't care*, she corrects herself: *He. He* doesn't care. Third person. Stop talking to him like he's still your eternal I-Thou after all this time. It's been five and a half years.

The plane plummets and she feels her stomach plummet, too. She clutches both armrests, her eyes shut tight. The plane drops again; it feels like it's diving, and she thinks she is going to vomit. Then the plane steadies itself. She opens her eyes. Gradually her stomach settles down. This thing with Jake, apart from everything else, is embarrassing. First of all because of its banality. The powerful older man at the peak of his career, and the young woman just starting out as a musician (or anyway the young*er* woman — fifty to his sixty-five). It's such a cliché. Secondly, it's embarrassing because she can't get over it. She's not a fool. She knew from the beginning that a relationship between a married man and an unattached woman couldn't last. But even so, here she is, stuck in this state and unable to move forward. It doesn't make any sense that she should be so fucked-up over what was, after all, just a five-month affair. She wasn't like this even after Brian died, and he was her husband and she'd loved him for over fifteen years. She did suffer terribly at first after Brian's death, but then she quickly recovered. She had no choice, in a way, ten years ago: Michael was ten and Ethan was eight; she couldn't just fall apart. Yet here it is five and a half years since she and Jake parted ways, and she's still obsessed with him day and night. There's something here she doesn't understand. Some mystery she can't solve.

Now the plane lands in a series of three rough bumps. Loud clapping erupts. Right. Israelis always clap whenever a plane lands. Celebrating survival — implicitly reminding you of all the possible disasters you have just narrowly escaped. The plane is still coasting along the runway, but already people are standing up, taking down coats and parcels from overhead compartments, phoning relatives and friends to say they've arrived, and squinting at hand-held devices to check their email. Good idea, thinks Eve. I should see what I've missed while up in the air. Probably ten or fifteen emails. Still sitting in her seat (practically the only person on the plane not yet standing up), she turns on her Blackberry. Maybe, she thinks, I'll have an email from Jake.

2. CAROUSEL

INSIDE THE AIRPORT, EVE IS WAITING impatiently in front of the carousel for her bags, when she hears someone call her name. She turns; it's Miranda Levy striding toward her with a smile. Miranda, who attended the same composition workshop as her three summers ago at the Toronto Conservatory. Ten years younger than her, Miranda is on everyone's lips these days because first she was paid a quarter-of-a-million-dollars to write the music for a big Hollywood movie, and then that music won "Best Original Score" this year at the Oscars. Eve, watching Miranda approach, can't help but feel a twinge — no, more than a twinge; a knife twist — of envy. Her own career is going nowhere. After her *Kaddish Concerto* won a prize seven years ago, people had high hopes for her. But these hopes have come to nothing, mainly because the past five and a half years have been a waste. All she has composed during this time is the second half of an oratorio, *Hallelujah*, that she had started years before, and two new works: her unfinished song cycle and a completed oratorio (actually, more than an oratorio; a kind of oratorio plus, like *L'Histoire du Soldat*) about Jake's life, called *The Life Story of a Man*. That's all she's done. She hasn't been able to create new music about anything other than Jake, and the older work that isn't about him, *Hallelujah*, has for some reason been rejected by everyone she has sent it to. It's been terrible. Especially since, during this period, more than any other in her life, she has longed — desperately longed — for success. If she won another prize, she thought, particularly one of the big ones like the Rossi Prize in New York, Jake would hear about it and maybe fall in love with her again. Because Jake always admired and respected celebrity. Now she smiles at Miranda and congratulates her warmly. She doesn't have anything against Miranda — she's a nice person: friendly and unpretentious. The two of them talk for a bit as they wait for their baggage to arrive. When they realize they were both on the same flight, they laugh.

"That's so funny!" says Miranda, and after they've finished laughing about it: "So what are you doing here, Eve? Did you come for the *Niggun* conference?"

"The *Niggun* conference? What *Niggun* conference?"

"What, you didn't know? *Niggun*'s hosting a three-day conference on Jewish music in Jerusalem this week. It starts two nights from now, on Tuesday. All the big names."

"You're kidding."

"No. I'm surprised you didn't hear about it. There have been ads all over the place for months now. Including in every issue of *Niggun*."

"I haven't read it lately," mutters Eve. She'd had to cancel her subscription to *Niggun* four and a half years ago — she'd had to stop reading it altogether — because Jake writes for them. He has either an essay or a music review in almost every single issue. At first, after they broke up, she liked reading what he wrote, even though it hurt. She imagined when reading his articles that he was talking directly to her, and this made her feel like he wasn't gone. But, after a while, reading Jake made her jealous. He has time to write these articles, she would think resentfully, but not a one-line email to me. (She was, at that point, still checking her email over a hundred times each day for an email from him.) And she nearly went mad with jealousy when, in one review, Jake lavished thick praise on the latest young, attractive, up-and-coming female composer,

Rebecca Milner, who had just won the Rossi Prize that year. She couldn't bear reading Jake after that. It made her feel too naked and vulnerable. Each word of Jake's was like a touch of his fingers on her skin.

Eve sees Miranda looking at her curiously. "So what *are* you doing here?" Miranda asks.

Eve, of course, doesn't tell Miranda about Jake. Or about her hope that being here, near Jake, will help her find an ending for her love-and-hate cycle, and maybe also an end to her obsession with Jake. Perhaps on this trip she will discover some clues to the mystery of why she can't get over this man.

Instead she explains about the advanced seminar in music therapy that she is taking. Every year at this time, the last week in December, she does a five-day seminar in Jerusalem. The Israeli Institute of Music Therapy is one of the best in the world after London's and New York's, offering some excellent international mini-courses, and this way she can meet the accreditation requirements for her clinical practice in Canada. Miranda nods vaguely. Like almost all the composers Eve knows, she can't relate to the music therapy thing that Eve does. Can't accept the fundamental idea of music as therapy. As if music were too pure to be used, or useful, for anything. Even helping people. It reminds her of how you're not supposed to use Chanukah candles, once you've lit them, for any practical purpose. I guess I'm not a pure musician, she thinks. Or anyway not purely a musician.

Miranda is rummaging through her purse. Then she holds something out to Eve.

"Here's the program for the conference," she says, and Eve takes it from her. "You should come. It'll be fun. Everyone's going to be there."

There's a loud, creaking, groaning sound. The carousel has started to move and the bags begin bumping down the chute. Eve, for the moment ignoring the bags, peruses the conference program. She doesn't see Jake's name on it, but she is sure he is in here somewhere. Her hands, to her embarrassment, are starting to sweat.

"I'm surprised you weren't invited to present," says Miranda. "You have so much to contribute. That *Kaddish Concerto* you wrote — I loved it. Everybody did."

Eve looks up from the booklet in her hand and, for the first time today, meets Miranda's eyes frankly, fully. Miranda is obviously speaking sincerely. She respects Eve. Admires her even. Eve thinks, I may feel like a failure as a composer. A nobody. But Miranda doesn't see me that way. "Thank you," she says.

Miranda has already turned toward the baggage. "That's mine," she says, and lifts off the carousel a small, tidy bag only slightly larger than a carry-on.

Eve, keeping one eye on the carousel for her own luggage, is again scanning the conference program. Miranda's right: all the big names are there. Except for Jake's. She must have missed it, though. The booklet is six pages long, all in small print, with lots of detail. *Oh! There's Miranda!* Miranda's listed as one of three people on a panel entitled, "What Makes Jewish Music Jewish?"

"I see you're one of the presenters," says Eve, trying to keep her voice neutral, rancour-free.

"Oh, yeah," shrugs Miranda, her long sleek black hair slightly jumping. "Nathan — you know Nathan Singelman?"

Jake's mentee. But also one of the people Eve wrote to about *Hallelujah* a few months ago, and who never answered back.

"I know *of* him," she says.

"Well, he and I were at an event together once at the 92nd Street Y, so I got to know him there. And a couple of months ago, he called and asked if I would come to his conference, and I said, 'Why not?'"

Why not, indeed. Eve feels her bitterness mount. Five and a half years ago, at the tail end of the after-glow from her concerto prize, she was invited, along with a generous honorarium, to speak at an international conference on Jewish music, where she was put on a panel with Jake. That's how they met. Now, not only was she not deemed worthy to present at this upcoming conference, she hadn't even been invited to attend as a paying member of the audience. She closes the program and hands it back to Miranda.

"No, no, keep it," says Miranda. "I have another copy."

"Really? Are you sure?"

"Yeah."

"Okay. Thanks."

Eve sees her bags, the two of them close together, coming down the carousel, and one at a time she wrestles them onto her wobbly cart. She feels ridiculous with her two huge, yellow, hard-shelled suitcases, each one looking almost like a trunk for a sea voyage, plus a carry-on bag holding her computer, next to Miranda with her one small, compact piece. This feels like a metaphor for something, but she can't put her finger on what. She and Miranda leave the baggage area together, walking without being stopped through "Nothing To Declare," and then outside to the taxi line. But just before leaving the building, Eve turns around and glances behind her with respectful acknowledgment and maybe even a little affection — a glance like the tipping of a hat — at the row of pay phones they just passed.

3. HOMEWORK

AT THE HOTEL, HER ROOM IS DIM and shadowy. One of the two light bulbs in the ceiling fixture is burnt out, and as a result, the four corners of the room are deep, dark pockets. Deep and dark enough, it seems to her, to each be hosting a large spider's web. She doesn't unpack. Instead she sits at the desk with the ugly, dull lamp to try and do some work before she gets too tired. Her music therapy seminar begins tomorrow morning, and last week she got an email from the instructor with a homework assignment due the first day. Each student has to bring a case to present — not necessarily a client they've worked with therapeutically, but someone the class can discuss as a potential case. Eve, over the past few days, has been frantically rushing around getting ready for this trip, and somehow this homework assignment kept falling to the bottom of her list. She decided, riding in the taxi to the airport, that there would be time to deal with this on the plane, but then, sitting there next to Born Again, his chubby body — his bum, to be precise — spilling over into her seat, she didn't feel like it. And she doesn't feel like it now, either. She sits glumly in front of a pile of folders: the packet of materials for the seminar and copies of her two recent compositions (her love/hate cycle and *The Life Story of a Man*), which she always brings with her wherever she goes. Then she brightens up. She doesn't have to create a case from scratch. She can use Jake. *The Life Story of a Man* is written in fifteen sections, each about a different period in his life, and in chronological order. They'd make a great case history.

She opens up the folder containing *The Life Story of a Man*. The fifteen pieces of music that make it up are of varying lengths and scored for different instruments. The first one, for example, is composed for a tenor accompanied by a lone recorder. (A lonely recorder. With a wandering, wondering tune, like that played by a shepherd wandering through the Judean Hills.) The second section is for tenor, soprano, and the same septet Stravinsky used in *L'Histoire du Soldat*: violin, double bass, clarinet, bassoon, cornet, trombone, and percussion. The third calls for the voice of a boy soprano along with five instruments from Biblical times: timbrel, cymbals, David's harp, flute, and a lyre. (A lyre because Jake is a liar.) *The Life Story of a Man* started out as an oratorio, but quickly took on a life of its own and evolved into something more than that, something like *L'Histoire du Soldat*, which, according to Stravinsky's instructions, was meant to be "read, sung, acted, and danced." As Eve began to move in that direction, she realized the word "oratorio" wasn't suitable for *The Life Story of a Man*; instead, she dubbed it a "storatorio," a term she invented, and the way she has thought about this creation ever since.

Now for a few minutes she scans her storatorio. Yes, this will do for her homework. Though even more suitable for a "case history" would be the original text that she first wrote out — just the words, no music — which she has a copy of somewhere here on her computer. That text, she recalls, was ten pages long, which was way too much to set to music. So she decided to take just a few sentences from each of the fifteen sections, and these, in the end, formed the libretto for her score. Ten pages, she thinks now, is far too long also for a class presentation. So I won't read the whole thing tomorrow; I'll just speak from it, extract the main points as I go along. I can wing it. I know this "case" inside out.

This case. She peers for a moment into the dark corner of the room to the right of her bed (which by now she is almost certain contains a spider's web). She has turned science into art before, but never art into science. When she was conducting the research on women with "borderline personality disorder" for her MA thesis, some of the women she interviewed she experienced not as clinical cases, but as songs. And some of these songs she even wrote down (and one day may make a collection of them). That's one sort of alchemy, it seems to her. But she has never before alchemized in the other direction: transforming music into scientific data. She bites her lip as she skims through *The Life Story of a Man*. Whatever she feels toward Jake, presenting him as a "case" tomorrow doesn't feel right. Turning his life into a psychological profile for public consumption. Meat for the lions' den. It isn't fair, it's dehumanizing. It's almost like killing his soul.

Killing his soul! She laughs. What is she — one of those superstitious old women who believe that if you take their picture, you're stealing their soul? Or that if you stick a pin into the heart of a voodoo doll, the person it represents will die? She gives a derisive laugh. Fuck it. If that's what happens, let him die. He's haunted me all these years. He almost destroyed my mind. It's time for him to go.

She flips quickly through a few pages of *The Life Story of a Man*, and then continues reading it more slowly. When she wrote this music four years ago, Jake's life — including his thoughts and feelings and perceptions of everything — were more important, and more real, to her than her own. She composed this storatorio sitting at the folding table in the basement, wearing nothing but her bathrobe, and the music flowed out of her like lava from a volcano. She wrote the essence of this piece — its burning core — all in one night, in a seven-hour marathon while her boys lay sleeping upstairs in their red-plaid flannel pyjamas. She thought then that she was doing this so she could write Jake out of her — empty him from her mind and body. Yet in retrospect, she was composing this music in order to preserve Jake. To keep him alive. The realness of his voice, and face, and the touch of his hand. She didn't want him to fade. She didn't want the whole thing to fade. For instance, the way they lay together in bed on that rainy afternoon back then. Lying there naked and him speaking to her nakedly. It was either before they'd had sex or after, she can't remember now. Though in a way, before and after were the same, because during those five days they just went back and forth constantly between talking and sex. Talking and sex and music, of course. There was music and sex and talk, and sex and talk and music, hour after hour during those seemingly endless days. And the music and talking felt like sex, and the sex and talking felt like music.

On that rainy grey afternoon, the two of them lay cosily in bed, watching and listening as the rain pounded against the large picture window, and the thunder crashed and the wind whistled like a duet alternating between percussion and woodwinds. And Jake started talking about himself. He talked and talked and talked. She just listened, loving him. All his words and stories etched themselves into her, like a wood-burning pen burning pictures into soft, ready wood. Because Jake didn't tell his stories just to her mind, he told them also to her body. His index finger while he talked drew languorous circles all over her naked belly with her bellybutton at its centre. So his words entered her body through her skin and her bellybutton. (That vestige of the umbilical cord, the primary cord of attachment. That primary, primeval chord formed by two notes joining.) Jake that afternoon inscribed his words, he inscribed himself, onto her wide-open, just-loved flesh, so that even one and a half years later, when she first transcribed his stories, she could still feel them inside of her. And I still can, though by now only faintly, she thinks. Because they've integrated themselves into me. Like those heart implants you hear about that knit themselves together with the body's natural skin until the two become indistinguishable. No wonder it's taking me so long to get over Jake. He's been in the cells of my body all this time. In every single cell.

She turns on her computer. She needs to read over the original text so it's fresh in her mind when she wakes up tomorrow. The seminar starts at nine o'clock in the morning, which will be two in the morning Canadian time, so she'll want to sleep in till the last possible moment, and not have to do this homework then. After briefly searching, she finds the original pages of text, makes a copy of them, and on this new version, changes the title from *The Life Story of a Man* to *The Life History of a Man*. Then she slashes the word *life,* and replaces it with *case,* so now it's *The Case History of a Man*. In less than a minute, she has changed Jake from a life to a case, and from a story to history. (*You're history, man.*) Good, she thinks approvingly. Now, in line with her profession's ethical requirements when publicly presenting a case history, she alters all the names. (These names she altered long ago on the storatorio, but not on this original text.) Jake now becomes Jerry, Fran Florence, Yael Yolande, and Dina Denise. She saves this case history and backs it up on her memory key. Then she reads the original over from start to finish. Reading one last time these words of hardened lava.

❧ *The Life Story of a Man* ❧

1

He knows there is something wrong with him. He's always known it, although he's never admitted it to anyone. He knows he's not like other people. He's missing something they all have. He doesn't know how to talk to people, how to really connect with them. He's always felt different, apart. Like there's a wall between him and everyone else. He tells himself that this is because he's so much smarter than they are, that it's because he's an intellectual. But in his heart he knows this isn't it. It's something else. Something deeper. He's just different. Weird. And he has been, ever since he can remember. Though he's kept it hidden as well as he could. He can't connect to other people. He's always alone, trapped inside his body.

2

There was a time when he wasn't alone. At the beginning. With his mother. They were glued together, they were inseparable, almost like one body. He clung to her, and she to him, and he was safe.

Then one day, when he was two and a half, for no reason, his mother unstuck herself from him. She unstuck herself from him and stuck herself onto somebody else. A wailing, screaming thing. A tiny red baby who was more important than him. He was nothing now. He tried to get his mother back. He tried everything he could think of, even wailing and screaming like that red thing, but even that didn't work — his mother just told him to stop acting like a baby. Which wasn't fair because when the red thing cried or screamed, his mother would pick it up and kiss it. He couldn't get her back. He tried and everything failed. So he gave up. If she didn't care, he didn't care. He stopped eating. He got sick. They had to hospitalize him for three days to keep him from getting dehydrated. His mother came back to him then. She picked him up and hugged him and said she loved him more than anyone in the world. She was sorry, she said, and she cried, and promised never to neglect him again. She stayed beside him every second he was in the hospital, holding his hand and stroking his forehead. She was his again. Only his. But as soon as he was better, the hospital let him go home, and once they were back home, there was that screaming red thing again. His mother rushed over and picked it up. And then she got busy with it. With his sister. That screaming red thing that took his mother away.

3

He was lonely all the time now. Lonely and angry. But he'd learned over the past five years how to act okay on the surface. He was a quiet boy, dark and serious, and highly intelligent. Simmering on the inside. Hating his mother. And his sister, too.

Every day his father came home from work before his mother. It was postwar, London was full of Jewish refugees, and Jake's mother, a part-time music therapist and a community volunteer, worked with them around the clock, always looking haggard. No more hot suppers with the family around the table. Jake would let himself in with a key after school and wait desperately, looking frequently at the clock, till five-thirty or a quarter to six, when his father would open the front door. The boy waited till he could hear the key turning in the lock. Then he flung himself at his father's short, slender frame. Clung to him. His father, a kind, warm man, a Hebrew school teacher whose students loved him, was kind and warm to his son for a couple of minutes, but then he had to go work in his study. He had papers to mark, things to do. The boy was alone again. Lost. Hugging himself for hours against the loneliness. Hugging himself by listening to music on the radio, and to the lectures about music that he sometimes heard in between. The warm voices and the music comforted him. As he listened, hugging himself and now and then rocking to the rhythm, Jake realized that when there was music, he wasn't alone.

4

Not only no hot supper; not even anything in the fridge. Nothing but a wilted leaf of lettuce. His mother was out with the refugees again. Caring about them, caring about strangers more than she cared about him. When she finally came home tonight at eight-fifteen or eight-thirty, she would be holding his sister's hand. She would leave the house with his sister every morning and return with her every night. He was never alone with his mother anymore. Never. He remembered what it was like when he was close to her. Laughing with her, having her freckled face close up to his. The smell of her and the warmth of her body when she held him. He wanted that again now. He still loved her. But now he hated her, too. Maybe hated her even more than he loved her. He'd never forgive her for what she'd done. Even if she wanted him back again, even if she begged him, he would never go back to her now. She had hurt him. She had betrayed him. And for this he would hate her forever. He promised himself this, secretly inside. And secretly inside, he promised her this, too. That was the least he could do. That was the most he could do.

5

Jake, once he discovered music, buried himself in it. Music would save him. He learned to play the piano and violin, he listened incessantly to music on the radio and on records, and he read everything about music he could lay his hands on at the local library. He especially loved two kinds of music: classical, and Jewish music from all over the world. By age thirteen, when he had his bar mitzvah, he had already started, with his allowance, a serious record collection, and taught himself Yiddish so he could understand the Yiddish songs he'd come across. (His father wasn't pleased about the Yiddish, being a Hebraist and a Zionist, but Jake persevered anyway.) At his bar mitzvah, Jake gave a brilliant talk on Jewish music, on the history, significance, and musicological structure of the *trop*, the musical score, for the Torah portion he had just chanted.

When years later he told people about what he had taught himself by age thirteen, they were extremely impressed, as were all the people present at his bar mitzvah. They thought he was a little genius. But the truth was, he had to do something. There was no one at home — he was bored. And he was lonely. He had no friends.

6

A black and white photo of Jake at that age. (*The one that Jake showed her when she was at his house.*) A dark, serious, brooding face. Thin lips, unreadable eyes. Eyes that soaked everything up, but gave nothing away. Secrets. He's full of dark secrets. At night in his bed, his hand working his cock, juicing it, making it squirt. Stifling his sounds, emitting only the quietest of moans. I'll be doing this all my life, he thinks. Cause no girl could possibly love me. Someone dirty like me.

7

He had no friends. He didn't know how to be with people, how to talk to people in a normal way. He gave off this dark loneliness. He told himself the problem was that everyone else was so much dumber than he was and he wouldn't bring himself down to their level. Making chit-chat, having superficial conversations. He wasn't shallow enough for that. The kids at his school had no depth or imagination; they weren't interested in music or the life of the mind. All they cared about was drinking, sports, and parties. He didn't have to lower himself to that just to try and fit in. Anyway, he had things they didn't have. Music, and books, and a rich inner life. Whereas all these people had was each other. Friendships.

Some of these friendships were with girls. He wanted that. He wanted to have a girl. But he didn't know how.

8

Starting fresh at a new school for high school, Jake got onto the running team. He discovered he loved to run. Discovered what it was to belong to a team. To have people to sit with in the lunchroom. To not be alone anymore. (*When she asked him fifty years later about his friends in childhood and adolescence, he told her about his running team. That was all he had. He counted them as his friends even though he never saw any of them outside of school.*) He felt like now he had friends for the first time. He wasn't alone. He ran and ran and ran.

9

He ran, too, when the bullies came. There was a gang of large bullies at the end of his block who picked on the Jewish boys coming home from school, and Jake was fast, so he could always get away. There was one time, though, when he was faced with three huge guys built like refrigerators coming toward him. Standing next to him was Bernie Stermac from his running team. Little Bernie, three inches shorter than Jake, and the smallest and slowest guy on the team. Jake looked at him. Then he looked at the bullies moving toward them. And he ran. He left Bernie alone to face the three bullies. Bernie got beaten up, of course. And badly. And Jake felt a little bad about this. But not that bad. After all, he thought, what choice did I have? It was him or me. And it wasn't going to be me. A guy has a right to save himself.

10

Jake's parents bought a new house. There were two rooms for the two children, and Jake and his sister both wanted the big room. They flipped a coin, his sister won, and Jake threw a tantrum. He wailed, he screamed, he sulked, he bargained, he bullied, he cried, and he argued, until finally he wore everyone down and got the big room. The deal they reached was that he would have it for the first year and his sister would get it for the second. But then, as the end of the first year approached, and his sister asked for the big room, Jake argued, sulked, pleaded, whined, bargained, and bullied until his sister, a good-natured girl, and more passive than her brother (*she was raised, after all, to be a girl, not a first-born boy*) rolled her eyes, shrugged, and gave in. That night in his bed Jake hugged himself with joy. He'd won. He'd beaten her. And he'd learned an important lesson from this. That if you play with time — if you pretend that something's temporary (*say a separation of three to five years*), when really you aim to make it permanent (*when you plan to never see this person again*) — people will give in more easily. And then, by the time the later date comes, they won't care as much anymore, and it's easier to modify the original deal. You can play for time, Jake told himself in his bed. You can play with time. Time is a weapon.

11

The first woman Jake ever slept with was a whore. He couldn't get sex any other way. He couldn't talk to girls. He didn't know how to form a connection with them. So after years of lonely horniness, he decided to go and pay for it.

The whore he slept with wasn't even the one he wanted. Standing next to the tall tough one that he got, there was another one, shorter and prettier, whom he liked but didn't have the guts to ask for. So he got the big, tough one. They fucked and he paid her. Afterwards, waiting for the bus in the rain, he hated himself. Hated his body with its needs and demands, its smells and urges, all of which made him ashamed. They had nothing to do with the life he wanted for himself, a life of the mind. The splendid life of music and books.

12

After the whore, he had two girlfriends in college. The first was a lot like him: dark, complicated, and tortured, and the relationship they had was dark, complicated, and tortured. They drove each other crazy — sexually, psychically, every way. Should they do it, or shouldn't they? What would it mean if they did? What would it mean if they didn't? This went on for two and a half angst-ridden years, and in the end, they broke up, never having done it.

Six months later Jake met Polly, who was far less intense. She was an uncomplicated person — kind, soft and sweet — and she loved Jake. He drank thirstily from her unconditional love and her generous, open, unashamed body, but he found her boring. There couldn't be much to her, he thought, if there was no *sturm und drang* — if she was never tormented or anguished like he was. And there had to be something wrong with her, a certain blindness in her, for her to love him with such unquestioning steadfast love. Not hating him even a little.

But just the same, Polly's love was powerful and real. And it filled, if not to the top, more than halfway, the well of loneliness inside him. They got engaged. And then he left to study in France for a year.

13

He'd won a scholarship to the Sorbonne. He and only one other person in England. It was a great honour, and Jake (who, after only one year of high school French, was perfectly fluent) went there with the highest hopes. At the Sorbonne, he was matched up with a tutor, a pleasant but no-nonsense woman who met him twice a week to guide him through his studies in classical music. Other than that, he was on his own — free to socialize, play sports with the other students, or join one or more of the many clubs. But he couldn't do it. He couldn't connect with anyone. He did his studying and went twice a week to meet his tutor, but other than that, he just wandered around the campus, feeling totally alone. After four months of this, he was so lonely that he crawled to the nearest psychiatrist, and had what in those days was called a nervous breakdown. The psychiatrist labelled it that way, but really it was just loneliness. Jake's loneliness wasn't just his inability to connect with anyone at the Sorbonne (with not even one of all the friendly students, club leaders and dormmates who reached out to him). He didn't even feel connected to Polly anymore. She was supposed to be his ultimate friend — his one-stop-shop friend: his best friend and girlfriend and fiancée, the woman he was going to marry when he got back from France — but she no longer felt real to him. After four months apart, he couldn't remember her voice and didn't even know if he still loved her. He asked his psychiatrist, "Do I have to marry Polly when I get back home?" (The psychiatrist didn't answer.) Jake also told the psychiatrist that he no longer knew who he was. That he felt totally unmoored and lost.

After two sessions with this psychiatrist, Jake returned to London, giving as his excuse that he didn't like the program at the Sorbonne. He said he didn't have patience for the academic game, and that he could live his life perfectly well without a doctorate in music. He told no one the truth. Soon afterward, he found a job covering the classical music scene for a mid-sized newspaper, and in time became their in-house music critic. Gradually he began writing for other newspapers as well, and then also for magazines and scholarly journals, producing weekly columns and articles and essays about music. Although Jake was recognized as an expert in both classical music and Jewish music, he was also quite eclectic, and could write about music of almost any kind. And unlike most of his colleagues, Jake could write in a homey, accessible way, so he quickly became a sought-after columnist, commentator, and critic.

Jake was feeling pleased with himself, especially when his first book, two and a half years after returning from the Sorbonne, became a hit, and put him on the map in the Jewish music world. But still there was something else he wanted to do: he wanted to write music. That was the real thing, he thought: not writing about music, but writing the music itself. That was the act of creation. The true, sacred thing.

But he wasn't able to do it. He tried, and couldn't. Couldn't get past his self-consciousness, his inner censor and critic, tearing apart every note he wrote almost before he'd written it down. He tried for months and then gave up, deeply disappointed. He felt impotent and acutely envious and resentful of the composers it was now his job to critique. But it was his bread and butter — he had to do it. So, feeling vaguely enraged, he continued judging all the new music being written.

He enjoyed this. He liked having the power of a judge. Ruling on what was and wasn't "good." Deciding, as they say on Yom Kippur, who should live and who should die. So Jake continued critiquing, and with his brilliance, his love of music, and his particular style (a unique mix of charm and superciliousness), his reputation began to skyrocket.

14

In college someone at his dorm had a friend named Fran, whom Jake had met a number of times. She was older than him by two years (twenty-three to his twenty-one), which made her seem to him like a wise, older woman. The day Jake returned from the Sorbonne, he spent an hour with his parents and then went over to see Fran. He asked her if he should marry Polly.

"Tell me about her," said Fran. "Tell me everything."

So Jake did. He emptied his mind, heart and soul — emptied himself totally — of Polly, telling Fran everything he could remember about her, even the most intimate details of their relationship. When he was finished, Fran said, "Sure, marry her."

Jake looked down at the ground and was silent for a moment. Then he looked up at Fran beseechingly. "But I don't want to," he said. "I want to marry *you*."

Fran smiled. Then she and Jake talked for a long time, well into the middle of the night, and the next morning Jake went to see Polly and told her it was over. Her tears and screams were uncomfortable for him, so he left as soon as he could, returning to Fran's place. A month later he and Fran were married. Jake liked the intensity of all this — the drama, the melodrama even. The torment, the darkness at the edges of his wedding happiness. And he knew that Fran, though she would never admit it, enjoyed the little soul-murder he had committed for her. A kind of wedding gift to her, sacrificing Polly, placing her, like a human sacrifice, on the altar of his new love.

Jake and Fran glued themselves together and, other than when working, rarely saw anyone else. The first three years of their marriage they spent almost all their free time in bed. They didn't just like being alone and intimate; they needed to be. No one and nothing outside of them was real. No one and nothing outside of them mattered. They shared everything and nothing was held back from the other: not a single thought that either one of them had was allowed to pass without being expressed, plumbed, and analyzed. Everything in each of them belonged to them both. One time, lying naked in bed, their feet got tangled, and for a few seconds Jake couldn't tell whose feet were whose. He was delighted by this and immediately told Fran, who was delighted by it, too. This proved something to them. They were closer than other couples. They had something special. They weren't really two separate beings — just one.

15

A few years later they moved to Israel, and when they got there, Fran said she wanted children. Jake didn't. But she did. This was their first major disagreement. And Fran won. Winning because Jake was so afraid of losing her and being alone again that he was willing to give in to practically anything she wanted. He gave in, but resented that she wanted children. To him this meant that he alone wasn't enough for her (whereas she was enough for him; she was all he needed).

Fran had a hard time getting pregnant, but five years after they started trying, they had a blond-haired girl, Yael. Fran loved her. Picked her up all the time, kissed her, hugged her, gazed into her eyes. Jake couldn't bear it. Fran seemed to love the baby more than him. She had glued herself to this baby; they were one unit now, Fran-and-the-baby, and he was left outside. So he stole the baby from his wife. Made the baby his. Made the baby love him more than her. (*He smiled smugly, triumphantly, when telling Eve about how he'd won. How he'd beaten Fran. Beaten Fran and the baby both.*)

A year and a half later they had a second girl, this time a dark-haired one, Dina, and Fran took this baby for herself.

Now they each had one, but Jake didn't mind. He didn't like the second one anyway. ("The dark one," as he called her.) From the beginning, he mocked this girl, derided her, and rejected her when she tried to climb onto his lap. Pushed her right off. He couldn't stand her. And couldn't stand to see all the love his wife lavished on her. Love that should have been his. He often felt lonely, neglected, and sorry for himself. There isn't enough love, he thought. There's never enough love to go around. Once, when the second baby was seven weeks old, he saw Fran cuddling it, and felt such rage he wanted to kill it. To smash its tiny head against the wall.

The years went by, and the blond-haired girl grew up quite well. But the dark-haired one, until the age of nine, screamed and tantrumed, often two or three times a day (tantrums that each lasted sometimes over an hour), pounding her fists and feet against the floor while her face turned bright red. At age nine the tantrums stopped, but the year she turned twelve she stopped eating and tried to starve herself. Neither Jake nor Fran even noticed that she had lost weight until she had dropped fifteen pounds out of eighty-five, and was so weak and anorexic she had to be hospitalized.

"It was so gradual, we didn't notice," they said to the intake staff at the Israeli hospital.

For the next six months Dina had to live in the hospital as part of its inpatient program, and Fran and Jake were supposed to go there once a week for family therapy. But Jake refused. Why should he have to go for family therapy — and "look at himself," as the social worker had put it — just because his daughter was fucked-up? But Fran prevailed upon him, and in the end, as usual, he gave in to her, and went. He went, but he went there hating his daughter. For this on top of everything else.

4. THE SEMINAR

"**W**OW! WHAT A DESTRUCTIVE, scary man," says a woman with dark hair when Eve finishes her presentation.

"Yeah," agrees a pale man with sandy hair.

Eve stands in front of the class, twelve faces from ten different countries, a blur around a large square table. She is the third student to present this afternoon, and these three case histories followed a long, tiring morning of self-introduction monologues and a review of all the latest theories. Now the students are supposed to use some of these theories to assess the individuals Eve and the others are presenting.

"Are there any other responses?" Hava, the teacher, asks in an Israeli accent.

Eve is glad her performance is behind her. She was surprised at how nervous she was presenting this "case history," since usually she is quite relaxed (she has presented dozens of case histories in her time). Today the room fell very quiet as she spoke, and her voice, as Jake became real for her again, took on a certain intensity and a deep timbre. She even felt dangerously emotional at a few points, but kept herself under control. Still, they could hear her passion for her "subject." She could tell by the way they listened to her, frowning and leaning forward in their seats.

Now her colleagues start making comments, mainly offering clinical insights about Jake that she has already arrived at over the past few years. But just the same, these colleagues' assessments are validating. She feels affirmed personally, and confirmed in her viewpoint, as she stands at the front of the class with her feet a foot and a half apart, in what Brian used to call her warrior position. After five minutes of this, a woman with a South American accent says, "I can't believe what he did to his second daughter. Such hatred. Such projection. She carries his inner darkness for him. She represents his dark side."

The "dark side." Eve pictures Darth Vader.

"And that maternal deprivation, that cutting off, that his mother did to him," says a grey-haired woman from Australia. "You see this again in the next generation, how he re-enacts this in his relationship with his 'dark' daughter. Imagine someone actually talking about a 'dark' and a 'light' daughter, and not understanding what they're doing."

"Well," says a young British man, one of only two men in the class. He is pale and skinny and reminds Eve of Darryl, a music therapist back home who has a crush on her and whom she keeps turning down. "Self-awareness does not seem to be this guy's forte."

Several people laugh.

Eve is starting to feel disloyal to Jake, maybe even dishonest. What they're saying is true, of course, but perhaps she has unfairly "stacked the deck" against him and misrepresented him, not sufficiently showing these people his beautiful side. He did have a beautiful side, after all. Otherwise she wouldn't have fallen in love with him.

"How is that daughter doing, by the way?" asks an Israeli woman with very short black hair. "What's her name again?"

It takes Eve a moment to remember her pseudonym for Dina. "Denise."

"Yes. How is she doing? Does she have a job? A relationship with a man?"

"Or a woman," says the British guy. "One shouldn't make assumptions."

"She has a job," Eve answers, recalling details about Dina's life that Jake told her. "A crummy job, selling lottery tickets, I think. Apparently, she is quite bright, but can't do anything better. For her" — and here she quotes Jake verbatim — "it's a major victory if she can get out of bed every morning. She finds life very difficult."

"Not surprising with a father like that," says a woman from France with a pretty blue hat.

A couple of others agree.

"What about her relationships?" asks the Israeli woman.

Eve shrugs. "Very sporadic. Just short-term things. Nothing more."

"As you'd expect," says the other man in the class, a good-looking Swede. "She has an avoidant attachment style."

"Oh, I wouldn't say avoidant," says a woman from the former Soviet Union. "I'd say ambivalent-resistant."

"No, no. Disorganized-disoriented," says the Australian.

An argument breaks out over Denise's attachment style. Eve stands there, feeling both superfluous and self-conscious at the front of the room. After a minute or two, Hava interrupts them.

"It seems to me that we are all very focussed on this 'dark daughter.' But in fact it is her father, Jerry, who is presumably coming to us for help. So let us now please turn our attention to him."

"Yes, but before we do that, we mustn't forget about the other daughter, too," says a blonde, sharp-nosed woman with a Southern drawl. "All this with Denise is obvious. The inner darkness that the father has banished and disowned. But when you have a parent who 'splits' the way this man does, projecting the good and bad parts of himself onto two different children, it's not only the child carrying the 'bad' part who gets damaged. The one carrying the father's 'goodness' is also at risk."

"True," says someone.

"How is she doing, actually, this 'daughter of light'?" asks

the Australian woman. "I doubt she's selling lottery tickets."
Someone chuckles.

"No," says Eve, "she isn't. She's followed in her father's
footsteps. She, too, is a music critic."

The class bursts into laughter. Eve is taken aback, almost
frightened. What are they laughing at? She didn't say anything
funny. At the same time she also feels affronted. So far, she
hasn't minded Jake being criticized or even condemned by this
group of people; in a way, she has enjoyed it. But to laugh at
him? How dare they laugh at this great man!

"Of course she is a music critic," says the Israeli woman. "She
has to be a clone of her father to get his love. A man like that
can only love a child who is a duplicate of himself. He can't
love a real, other, separate person. Only a copy of himself. If
he can love at all."

"Exactly," says a woman from Romania in a bright green
dress. "Narcissists aren't really capable of love. Especially when
they're perfectionists, like this man seems to be. Perfectionists
essentially hate life. Because to love perfection and hate imper-
fection means that basically you hate people. Because people
are never perfect."

Eve stares at this woman. Yes. Precisely. When things were
perfect between her and Jake, he loved her more than anyone
in the world. But the second she wasn't perfect anymore —
meaning she no longer matched his fantasy (she didn't exist just
when he wanted her to, she didn't totally worship the ground
he walked on, and she started to act like a real person, with a
mind of her own, and needs) — then he hated her. Hated her
more than anyone in the world.

"Okay," says Hava, "enough about these daughters. But
before we move on to Jerry, just very briefly, what about his
wife? We haven't talked about her yet at all."

Hava looks inquiringly around the class. No one says a word.

"Well," Eve volunteers, "she, too, projects a lot onto their
daughters. Florence has two sisters, one that she and Jerry

like, and one they despise. And at least once a week Florence calls Yolande by the good sister's name, and Denise by the bad sister's."

This time nobody laughs. "Wow," the British guy says. "This is so sick. Talk about no boundaries."

A couple of people nod.

"And this woman calls herself a therapist," says the South American woman.

Someone snickers. Others laugh or shake their heads.

"Well, not a real therapist," Eve explains. "A 'bodywork' therapist. There's this special approach she follows, I don't remember what it's called. But she has a teacher, a sort of guru in Holland, she studies with."

Jake told her with a sneer about this "teacher" of Fran's. A total charlatan, apparently, with ten acolytes from around the world, who once a month paid him a mini-fortune to get on a conference call with him and the rest of the group to discuss their cases. Afterwards they all did slavishly whatever he told them to. It's almost like a cult, Jake said, how blindly they follow this guy.

Now she recollects something else that Jake told her, and this he told her as a way of praising Fran's generosity. "In this approach," Eve says to the class, "they believe in 'flexible boundaries.' So if one of Florence's clients is going through a hard time, she'll let the session go on for longer than the usual hour. She'll give them an extra quarter of an hour, or half an hour, or even a whole hour, whatever she thinks they need."

"Oh my God," someone says.

"Well, that fits, doesn't it?" says the Australian.

"All *right*," Hava says, and this time there's a firmness, some of the hardness of flint in her voice, that gives Eve a jolt. Hava till now has seemed like a dumpy, maternal, rather non-directive type of person, but apparently (unlike Fran) she does have clear boundaries. "It's time to move on to Jerry," says Hava, "much as some of you seem to want to avoid this. I can't help wondering if there is something about this man that is putting you off." She pauses and waits, but no one says anything. "In any case, a number of you have already mentioned this man's splitting, projection, and perfectionism. Is there anything else, diagnostically speaking, that you notice about him?"

Silence. Everyone seems talked-out and tired by now. It's been a long day, and most of them, like Eve, arrived in Israel just yesterday and are jet-lagged. One of her colleagues half-heartedly throws out a lacklustre idea about Jerry maybe having an addictive personality, but Eve explains that he doesn't drink, do drugs, or even smoke cigarettes, so there is no evidence for this. Then there's silence again. Hava's laptop is open on the table in front of her, and now she types something on her keyboard, fiddles with her mouse, taps a few more keys, and then looks up at the big screen on the wall at the front of the class. Some text fills what a second ago was a blank screen. It's a list of some kind.

"Tell me, Eve," says Hava. "Are any of these items characteristic of Jerry? Do any of them remind you of him?"

Eve reads what's on the screen:

1. *Need for stimulation/proneness to boredom.*
2. *Parasitic lifestyle.*
3. *Poor behavioural control.*
4. *Promiscuous sexual behaviour.*
5. *Lack of realistic, long-term goals.*
6. *Impulsiveness.*
7. *Irresponsibility.*
8. *Juvenile delinquency.*
9. *Early behavioural problems.*

"No," says Eve. "These aren't like Jerry at all."
"Not even a little?"
"No."
"Then how about these?"

Hava moves her mouse again, and now there's a different list of items up on the screen. Eve is starting to feel put upon: how many more pages like this is she going to have to comment on? She is tired and her legs hurt; she wants to sit down and be done with her turn. But for the moment she has no choice, so she looks up at the screen. One at a time she considers the items listed.

She asks herself, Does Jake have:

1. *Glibness/superficial charm?* Yes. At the Jewish music conference where they first met, she watched Jake at one of the breaks chatting up one of the other presenters there. (He was so charming it would have been called flirting if that guy were a woman.) Though afterwards Jake told her this guy didn't have an original thought in his head.

2. *Grandiose sense of self-worth?* Oh yes. Jake always felt he was smarter than everyone else in the room. Much of the time this was true, but not always. There was something a bit exaggerated, distorted, about his self-image. He was brilliant, yes, but not the total genius he thought he was.

3. *Pathological lying?* Definitely. With Nathan Singelman. And with Fran. (Once he swore to Fran, looking her straight in the eye, that he was no longer in contact with Eve; then the next day he laughed with Eve about this on the phone.) And of course he also lied to her. He said they'd meet again, he promised her that, when he knew full well they wouldn't.

4. *Cunning/manipulative?* Oh, yes. That story with his sister and the good room is a classic.

And he used this same trick with her — the trick of time, of deferment — when he asked at one point for a three-week hiatus in their relationship ("Just give me a couple of weeks away from you to cool things down with Fran"). But at the end of those three weeks he had learned to live without her. This "brief hiatus" was the beginning of Forever. And of course he'd planned the whole thing out.

5. *Lack of remorse or guilt?* Absolutely. He never felt either

of these. That time he said to her with an apologetic, helpless, what-can-I-do?-I'm-a-bad-boy look, "Fran keeps telling me I should feel guilty about what I've done to Dina. But I don't. I never have."

6. *Emotionally shallow?* Yes. He seemed to have deep feelings for people, he'd seemed to love her, but he hadn't. What looked like love was actually just need. He didn't feel anything for anyone else. Really he was dead inside.

7. *Callous/lack of empathy?* Oh, yes. That time they were talking on the phone, and Jake told her that at that very moment, Fran was lying sprawled out face-down on their bed, and he could hear her sobbing her eyes out, because she felt he didn't love her anymore. He said this in quite a pleased tone, flattered that two women wanted him and were fighting over him. He felt no empathy for his wife of thirty-eight years. Eve was so frightened by his callousness at that moment, so chilled by it, that she told him on the phone, "You should be kinder to Fran. She loves you and this must be hard for her." And he said, "You have more compassion for her than I do." Which was true.

8. (Last on the list:) *Failure to accept responsibility for own actions?* Yes. He never took responsibility for anything he did. Not with Dina. Not with the boy from his running team. And not with her. If someone had to suffer, it wasn't going to be him. "A man has a right to save himself."

She has finished the list now. Quickly she scans all the items: Glibness/superficial charm, Grandiose sense of self-worth, Pathological lying, Cunning/manipulative, Lack of remorse or guilt, Emotionally shallow, Callous/lack of empathy, Failure to accept responsibility for own actions.

Wow. That is Jake exactly.

The room is totally silent. She notices this, and notices that everyone's looking at her, waiting for her answer.

"Well?" asks Hava.

"Yes," says Eve. Her mouth is dry and she has to push the

next words out with her tongue. "These sound like Jerry. But what is this list? Where is it from?"

"In a moment," Hava says calmly. "But first, tell me: which ones fit with him? And would you say these items characterize him 'somewhat,' 'moderately,' or 'strongly'?"

Eve hesitates. She feels like she is being tested, but she doesn't know for what. She forces out the words: "All of them fit. And all of them strongly."

"All of them, and all of them strongly? Aha!" cries Hava to the class. "Just as I thought! Take a look at this." She bends over her computer again, the screen lighting up her face, giving it a strange glow. "I hope you don't mind," she says as she fiddles with her mouse, "that this article is just from Wikipedia. But lately I have found many of their articles provide excellent, accessible summaries, and they're quite up-to-date."

Eve, together with the rest of the class, looks up at the new text now on the screen, and follows along as Hava reads aloud.

"Psychopathy. Psychopathy is a personality disorder whose hallmark is a lack of empathy."

Psychopathy? Why is Hava showing them *this*?

"Researcher Robert Hare, whose Hare Psychopathy Checklist is widely used, describes psychopaths as 'intraspecies predators who use charisma, manipulation, intimidation, sexual intercourse, and violence to control others, and to satisfy their own needs. Lacking in conscience and empathy, they take what they want and do as they please, violating social norms and expectations without guilt or remorse. What is missing, in other words, are the very qualities that allow a human being to live in social harmony.'"

Eve is getting impatient now. What is Hava doing? Why is she wasting their time like this? They're supposed to be talking about Jake, and Jake is not a psychopath.

"Psychopaths," Hava continues, "are glib and superficially charming, and many psychopaths are excellent mimics of normal human emotion; some psychopaths can blend in, undetected, in a variety of surroundings. There is neither a cure nor any effective treatment for psychopathy; there are no medications or other techniques that can instill empathy, and psychopaths who undergo traditional talk therapy only become more adept at manipulating others. The consensus among researchers is that psychopathy stems from a specific neurological disorder which is biological in origin and present from birth."

Someone's hand goes up. "Just a moment, please," says Hava. She scrolls down further in the article, and starts reading to the class about the clinical assessment of psychopathy. Eve turns her back to the screen and stares at Hava. Hava is explaining that the Hare Psychopathy Checklist, or PCL-R, is the instrument most commonly used, and it yields scores on two factors. Hava is blathering on about one of these being associated with anger, anxiety, criminality, and violence, and the other with extroversion, positive affect, and core psychopathic traits. Hava pauses and looks around the class, her glittering eyes lingering on Eve for a few moments. Eve looks back at her as evenly as she can, hoping that her impatience and annoyance don't show.

"You see," says Hava, "the two scales that Eve used just now to assess Jerry were the two scales from the PCL-R. First I put up Factor 2, and then Factor 1. Jerry does not fit the profile of a Factor 2 psychopath: angry, violent, and with criminal tendencies. But he did score high, in fact he achieved the maximum possible score, on every item of Factor 1. Which means that he has all the core personality traits associated with psychopathy. In other words, Jerry is a classic psychopath."

What? thinks Eve. This is ridiculous. Impossible! Jake's not a psychopath!

As if answering her silent objection, Hava looks away from Eve and says patiently to the rest of the class, "Most people think of psychopaths as serial killers, murderers, kidnappers, or rapists, but actually this isn't the whole story. Psychopathy is a much broader category than this. The murderers, rapists, etc., manifest the Factor 2 traits of psychopathy: impulsivity, irresponsibility, lack of long-term goals, a proneness to boredom, and so on. But primary psychopaths manifest mostly Factor 1 traits: arrogance, lying, callousness, and manipulativeness. So Jerry is the perfect example of a primary psychopath."

Eve is feeling dazed. She can't really take in what Hava is saying. It's unbelievable. Almost like hearing that she herself has just been diagnosed as a psychopath.

"Of course, in order to diagnose Jerry properly," Hava is saying, "you'd need to do a full and proper assessment of him. A checklist alone is never sufficient. But there is no question, no question at all, based on what we've heard here, that we are dealing with a dangerous man. Someone very, very dangerous."

Eve is feeling more disoriented by the second. A couple of students are starting to respond to Hava. The Australian woman disagrees with her: she is convinced that Jake isn't a psychopath, but a sociopath instead. There is some lively back-and-forth between three of the students about the differences between psychopaths and sociopaths. The woman from the southern U.S. believes psychopathy and sociopathy are essentially the same phenomenon. The British man and the Australian woman think these are two distinct types of antisocial personality disorder: psychopaths are born with temperamental differences such as impulsivity and fearlessness that lead them to risk-seeking behavior and an inability to internalize social norms, whereas sociopaths are born with relatively normal temperaments, and their personality disorder is an effect of negative environmental factors like parental neglect, delinquent peers, and poverty. These three students go on for quite a while, until the woman from South America, who sees Jake as a psychopath, says that in the Hare Psychopathy Checklist there is often a lot more overlap between Factor 1 and Factor 2 psychopathy than is usually recognized.

"We shouldn't rule out the possibility in this case," she says, "of criminality or violence in the future."

Eve can't believe this conversation. This isn't Jake they're talking about. Or anyway not the Jake she knows. She is starting to feel quite dizzy. "If you don't mind, I'll sit down," she says, and returns to her seat. But nobody notices or cares. They are all too busy interrupting each other and arguing over exactly in what way Jake is mentally ill.

5. TALBIEH

THE SEMINAR ENDS NOT LONG AFTER, at three o'clock. Eve's mind is spinning and her emotions are churning, so, too agitated to return to her hotel, she goes for a walk instead. The Israeli Institute of Music Therapy is located on Chopin Street (how apt), and without any particular destination in mind, she starts walking, at first briskly and then at an amble, through the old neighbourhood of Talbieh. It's almost silent now in the mid-afternoon with all the old people still napping. She pictures them asleep in their beds, like she and Jake used to nap together in the afternoons. They'd be half-dressed and sweaty in the Jerusalem heat, lying in the tangled bedsheets, so full of love for each other they were defenseless. She now passes a yellowish wall at least twice her height, curving with the street for almost an entire block. What's that there for? she wonders. What's it protecting or concealing? A consulate? Some clandestine base for military defense? A secret garden? So much is hidden, she thinks. Even from ourselves. Or, as her father used to say darkly, from ourselves most of all.

Reaching the end of this wall, she sees a few modest houses of worn brick and instantly recognizes one of them. This is where she used to meet her therapist when she lived here thirty-two years ago. She pauses in front of this house with the prickly bushes in front, paying it a minute of silent respect as she gazes at its faded blue window frames. She wonders what Nadav would make of Hava's diagnosis of Jake. Nadav was psychoanalytic in approach, so she thinks he'd probably agree with Hava. But Eve isn't sure what she herself believes. Even though she knows something is wrong with Jake. (And she knew it then, too.) He had the ability to drop a wall down between them from one second to the next — a steel wall six feet thick, like the ceiling-to-floor doors in prisons that crash shut and make the ground under you tremble with their weight and finality. One minute you were the closest person in the world to Jake. You were his best friend, it was you and him against the world, you and him together and warm inside a womb-like cocoon. And the next thing you knew, you were completely alone, outside in the cold.

The first time this happened, she was at the airport. He had dropped her off an hour and a half before, and in ten minutes she would be boarding her flight back to Canada. But unable to bear parting from him without hearing his voice just one more time, she dialled his number from the departure lounge.

"Hi," she said, expecting the usual warmth and love. The long, drawn-out "Helloooooo!" that always showed her, by the music in his tone, how happy he was to hear from her.

But this time he just said, "Yes?" Almost as if he didn't recognize her voice. So business-like and brusque that for a moment she thought she had dialled the wrong number. But no, she knew Jake's voice and English accent. It was him.

"I just wanted to say goodbye again," she said lamely, almost stammering she felt so awkward. "Since there's a pay phone in the lounge."

"Oh," he said. And there was silence. There had never been silence between them before. Or anyway, not this type of silence. She forced herself to say a few more things, and Jake, sounding very distant, responded. But she got off the phone in just a minute or two. It was clear he didn't want to be talking to her. He was done with her. He'd dropped her off at the airport, he had finished with that project and now he was on to the next one. The next one being how he was going to cope with Fran's return from England in less than ten hours.

After they said goodbye and she heard the click on the phone of Jake hanging up on her, she stood perfectly still, holding the cold metal receiver in her left hand, frowning. She just stood there like that until the loudspeaker boomed out the boarding announcement for her flight. For the entire ride home, she doubted herself. Maybe I'm crazy, she thought. Maybe what I thought happened between me and Jake on this trip never really happened. Maybe I imagined the whole thing.

And she doubted Jake, too. Did he love her or didn't he? Was she something to him — in fact, the person he loved most in the world — or nothing? Maybe she was nothing to him.

But then she got home and found a tender, loving, passionate email from him, and all her doubts disappeared.

Until the next time it happened.

There must be a name for this, she thinks, gazing at Nadav's old building. It wasn't personal to her, she knows (much as it felt totally, agonizingly personal at the time). Jake did the same thing to Fran. Maybe he did this to all women. Or all people. This cutting-off thing of his. Turning ice cold on you, and lacking in all feeling or empathy when you least expected it. Like you're swimming in the warm bath-like waters of the Gulf Stream and suddenly you hit a frigid current from Iceland. But so what? she argues with Hava and Nadav. This is true of lots of people in the world. All sorts of people are self-centered and unfeeling. Since when does this mean that someone is mentally ill? Where exactly does the moral meet the psychological? Maybe all these people aren't mentally ill. Maybe they're just shmucks.

Eve resumes her walk now through Talbieh's peaceful, sun-mottled streets, a little surprised that she is defending Jake. But she doesn't want to accept Hava's diagnosis. What would it say about her, after all, if for the past five and a half years she has been in love with a psychopath? Now she stops walking. A powerful, sweet scent is assailing her nostrils. It's honeysuckle, her favourite fragrance, wafting from a beautiful flowering bush on her right that's exploding with delicate white blossoms. Gently she tugs at the lowest branch and sniffs. Then she stands there for a while, repeatedly inhaling the aroma in a kind of ecstasy. As sweet as a narcotic, she thinks, that you can't resist.

Like Jake. Jake whom she couldn't resist. She stayed with him, sniffing him, licking him, kissing him, even when she knew he was disturbed. (Yes, she had known. Of course she had known.) The first time she had an inkling of this, they were lying in bed in the hotel. It was their third day together there, their third day of non-stop talk and sex and music, and she, exhausted and needing something un-intense and brainless, reached for the remote and clicked on the TV. The man on the screen hadn't finished a single sentence before Jake, who had grabbed the remote from her, clicked it off.

"We're not going to waste our precious time together on that nonsense, are we?" he asked, while she gazed longingly at the dead screen. She knew about Jake's contempt for TV, but she also knew that this wasn't just that. He was jealous. He wanted all her attention for himself. She had noticed already that whenever she talked to him about her boys, he would fall frostily silent or abruptly change the topic. It was like she wasn't allowed to love, or enjoy, anyone or anything but him. Continuing her walk now, she sighs. She could understand — though she didn't like it — Jake being jealous of her two marvellous boys. But to be jealous of a TV set? Crazy.

Crazy. And controlling, too. She had to share everything with him — everything, however minute — whether in her mind, heart, or body. What she was thinking and feeling every single moment. He even wanted to know where in her body — where exactly — her desire for him began. At first she enjoyed this. She was flattered by his ardent interest, his hunger to know everything about her. She found it romantic, and she loved the way he listened to her — as closely, raptly, and admiringly as if she were a piece of beautiful music. But once she had been back in Canada for a few weeks, it started to feel claustrophobic. They emailed each other at least four times a day, long elaborate letters describing everything they did, thought, and felt, and this took hours out of her day, and much effort. Everything she experienced had to be described, documented, and analyzed. If she went out for a walk, met a friend for lunch, or attended a concert, she needed to tell Jake every single detail. What she saw on her walk. What she ate and talked about with her friend. Who performed at the concert, what they played, and what her assessment was of the music. What she thought about when she got home and was lying in bed. (Did she think about him? And if not, why not?) She wasn't allowed any privacy at all.

Eve strolls along the silent street, oblivious to the chill in the air. What did that man say in class today? "No boundaries." Exactly. There were no boundaries. That's actually what she liked at first. Wasn't that what being in love was all about? But after a few weeks of spending two to three hours a day writing letters to Jake, she began to feel strangulated, like a calf with a rope around its neck. Tightening. Tightening. Everything she had, everything that was hers, had to be shared, had to be given away to Jake. Nothing could remain just hers anymore.

Even her own music. Even there he invaded. One day he started taking an interest in *Hallelujah*, the oratorio she was composing, and began making comments and suggestions.

"We can make it our project," he said enthusiastically on their first transatlantic call, two and a half weeks after Eve's return to Canada. (A call she paid for, like all four of their phone calls, since she had bought a cheap calling card for this purpose.) "I can't compose by myself," he said, "but together we can. And since we're not going to have a real baby together, we need some other joint project. Some other 'baby.' So *Hallelujah* can be it."

She didn't want to compose with Jake. She had never composed with anyone else, and couldn't even imagine how that would work. But she didn't want to disappoint him. So she allowed him to give her feedback, and she began shaping her music to bring it in line with his suggestions and taste. Pretty soon she wasn't writing her own music anymore. And after a while, for the first time in her life, she found she couldn't compose at all. It was also around then that she became frequently short of breath. As if she were literally being strangled.

So on their second phone call, four and a half weeks after she left Israel, as gently as she could, she told Jake that although she was still in love with him, and he was still everything to her, she needed a little more breathing space in this relationship. She was feeling somewhat strangulated. And then, since he liked rhymes and always laughed at her cleverness with them, she gave him a rhyme to lighten things up.

"Strangulated and triangulated," she said.

"Triangulated" was what she picked as her rhyme-word because, over the past few weeks, he had started dragging Fran, one way or another, into every single conversation, whether on the phone or in their letters. Not only did Eve not want to have to tell Jake everything about her life anymore; she also did not want to have to be hearing everything about his, either. He was sharing the most intimate details about his life with Fran, details that made Eve cringe or blush. About their sex life, for instance — or more precisely, the gory details of the lack thereof. He also told her about Fran's fierce and hopeless struggle with her body (she was seventy-two pounds overweight), and about her tears and tantrums over Jake's love for Eve. (Fran had guessed fairly quickly what was going on, and Jake hadn't denied it.) On their first phone call, he had told Eve that on the previous day, Fran had thrown a dish at him and said he'd destroyed her self-esteem as a woman.

Eve winced. "I really shouldn't be hearing this," she said.

"But who else can I tell?" he asked her. "I have no one else to talk to but you."

And she, fool that she was, had felt touched by this, and said nothing. So he kept on doing it. And the truth is that although it was embarrassing to hear all about Fran, it was also gratifying. If Jake was talking to her like this about Fran, then it meant that she (Eve) was his #1 woman, and Fran merely #2. It pleased Eve to hear about Fran's vulnerabilities and most intimate secrets, so she accepted the triangle game.

Until, that is, Jake started telling Fran about Eve's vulnerabilities and most intimate secrets. About her childhood, for instance, or what she was like in bed — exactly what she said or did when she came.

"You told her that?" cried Eve. It was unbearable. Humiliating. She begged him to stop sharing personal information about her with Fran. She entreated him to promise he wouldn't do this anymore. She told him it made her feel violated, as if he had left the door open while they were making love so Fran could peek in and watch. Or worse, as if the three of them were in bed together.

But Jake made light of it. He even joked once that having "two wives" was no big deal, since his namesake, Jacob in the Bible, had had not just two women, but four (two wives and two concubines).

"Imagine that," he said with admiring wonder.

So now, with all this between them, Eve complained to him about triangulation and strangulation. Jake, for the first time ever, didn't laugh at one of her rhymes. There was silence on the phone. (Their second bad silence.) Then he told Eve coldly that if their relationship wasn't to her liking, she was free to leave it at any time. He said that from his point of view, they could end it right then and there. She was so shocked, and so frightened at the prospect of losing him, that she never criticized him again.

6. THE PARKETTE

S HE FINDS HERSELF NOW OUTSIDE of Talbieh, in front of
a neighbourhood parkette. She is bored and fed up with
herself and with thinking about Jake. Enough already,
he's not the whole world, she tells herself as she sits down
near the entrance to the parkette on a bench. Two dogs, one
white and one black, frolic together on the sparse grass next
to the slide. Darkness and light. Yael and Dina. A man and a
woman standing a little way apart (apparently each the owner
of one of the dogs) watch their pets with indulgent smiles. Then
the man and woman smile at each other and exchange a few
words. They look away and then smile at each other again.
Perhaps they'll hook up. Eve has heard of dogs bringing their
owners together. The man looks pleasant enough, but who
knows? Maybe he's a psychopath. Maybe the woman is, too.
After all, it takes two to tango.

I knew, she thinks, watching the dogs. I pretended not to,
but I did. *Take responsibility*, as her friend Reut always says.
Eve did try to save herself, though. She wasn't a total passive
wimp. But, by the time she realized something was wrong, it
was already too late. She could only watch helplessly as, re-
volving her life around Jake's, she gradually lost not just her
sense of self-confidence, but her very sense of self. It was like
watching someone in a movie, someone who (no matter how
much you care about them) you can't do anything to help.
Jake, inch by inch, took her over. He moved into her mind

and soul as swiftly and casually as if he were moving into an apartment. Settling in, inhabiting her, all the floor space, and walls, and air inside her, filling up all her inner space with himself. He replaced her, replacing her blood with his, like in a blood transfusion, until there was nothing left of just her anymore. There was no more Eve-without-Jake.

Because of this, there was also no more music in her. Not just no composing; there was no music at all. Only silence inside her. Not the living, breathing, fertile, creative silence that she sought, and found, in solitude, and loved. No, this was different. It was dead silence. And she herself felt dead.

But Jake, she believed — Jake and only Jake — could bring her back to life.

A new dog, a Doberman Pinscher, enters the parkette, ignoring, even snubbing, the two dogs that are already there. It trots in, head high, carrying in its mouth a limp doll that at first Eve, with shock, mistakes for a dead baby. The Doberman Pinscher stands perfectly still in front of its owner, a small, round-cheeked old woman. Gently she removes the doll from the dog's mouth and, with a surprising show of strength, hurls it far away for him to fetch. The dog comes running back, panting, his quarry between his teeth, and again stands perfectly still before his mistress. Eve watches this scene repeat itself over and over, five, ten, fifteen times, mesmerized by its rhythm. I did try to save myself, she thinks. I did.

Six weeks after returning to Canada, she tried to take a day away from Jake. She had to extricate herself, she decided, before all the life in her leaked out like blood onto the ground, leaving nothing there but an empty sack of flesh. So on a Tuesday afternoon she emailed him that until Thursday morning she was going to be incommunicado — away from her computer, her phone, everything. She was going to spend all day Wednesday at Toronto Island, she wrote him, just to be alone and think.

"How I envy you," he immediately wrote back.

But she couldn't do it. After an hour and a half of kicking stones along the gravelly beach, of feeling her pale skin burn in the almost-midday sun, of gazing at the thrashing ugly grey water and listening to the anguished cries of sea gulls, she stopped pretending to herself that she was doing anything other than writing letters to Jake in her head (describing to him every rock and person she passed, the exact colour of the sky and sun, and the way the beach smelled: dryness and wetness mixed together because of the sand and sea; suntan lotion, French fries, and sweat). She raced back home to her computer to devour the letter he had written during her absence: a long, flowing, eloquent letter about how achingly he missed her. And then she wrote him back, an especially long letter (five pages single-spaced), writing it anxiously, apologetically, with all the passion she could muster, to compensate Jake for abandoning him.

The Doberman Pinscher once again delivers the doll obediently to the old woman. Back then I couldn't be separate from Jake, thinks Eve. I couldn't be away from him for even a full morning. I was completely dependent on him, like a heroin addict. As if Jake and I, through needles in our arms, were attached to each other by the same rubber tube, and I thought of this tube as my lifeline (my umbilical cord), when in fact it was draining all the life out of me and transferring it over to Jake. Sort of like a joint bank account where one person keeps depositing into it at one end, and the other person keeps emptying it at the other. Jake got stronger by the day through our relationship, and I grew weaker and weaker. As though we'd made a devil's pact: I would carry all the weakness that was in both of us, and he'd carry all the strength. By the time he finally threw me away, there was almost nothing left of me. I was a starving mangy dog, nothing but skin and bones. A starving mangy drug addict. But still I clung to him around the knees. *Please don't send me away. Please, I'll do anything. Just don't leave me or send me away.*

7. TO GO OR NOT TO GO
(TO THE CONFERENCE)

A T ONE EDGE OF THE PARKETTE, on the corner of a street facing a row of houses, Eve spots a silver pay phone. She glares at this phone. It glares back at her daringly. "Come on," it's saying to her. "Here I am. *Hineni*. Use me."

I could, thinks Eve. I could call Jake right now. I could call and then hang up on him, as usual. Or I could even call him and then stay on the phone for a while, actually talk to him. She gives a little laugh. What would she even have to say to Jake — the real Jake, not the one in her head — after all these years? I love you? I hate you? Neither of these is precisely true. She doesn't even know exactly what she feels anymore. Mainly she's just tired of all this now. She wants this to be over and done with, once and for all.

She approaches the pay phone. It watches her with gloating. It knew it could break her resistance. She inserts her tiger phone card and dials.

"I'm here," she says.

"Eve!" cries her friend Reut. The two of them have been friends since the old days when Eve used to live here, when they were both single. Reut is delighted to hear Eve is in Jerusalem.

"Come for supper tomorrow night," she says. "Tonight I'm working, but tomorrow's fine."

Eve says, "I'm not sure, I'll have to see." While Reut chatters on, bringing her up to date on everything, Eve, though she meant to listen to Reut, finds herself extracting from her purse, and then scanning, the conference program Miranda gave her at the airport (dog-eared and crumpled by now from all the times she has looked at it since then). The conference starts tomorrow evening with an opening banquet. As she examines the rest of the schedule, she sees that Miranda was right. Everyone's going to be there. Everyone who's anyone in Jewish music. Including a couple of people she has been admiring for years from afar and would love to meet. (And who, if they wanted to, could also help her get *Hallelujah* performed.) Reut is telling her all about her husband's new job and her horrible stepmother — who sounds quite a lot like Eve's stepmother Julia — and Eve is half-listening, but with the other half she is thinking, I should go. I really should. What an amazing coincidence that this international conference on Jewish music is taking place right now when I just happen to be in Jerusalem. This could be the breakthrough opportunity I've been waiting for.

"Why can't you come for supper tomorrow?" Reut's now asking bluntly.

Eve tells her about the opening banquet of the conference. Meanwhile her stomach is curdling. What if Jake is there? she is thinking. She can't go if Jake is there. True, he isn't listed in the program. But there's no way he won't show up at least once during the whole three days of this conference. It's impossible: the world's leading authority on Jewish music, living just one hour away.

"I may not go, though," she says.

"Why not?" asks Reut. When Eve doesn't answer, she says, "Not because of Jake, I hope." When again Eve doesn't answer, Reut groans, "Oh, Eve. Come *on*."

Eve is seeing herself now at the Van Leer Institute, standing among the throngs in the sophisticated, elegant, spiralling lobby where everyone will congregate before the banquet starts. She is standing there by herself when Jake appears before her.

She won't be able to handle it. She won't be able to look into those sharp icicle-blue eyes. They'll drill right through her. And his mouth — that mouth so strangely familiar to her from the first time she saw it — she'll stare at it like an idiot. At his lips, and his tongue while he speaks, and she won't be able to hear a word he's saying. Or answer him, either. She'll be speechless, unable to utter a single word. She'll drop her eyes to the ground like an abashed (or a bashed) child.

"Eve," Reut's now saying indignantly. "You can't not go because of Jake!"

"Sure I can," says Eve, annoyed, almost angry, with her old friend.

"No, you can't," insists Reut. "You're shrinking your world smaller and smaller each time you come here, in order to avoid seeing him. Soon you won't even be able to leave your hotel room, and then you'll stop coming here at all. You're turning into an agoraphobic."

To herself Eve admits that Reut has a point. She's had to miss out on dozens of events while visiting Israel over the past five years. She has had to avoid going to Tel Aviv, especially to anywhere near Jake's neighbourhood (which is not far from where some of the trendiest restaurants and theatres are) in case she bumps into him there. She has also had to avoid all musical events, and not just in Tel Aviv, but anywhere in the country. Including, last year at this time, a fabulous concert that she had wanted to go to, not least of all because of the post-concert party that followed it, which was supposed to be attended by some great Israeli musicians and composers, among them a few celebrities. It was Reut who had invited her since she was on the fundraising committee for this event. And even though she knew all about Jake, she was still astounded when Eve refused to come because she was afraid he'd be there.

"I'm only like this in Israel; in Canada I'm fine," Eve says reassuringly to Reut, though she knows this is only half-true. Sure, it's harder here in Israel than in Canada. Here she is just an hour away from Jake's house. But even in Toronto she has to avoid things. Any lecture on Israeli or Jewish music, for instance, in case he gets quoted there, which he very often does. Ditto for Jewish music shows or interviews on the radio, TV, or Internet, for the same reason. And she has not only had to cancel her subscription to *Niggun* because of his articles there; she has to be extremely cautious when she reads any Jewish newspaper or magazine: the *Canadian Jewish News*, the *Jerusalem Report*, *Ha'aretz*, and any one of a dozen more. Because at least half a dozen times in recent years, Jake has ambushed her, leaped at her off the page, and he could again at any moment. Either with words or with the picture that all these newspapers were carrying a few months back to promote his latest book. Jake in a black t-shirt and brown corduroy jacket talking animatedly, Jewishly, with his hands. Reaching out beyond the photo, trying to persuade the person viewing it of something. His hands outstretched beseechingly toward her.

Reut knows better than to be reassured. She stays on the phone for a while longer with her friend, trying to convince her to attend the conference.

"You can't not go," she urges Eve. "You can't give Jake this power over your life. Think of all the interesting people you can meet at this conference, and the professional opportunities this could open up for you. It's a gift from heaven."

Eve just grunts in response.

Reut is silent for a moment and then tries a new tack. Gently she says, "There's nothing to be afraid of, Eve. If you see him, you see him. You say hello. Or you don't say hello. That's all there is to it. End of story."

When Eve still doesn't answer, Reut adds, in blunt Israeli fashion, "Don't come over for supper tomorrow night. I'm disinviting you. I don't want to see you here. On the weekend, sure. But tomorrow night you be at that banquet."

"I love you, too," says Eve, smiling, and hangs up.

8. KING DAVID STREET

VE, WITH NO DESTINATION IN MIND, resumes her stroll. Half a block from the parkette, she steps down onto the road to make room on the sidewalk for a religious woman with a double stroller bearing twin babies, and next to it, a whiny little boy dragging along reluctantly, wanting to be picked up and carried. In Hebrew the woman says, "Thank you" and Eve says, "You're welcome." Then she continues her walk more cheerfully, feeling less alone, and seven minutes later she turns onto King David Street. The centre of that street is jammed with stalled, white, honking cars that remind her of stupid, ornery, bleating sheep, but on both sides of this white herd, the sidewalks vibrate with colour and life. There are South Americans in bright striped ponchos, Greek Orthodox priests in flowing black robes, and a pale young girl in pink shorts. There are also Arabs and Jews, Ethiopians and Druze, and she hears, along with Hebrew, Arabic, and English, smatterings of French, Russian, and Amharic. All these people, filling the sidewalks, bob up and down and sweep forward together.

She is surprised at how congested the sidewalk is; she doesn't recall King David Street this way. Then she remembers her neighbour on the plane. Ah! It's Christmastime, it's all the Christian tourists, and there are undoubtedly some Chanukah tourists here, too. Like this thirty-something couple now walking toward her: the man with a knapsack on his back and the woman wearing a *Magen David* on her necklace, each of them with a camera slung over the shoulder. Now they're entering an art gallery with a sign on the door welcoming tourists and promising them a tax rebate when they leave the country. Eve steps toward this gallery and, grateful to be out of the maelstrom of people she can feel rushing now behind her back, gazes into the window. Junk. Kitsch. The sort of crap she wouldn't put up on her wall even if she got it as a gift (much less being willing to pay for it). Three thousand five hundred dollars they're asking for that monstrosity in the window: a dog over a moon, a third-rate — no, seventh-rate — imitation of a Chagall. Poor Chagall, he must be turning in his grave, she thinks. God, people are stupid. They'll buy this shit in the window — they'll even consider it "good" because it costs a lot of money, or because someone told them it's good — but my beautiful *Hallelujah* nobody wants. Disgusted, she leaves the window and walks on. It's very discouraging. But at least she knows the true value of her music.

Thanks, most recently, to Jake.

"You have great talent," he said to her. "You have the potential to be a world-class composer."

They were at the conference. The conference on Jewish music where they met. The two of them had been on a panel together that morning. Jake loved her presentation, and presenting right after her, had praised her originality and courage, and the innovative approach she took to exploring new forms of Jewish music. Then they strolled together, chatting, to the dining room and sat next to each other at lunch, and partway into the main course (finding the dining room so noisy they couldn't hear each other), they slipped down the hall to the music library, where they talked for three hours straight. After about forty-five minutes, they noticed that the first session of the afternoon was about to begin, and with self-conscious little laughs, feeling naughty, they decided to skip it so they could continue their conversation. They skipped the next session, too, and then the one after that. As the afternoon progressed, they talked more and more eagerly and intensely, leaning closer toward each other, both of them slightly flushed, and once in a while she, in her enthusiasm, would touch Jake on the arm. By this time she was feeling very comfortable with him. Early on in their conversation, he had asked her to call him Jake because that's what his friends called him, and she had been ever since. She felt like they'd met before and knew each other somehow, even though she knew they hadn't. All afternoon they talked and laughed. Then, in the late afternoon, the light in the room slightly greyed as it slanted downwards from the elegant high windows, and she asked him if he'd like to see something she had written.

"It's a *Kaddish Concerto*," she said.

"A *Kaddish Concerto*?" he asked, a flicker of interest in his eyes, like a match suddenly struck. They were sitting quite close to each other in two black armchairs almost touching, positioned at ninety-degree angles to each other, and he, in his eagerness, leaned forward even closer.

"Yes," she said. "A fusion of Jewish purpose with classical form."

"Sure!" he said. "I'd love to see it."

She knew that this music library had a copy of her *Kaddish Concerto,* because a year and a half before, when it won that Jewish music prize, she had come here to give a talk about it. "I'll be right back," she said, and hurried down to the stacks to find it. Five minutes later she returned with the manuscript in hand, but Jake wasn't in his seat. He stood in the middle of the library, searching anxiously all around the room. When he saw Eve approach, he looked visibly relieved.

"I thought you weren't coming back," he said.

"What do you mean?" she asked, confused. Why would he think she'd run out on him like that? "I just went to get this from the stacks." She handed him her *Kaddish Concerto* and he took it back to his seat and began to read. Too nervous to sit in her chair and watch his face while he read her score, she waited at the far end of the library, near the bathrooms. When she had first heard she was going to be on the same panel as Jacob Gladstone, she was totally intimidated. For twenty years she had been listening to his radio programs and reading his books, articles, and essays on Jewish music, and she had even used his classic *What's Jewish About Jewish Music?* as a key reference in her Master's thesis. So for her, Jacob Gladstone was almost Jewish music itself. Watching him now from the furthest end of the library, she could barely believe that this great man was reading her score. She had thought of this idea, of showing him her *Kaddish Concerto*, in the days leading up to the conference. Back then, when the name Jacob Gladstone just meant someone extremely famous and powerful. Whereas now he was (well, still that too, of course, but also) her new friend Jake: a white-haired man with warm, twinkly eyes in a lined face.

Now the lines in this face were frowning. He was reading very intensely and there was no way to tell from his expression whether he liked or disliked what he was reading. She watched him, barely breathing. Finally he closed the red volume, threw it down on the table in front of him, and sat back for a minute with his eyes shut. Then he opened them, scanned the room for Eve, strode over to where she was standing, and gave her a very quick kiss on the lips — a kiss that was forceful, though, and in a certain way, passionate.

"It's wonderful," he said. "*You're* wonderful."

She, stunned by the kiss, just stared at him.

"You have great talent," he said. "You have the potential to be a world-class composer."

Still she just stared.

"You're a real musician," he said. And then, with hunger, he searched her eyes: "But you know that already, don't you?"

She smiled, shrugging, and lowered her eyes to the floor. Of course she knew that. And not only because her *Kaddish*

Concerto had won a prize. But still it was deeply gratifying to hear it, especially from the great Jacob Gladstone. Now she looked up at him again. They were standing close together right in the middle of the music library, and for what felt like a long time they gazed at each other. Then she was aware of the people all around them, some of them from the conference. She wondered if anyone had seen Jake kiss her.

"I have one small comment, though," he was saying.

Now she recognized, not far off, the man who had sat next to her at the banquet the night before. He had tried flirting with her a little bit, and now he was lingering nearby and watching her, as if waiting for Jake to finish so he could have his turn. Jake, following her gaze, said, "Poor Cadjman. He looks like someone who's had his cookie stolen away."

She laughed. That was exactly what he looked like. "You're right," she said. Then, more soberly, "What's your one small comment?"

Jake paused for a bit, studying her carefully before answering. "The second repeat," he said, watching her, gauging her reaction. "It wasn't necessary. You were fine without it."

He was smart; he'd put his finger on the one false note in her whole *Kaddish Concerto*. The one self-indulgence. "I know," she said. "It was silly." And she grinned at him and shrugged.

Jake, after a few seconds, laughed with relief and joy. "I *knew* it," he said. "I knew that with you I could say exactly what I think. That I don't have to hold anything back." Then he added, "You know, with someone less talented, I wouldn't even have mentioned something so small. But you..." — he leaned closer to her — "you I will always hold only to the highest standard."

Eve felt entranced. *You I will always hold.* Would he always hold her? And what did he mean by *always*? She was a bit dazed and disoriented by his compliments (which were much more than she had even dared hope for), and also by his intimate, affectionate tone.

Now he looked at his watch and said, "I need to get my things. I have to go to the airport soon."

Numbly she nodded. Still feeling on her lips the reverberations of his kiss, she followed him out of the library and down the hall to the cloakroom, where he picked up his bag and overcoat, and then around the corner to the front desk, where he ordered a cab. Then the two of them stood on the curb of the busy street with the cars whizzing by, while they waited for his taxi to come. Standing there, she felt safe, the way she'd felt as a little girl at the curb with her father, waiting for him to take her hand and lead her across the street. But now she also felt surprisingly emotional. At one level she understood perfectly well what was going on. This man had come to Toronto for a three-day conference, and now he was going home to Tel Aviv. But at another level she couldn't understand it at all. They had just had this amazing conversation, the kind you have only a few times in your life. There had been almost immediately an unusually deep connection between them. They'd just begun to get to know each other. How could he be leaving her now?

Jake was anxiously scanning the street for his cab. He kept glancing worriedly at his watch and seemed to have almost forgotten she was there. Honking cars raced by, splashing mud from the rain puddles up toward the curb, and she instinctively stepped back a few inches, without even noticing. She was so overwhelmed by intense emotions that she couldn't think of a single word to say to Jake. But then she blurted out, "Will I see you again?"

Jake, who had been looking up and down the street, smiled first at the street, and then turned his smile on her. "I certainly hope so," he said, looking down at her from his height. "I would like that very much." He fumbled around in the inside pocket of his coat. "Here," he said, and held out to her one of his business cards. "If you ever come to Israel, give me a call. I'd love to hear from you."

She stared at his mouth (that familiar-feeling mouth) and then took his card. But she felt strange now, like none of this was really happening. Slowly she began to read the words on his card. Very slowly, one at a time. Then, sensing something, she looked up. His taxi had arrived. And half a minute later he was gone.

*

Eve, tramping now down King David Street, is smiling. Even after all these years, it gives her pleasure to remember that first afternoon. How he praised her. How he said she was wonderful. But how ironic that out of everyone in the world, the one person who knows the true value of her music is Jake. It's like Salieri and Mozart in *Amadeus*. The one person capable of appreciating Mozart's genius was his enemy who constantly obstructed his success. Not that she's Mozart, and Jake isn't actively obstructing her. But he is also not helping her. And the music world being what it is, that's almost the same thing. Now a dirty, dishevelled man, staggering toward Eve, nearly crashes into her. He veers to the side and violently spits out something into the road, making a retching sound, and then stumbles toward her. Nauseated, she gives him a wide berth, but she can smell him as he passes her: a mixture of tobacco, dried sweat, urine, poverty, and despair.

She hurries on, and soon after, panting, sits down gratefully on a black wrought-iron bench that she knew somehow would be there. She can feel the iron digging into her thighs through her thin slacks. From somewhere there's a smell of perfume in the air, nearby a man is shouting, hawking hot twisted bagels from a box around his neck, and across the street, exactly facing her, stands the noble King David Hotel. The hotel that was bombed in 1946 by the Irgun, snapping off its entire right wing like a piece of matzoh. Yet here it still stands in all its elegance. She squints in the late afternoon sunlight as she watches the people coming out through the hotel's stately front door. A dark-skinned man with a fez. Then a sunburnt, pudgy man of about forty, looking like a child with his round pink cheeks and chubby legs and his huge lime-green shorts with pink flowers splashed all over them. Probably American. Then an attractive woman emerges, wearing a snug little black dress and glamorous sunglasses, looking remarkably like Sophia Loren.

How, wonders Eve, could I ever have believed that a man could make me into the person I wanted to be? Beautiful. Sexy like Sophia Loren. Not to mention a world-famous composer. She gives a bitter little laugh (causing the old woman next to her on the bench to glance at her and then look away). It's so stupid, it's almost funny, she thinks. Prince Charming will make all your dreams come true. How could I have fallen for something so idiotic — a woman of my intelligence? But no, that's not the right question, she answers herself, facing the hotel across the street. It's: How could I *not* have fallen for that? I was raised — all of us girls were raised — to believe this nonsense from the day we were born. They were reading us *Cinderella, Sleeping Beauty*, and *Snow White* from before we could even talk. *Some day my prince will come…* She had actually sung that solo in a school play. Eve moves over on the bench to make room for a large woman and her skinny boy and girl. *Some day.* Some day a man will press the magic button on the doll (on her back, or her neck, or her clitoris), and she will start to move jerkily in time to the man's music, dancing to his beat (or his beatings), and only then will her "real life" begin. The man's touch, or magic kiss, will awaken her from death, or from sleep, or virginity, or from just plain waiting. Which are all the same thing. Since waiting is a form of death.

The doorman of the King David is wearing a dark blue uniform with gold buttons, and all this time he has been standing at attention to the right of the front portal. Now, with a slight bow, he pulls open the door for a man hurrying up the steps toward the entrance. The tall, dark doorman looks familiar; she studies his face. Maybe he was the doorman back then, too. When she and Jake were in room 1008. A room that had forest green walls, and when the moonlight came pouring in through the floor-to-ceiling window, it felt like she and Jake were in The Forest of Arden, in *A Midsummer Night's Dream* or *As You Like It*. Their first night in this room, there was a full moon, and it lit up the forest-room so brightly that even when they closed the heavy damask curtains, it felt not like night, but daytime. She and Jake by then had been in frequent contact ever since she had arrived in Israel nine days earlier. They had seen each other four times in person, for a few hours each time, when Jake drove in to Jerusalem to see her, and they'd talked on the phone at least twice a day, often three or four times. But this was their first time sharing a room or making love. They'd fooled around together, of course, but she had wanted to wait to make love. She'd needed to feel ready, she said. Then she was, and on the ninth day, Jake drove from Tel Aviv to Jerusalem with an overnight bag, to spend the last four days with her before she returned to Canada.

That night, when she stood before him naked, he said, "I want to kiss every inch of your body."

And he did.

After they'd made love, they talked and made love again and talked some more and then he sang to her and then they made love a third time. Afterwards, while he slept, she lay in bed, staring at the moon. She wasn't someone who had ever had sexual problems. She had always thought of her sex life as satisfactory. But now, lying next to Jake, she understood that she had never really had sex before. Until this night, she had, in a sense, been a virgin. A married-for-fifteen-years fifty-year-old virgin.

Not that Jake was a particularly experienced lover. On the contrary. She had just discovered to her astonishment that he had never in his life done anything but the missionary position. "Fran didn't want to," he explained, blushing, when Eve, obviously amazed, asked him why.

Ultimately, though, his sexual inexperience didn't matter. Lying in bed on that moonlit night, she felt that all this time, all through the years of her adult life, she had just been waiting. Waiting, without even realizing it, for someone to come along and touch her the way Jake had. Because when he touched her, she felt like he wasn't touching just her body; he was touching *her*. Why it was like this with him and not with anyone before, she had no idea. But it was undeniable. They knew each other's bodies somehow, without saying a single word. Everything she felt, and wanted, he, without being told, understood and responded to. And she felt everything that was in him, too. They were like one body.

*

The next morning they ate breakfast in their room, sitting in gold-coloured armchairs across from each other, naked. Included in the price of the room was an all-you-can-eat buffet, an elaborate, generous interpretation of the traditional Israeli breakfast. Since Jake was afraid of bumping into anyone he knew at the hotel, it was Eve, that first morning and every morning thereafter, who took the elevator downstairs to the dining room and shlepped back up to their room a tray piled so high and so heavily with food that it kept them sated till the mid-afternoon. She brought them a little of everything from the beautifully laid-out buffet, the "*shulchan aruch*," in the hotel dining room. There was smoked salmon, herring, whitefish, and carp, cut-up carrots, radishes, onions, cucumbers, and tomatoes, breads, rolls, and pastries, jams, jellies, marmalades, and spreads, four flavours of yogurt, seven varieties of cheese, olives green and black, eggs prepared any way you wanted, pancakes, waffles, and moussaka, fresh-squeezed juices (orange, grapefruit, or apple), a bowl of dates, figs, raisins, and sunflower seeds, an enormous platter of pineapple, melons, and berries, and coffee, tea, or hot chocolate. That buffet was the epitome of Abundance, Beauty, and Diversity. Not unlike the sex they had over those five days. Abundant, diverse (they tried, starting on the second evening, lots of different things), and beautiful. Always beautiful.

When she got back to the room that first morning with the tray, she and Jake ate hungrily without speaking, the only sounds being their cutlery clattering against their plates, the gentle slurping of sweet cocoa and strong, fragrant coffee, and the occasional grunt of appreciation for the food. They ate facing each other, sitting in the two gold-coloured armchairs with the round coffee table in between them, and Jake's long, lanky legs stretched out before him like a cowboy's. As soon as they'd finished their breakfast, the two of them climbed back into bed. Bed for them was the place for everything except food. It was for sex, of course, but also for listening to music and talking. The previous evening, before making love for the first time, they'd been sitting on the bed, talking, and he asked her what her father did.

She laughed. "You mean, 'Does the girl come from a good family'?"

Jake, a little embarrassed, chuckled and shrugged. "Something like that."

Eve didn't like this question at the best of times, but she especially did not like Jake asking it now. His timing made this feel like a test, as if her father's status were her entrance ticket (like the entrance ticket into a movie) to Jake's body and love.

She sighed. "All right, let's get this over with," she said. And she told him what her father did for a living before he retired.

Jake's eyes opened wide. "Wow!" he said. "Really?"

Eve hated how people always got so impressed by this. So what that he was once the national Minister of Health? she thought. Someone has to be the national Minister of Health. Jake was going on and on now about her father, clearly excited by his prominent position. She put up with it for a while, and then said, "Can we stop talking about my father now? Isn't there anything more interesting that we could be doing?"

Jake stopped talking about her father. They kissed. And then started to make love.

Now, after their first breakfast, they lay in bed and talked about Israel. Jake was surprised and delighted to discover that she, like him, loved Israel passionately, and that thirty-two years before, she had made *aliyah* the very same month that he had. He'd been thirty-four then, not twenty like her, and he'd been married and financially independent, so his father, unlike Eve's, hadn't been able to make him come home. You got to stay in Israel, she thought, looking at Jake. You did what I wanted to do. What I should have done. You fulfilled the dream.

Just then the phone rang. It was the front desk calling to clarify her departure date, and of course she answered the phone (the hotel didn't even know of Jake's existence). After she hung up, Jake, his face full of admiration, said he was very impressed by her Hebrew. She spoke it beautifully, he said, better than many people he knew who'd lived here for the past thirty years. She glowed. Jake was pedantic, almost fanatical, about the Hebrew language, so coming from him this was a high compliment. They talked about languages then: they both knew French, Hebrew, and Yiddish, and it pleased Jake to no end that she had Yiddish. They chatted for a bit in Yiddish, which she had rarely spoken with anyone but her father, whose first language it was. Then she told him she also knew Latin and Greek (she had studied them in high school), and he was again very impressed. Even envious, he said.

After that they listened to music together. Jake had brought some CDs from Tel Aviv that he wanted her to hear, and it turned out, to her surprise, that he had precisely the same taste in classical music as her father (Mozart, Schubert, and Brahms being favourites). She had been brought up on her father's tastes, so this first time that she and Jake listened to music together, they already loved and knew intimately many of the same pieces. This was also true of the Jewish music they listened to that day, some of which was Pesach music since Pesach was around the corner. They both loved Srul Irving Glick's *Music for Passover*, and agreed that this album and his his *Triumph of the Spirit* were "in a class of their own." But it turned out that they had also both been listening to other works that the other didn't know anything about. Jake told her about the latest hot composer in Israel then: a thirty-something "bad boy" from Haifa, Doron Hareli, who described his new politically-charged version of "*Dayenu*" as "a pro-peace, anti-war anthem." Hareli had made a few minor changes to the words of the traditional song, so that his "*Dayenu*" no longer meant "What we have is enough," but rather, "We have had enough!" Jake recommended that she listen to it. He thought she would find it interesting musically "despite its political naïveté."

She registered these last four words. She knew there were significant political differences between the two of them. Jake was right-wing, and was seen as anti-feminist by many women composers, musicians, and music students. With feminism in mind, she told him now about Malka Hornstein's latest composition: a splendid, light-hearted romp of a "*Echad Mi Yoda'at*" ("Who Knows One?"). To her amazement, she discovered that he had never even heard of Malka Hornstein, the Australian Jewish feminist composer. In fact, it turned out that he was ignorant about Jewish women composers in general. She told him a bit about Hornstein, and what an admired role model she was for so many Jewish women composers, especially feminists, but not only.

"Let me ask you something," he said, "since you keep using the term 'feminist.' How do you define that? I've never understood it exactly."

She had been asked this many times before, and she had answers prepared at various levels. She wasn't sure, though, how deeply into this Jake wanted to go. Tentatively she asked, "You mean generally, or in relation to music?"

"Both."

She began hesitantly, but then seeing that he was listening attentively, she gave him a serious answer. Soon she was in high gear, speaking passionately and eloquently about sexism in the music world, gender bias in music education and performance, and the importance of finding strategies to empower more teenage girls and young women to pursue careers as conductors and composers. As she expounded on all this, she was half-consciously operating on the benevolent, generous assumption that, like many males of his generation, Jake's sexism wasn't due to evil intent on his part. His sexism was just blindness, the way that people sitting on the powerful side of the desk are often blind about the impact of this on those sitting on the other side.

"Now about the F word..." she said.

He gave a little laugh.

"First of all," she continued, "what feminism isn't: It isn't 'anti-men'."

"Oh, come on."

"Really. That's just a stereotype. Feminists don't hate men; we just see women as men's full equals. Therefore we believe that women deserve full equality — economically, legally, in every way."

"Well," he said, "that seems reasonable. But surely this isn't all there is to feminism?"

"Yeah, pretty much." She shrugged. "If you want it standing on one foot."

"Well, give it to me on two."

She was about to start elaborating when Jake burst out with vehemence, "What you're saying is all well and good. But it's those bra-burning types I can't stand; they're something else entirely. Those Women's Libbers want to destroy the family."

Women's Libbers? She had never heard anyone use this term aloud except her father; it had been out of usage for decades. This made her feel alienated from Jake, like he was from not just another generation but another world. But then, precisely because of how out of it he was, she felt a rush of protective affection for him, like she sometimes felt toward her father. It's generational, she thought; it's not his fault what year he was born. So she said to him evenly,

"Those, too, are both just myths. For the sake of historical accuracy, no feminist ever actually burned a bra. And more importantly, feminists do not want to destroy the family. Most feminists, like me, are married and have kids, and we love our families as much as anyone else. We do ask questions, though, about family life, the same way we ask questions about all other social institutions, and how each of these affects women. For instance, the research shows clearly that marriage is good for men — it's beneficial for men's physical and mental health — but it's bad for women's. So, of course, feminists ask why. And according to our analysis, it's because of how family life is currently structured and arranged. For example, who in the family does most of the childcare and household labour, and who holds most of the economic power."

She paused, watching Jake's face as he thought about what she had said and absorbed it. She continued, "To address these inequities, feminists also research and imagine different ways that families could organize themselves that would be better and healthier for women. So we support alternative models of family life, where both the responsibilities and resources in the family are distributed more evenly between the women and men. We seek ways to make families more supportive environments for all their members. But that doesn't mean we're 'against the family.'"

She stopped and waited for his response.

"Well," said Jake a few moments later, "if this is truly what feminists believe, I see nothing objectionable in feminism at all. What you're saying sounds eminently reasonable to me."

"It is."

"I mean, I have two daughters, and I wouldn't want either

of them being paid less than the guy sitting next to them doing the same job just because they're female."

"Of course you wouldn't. It's a matter of women having self-respect and not undervaluing themselves. And employers treating women and men as equals."

"Well, that seems fair enough," he said. Then he added thoughtfully, "Yes, I could live with that."

She looked at him sharply. There was something in the way he said this that sounded like he had been asking himself, for the past few minutes, not just whether he could live with feminism, but whether he could live with her. As if the two of them, without her being aware of it, had been in negotiations over their future living arrangements.

"It's a pleasant surprise, and a relief, I must say," he went on, looking like a worry had been lifted from him, "to hear that feminists aren't anti-men."

"We're not."

"Well, you certainly aren't. Not in the least. You're a lovely woman, and nothing like how I've always pictured a feminist." Now he gave her a sly sideways smile. "You hardly seem to hate men at all."

"I don't hate men," she said soberly. Then she said, imitating his expression, that twist of his lips, "Some of my best friends are men."

He laughed.

"Let me sing you some feminist music," she said, and sang for him by heart the first few verses of Hornstein's "*Echad Mi Yoda'at.*" When she finished, he said he liked the music, but what he found most moving was hearing her sing. "I didn't know you could sing," he said. "You have a beautiful voice."

"I love singing. Sometimes I lead the services at my *shul.*"

"Really?"

"Yes. We don't have a *chazan* at our *shul*. We rotate; whoever wants to can lead."

"Really?"

"You sound so surprised. But it isn't that unusual. Lots of *shuls* are doing this now, and many women lead *davening*."

"I know," he said. "I've heard about this, obviously. But I've never personally known a woman who was doing it." He considered her for a bit. "I always opposed the female cantor thing myself. Not that I'm at all religious anymore. I left all that behind when I left my parents' home. But you know the old Yiddish joke: The *shul* I *don't* go to has to be the right kind."

She chuckled. "I know that one."

"Actually, it's funny," he mused in a puzzled voice. "Now that I think about it, I'm not sure I can even recall what all the fuss was about — why I was so opposed back then to women leading the *davening*. When I think about it now, well, I'd love to hear you sing sometime in your *shul*. I'm sure it would be beautiful."

"Anytime. Come to Toronto."

"I wish I could," he said, and gazed off into the distance.

They were sitting on the bed just a few inches apart; the sun from the window slashed across the bed in a triangle, warming her feet. Now he studied her, looking perplexed. "You know," he said, "this is only the sixth day I've ever seen you, and already you're overturning my beliefs of a lifetime!"

She laughed. She was happy, flattered to be having an impact — an intellectual impact — on this great man of ideas.

Though it turned out, in fact, that she didn't. Eight months later she unexpectedly came across an interview with him in *The New York Times* where he dismissed Jewish feminist contributions to Jewish music as "insignificant." "Perhaps in another ten or twenty years, it will be worth listening to," he said. This was no different than the sort of thing he'd said numerous times before meeting her. It was no worse, but also no better. She had had no impact at all, she realized with shock.

But now she played for him on her iPod Malka Hornstein's "Miriam's Song with Timbrel," and then he played for her an esoteric work by Salamone Rossi that she had never heard before. He worshipped Salamone Rossi, and throughout their five days at the King David, he told her all sorts of anecdotes and stories about him, most of which he planned to include in the book he was writing, *"Dear Papa": The Letters of Salamone Rossi to His Father, 1586-1610.*

Dear Papa. Lying with her head on Jake's bare stomach, and occasionally kissing his hand, arm, or cheek as she listened to this music, she remembered listening to music with her father on Saturday afternoons, curled up in his lap. Other than with her father and now with Jake, she had never listened to music with someone else. She had been to concerts, of course, but she had never listened to music with just one other person. That felt too intimate, in a way. In college, for instance, she had boyfriends she made love to, but she had never allowed them to listen to music with her. Yet here with Jake it felt completely natural. Perhaps because they had such similar sensibilities. After they had listened to a piece of music together, their responses were often uncannily alike. Like on that first day, when after listening to some Brahms, he asked her, "What did you think of the way he played those opening bars?"

"Too emphatic."

"Exactly."

"It should have been played with tenderness, with some delicacy, the way van Cliburn did. You know that recording?"

"Of course! Wasn't it perfect? No one could play Brahms like van Cliburn."

"No one. Never was and never will be..."

Or, a little later, she said,

"That transition to the theme in the second movement..."

"They came in too abruptly. Like they were running to catch up."

"Precisely. You heard that, too?"

It amazed her to discover that someone else could hear exactly what she had heard, pick up on every nuance that she had. She had always felt alone with these feelings and thoughts. She had started composing just ten years before and wasn't connected to the local music scene in Toronto. The music she wrote wasn't rooted in that soil. She had felt lonely for a long time, not personally, but musically. She was musically lonely even when Brian was alive. He was a wonderful man, but he found her sort of music boring. He'd accompany her to concerts to please her, but once there, he'd fall asleep. Or else he'd use that time to think about his clients' portfolios, and in the middle of a concert that took her breath away with its beauty, Brian would be jotting down ideas for work the next day.

Jake, on the other hand, felt music as vividly as she did. It first entered him through his ears, but then flowed into his bloodstream and swam throughout his body, filling every cell. A few hours after their first breakfast at the King David, sometime in the mid-afternoon, she showed him a short piece she had written three days before, titled *God's Song*. It was a crazy piece of music, something she was sure that no one, not even he, could understand. But he did. Not only did he understand it; he loved it.

"It's nothing short of brilliant," he declared. "You're building the grammar of a new language for Jewish music."

She shrugged modestly at first, and then grinned ear to ear and threw her arms around him. He alone, out of everyone she had ever met, understood her musical language. What she had always thought of as her craziness. This weird thing inside of her. But now she didn't feel odd or abnormal anymore. With Jake she was okay. More than okay. She was unique. Talented. Beautiful. Jake loved and understood her music, which meant he loved and understood her.

Around six o'clock that evening, after they'd decided to order room service for supper, Jake turned on Beethoven's String Quartet in C, Op. 59, No. 3 (the third Razumovsky). And in the middle of the hypnotic, slow, and profound second movement, Eve, lying naked next to Jake, turned on her side and began to play the theme on his belly as if he were a piano.

She played about half of the second movement this way, and after that, bits and pieces of the third. Then she came in again toward the end of the fourth movement, pounding out on Jake, gently pounding, the triumphant finale. The triumph in this music, she knew from her studies, mirrored Beethoven's feeling of triumph at that point in his life over the limitations of his deafness (and more generally, the victory of the capacity to create art in spite of all the obstacles of life). When she played this finale on Jake's belly now, she was laughing and feeling victorious. Music would win. Music would triumph in the world. And she felt, playing this music now, like she was somehow making love simultaneously to the music and to Jake. She played the finale, with all its ascents and descents, its rhythms and rhymes, first on his belly, and then not just on his belly, but all over his body. She could play Jake, she discovered, like any other instrument she had ever used for composing on. So when the finale ended, she didn't stop, but continued playing on him, playing whatever notes or tunes came into her mind, and playing them with whatever parts of her body she felt like (her hands, her elbows, her nose, her mouth, whatever). Eve, who was usually quite shy about sex, now felt totally free. With music accompanying her, she could touch Jake anywhere she wanted. Nothing was wrong, nothing was dirty or shameful. It was all just music.

Then Jake whispered something to her, so quietly at first that she couldn't hear and had to ask him to repeat it. Blushing, he forced out two words, looking agonized. *Oral sex.* She was surprised, and also slightly confused by this rather formal term, but she didn't mind giving Jake what he'd asked for. It was all just playing, and as she played the music on him the way he'd requested, she enjoyed seeing his pleasure. His astonishment. His gratitude.

Nothing they did was wrong or ugly. Everything was music.

9. HEBREW UNION COLLEGE

EVE STANDS UP, WINCING as the backs of her thighs rip away from the iron grooves in the bench. The pants she is wearing are almost as thin as a layer of skin, and she can feel the bench's pattern of circles and curlicues engraved into her flesh. She steps forward, away from the bench, and leaping back, narrowly escapes being run over by a baby carriage. She stares in amazement at the back of a woman barrelling down the street, pushing her baby carriage as forcefully as a lawn mower, but much faster, clearing the sidewalk of pedestrians as if they were weeds. Shaking her head, Eve starts walking toward the Old City. Yes, she thinks, what I remember about me and Jake at the King David, that's how it was. It was beautiful and we had a real relationship. I'm not crazy. I didn't just imagine the whole thing.

As if arguing this before an invisible judge, she brings forth proofs. He did say that:

She was the best friend he'd ever had.

He loved her as much as his own daughters or wife.

Some of the things he told her he'd never told another living soul, including Fran.

Only now that he'd met her, did he understand the point of living.

Before he met her he hadn't been unhappy; he had just been dead. And if he ever were to lose her, he'd go back to being dead.

Yes, all this is true. He did say these things. These words

are proof as solid as cement. As solid as the sidewalk she is walking on now.

But now Eve stops walking. She is standing in front of a construction site next to Hebrew Union College. A large sign tells her that a building is going to be built here, but right now they're obviously in the process of pure demolition.

Prooftext: *He told you things he'd never told anyone else.* It was on their fourth day together in the hotel that Jake told her what had happened to him at the Sorbonne. Then he paused, looked at her anxiously, even warily, and said, "You're the first person I've ever told about this. Even Fran doesn't know."

Eve was flattered but shocked. She couldn't imagine having kept a secret from Brian for thirty-eight days, much less thirty-eight years. "How could you not tell her?" she asked.

"She wouldn't have understood," he said. They were sitting on the bed, both cross-legged, Jake just in boxer shorts. She had on nothing but a long black T-shirt (one of Jake's that she had borrowed) that pulled tight across the two bumps of her knees. She gave it a yank now and then so it formed a modest flap over her private parts. Jake looked at her searchingly now. "Fran's a very conventional person," he said. "Everything with her is black or white, normal or abnormal. Last week I told her something that popped into my mind and she said I was crazy."

"You're not crazy," Eve said warmly. "You just have an inner life."

He looked at her gratefully. "You understand that, but she doesn't. I don't want to speak ill of Fran. She means well and she's the mother of my daughters. But there's so much inside me I can't share with her. I've been lonely for a very long time. Pretty much since the girls were born..." Wincing, he touched his cheek and then gaped at his hand. "Look at me," he said. "I'm crying. I haven't cried since I was seven years old. I didn't even cry at my parents' funerals. But here I am, crying with you." Tears ran into the deep wrinkles in his face. One trickled onto his lip, but he didn't seem to notice. "How could I have met you only now?" he cried with anguish. "I feel like I've wasted so many years." He covered his face, sobbing like a child.

She put a hand on his arm. After a while he grew calmer. Then he looked up at her.

"I'm not the same person who walked into this hotel four days ago," he said. "I'm a new man. And I don't want to go back to being the old one."

She didn't say anything; just listened.

"You know," he said, "the night before I married Fran, she asked me if I had any regrets about getting married, and I told her my only regret was that I had just one lifetime to spend with her. But now" — he looked at Eve, pleadingly — "I want another lifetime. To spend with *you*."

This did happen. She didn't invent it. I wasn't nothing to Jake, she thinks. I mattered to him. She watches as a huge crane, high in the sky (a sky that is grey and end-of-the-day tired) slowly descends all the way down to the ground. It does this gradually, gracefully, and then at the bottom scoops up a pile of boulders and stones, swings off to one side, and dumps them somewhere out of sight.

One last prooftext she summons. From later the same day. They were both next to their overnight bags, on opposite sides of the room. They'd just showered and were dressing to go out for dinner. She was sitting on a fake-leather hassock, putting on her socks.

"Thank you," Jake said out of the blue.

She finished pulling on one sock and looked up at him with curiosity. "For what?"

"For listening to me. For loving me. I can scarcely believe that someone wonderful like you could love me."

She was surprised. Such low self-esteem, she thought. He doubts his own lovability. But this didn't repel her; it only made her feel more tender toward him. "There's no need to thank me," she said. "We're friends."

"Yes," said Jake, looking as if he'd never thought of this before. "We are." He'd been about to button up his shirt; now he stopped. Between the two light blue panels of his open shirt, his chest was a thin, pale stripe.

"You know," he said, "I don't think I've ever had a friend like you before. I think you're the best friend I've ever had."

"I hope we stay friends."

He looked surprised. "Well, of course we will." He started to button his shirt. "How could we not?"

She was finished getting dressed and came over to sit on the edge of the bed nearest the window, not far from where Jake was standing, tucking his shirt into his pants. "Well," she began, feeling like some Wise Older Woman instructing a less experienced, younger man. "Sometimes two people fall in love, but they're not actually friends. There's nothing underneath the erotic passion, so when that's gone, there's nothing left."

Jake looked shocked. "That could never happen with us," he said. "This is real. It's deep. We're friends, Eve, and always will be."

"Do you think so?"

"Of course I do. Don't you?"

"I don't know." She shrugged. "I'm not as certain about things as you are. Life is … unpredictable."

Jake looked troubled for a few seconds. Then he said softly, "Spoken like someone whose husband died at the age of forty-two."

She glanced sideways up at him and shrugged again. He sat down next to her.

"I'm not planning to have a heart attack, Eve," he said. "I'm not a young man, but I don't have a heart condition, or any other condition, and I'm planning on sticking around for quite some time."

She didn't say anything.

"Eve, listen to me." Jake took her hand and she looked at him. "Who knows what exactly will happen between us? Obviously things will be different when you return to Toronto and Fran comes back from visiting her mother. But one thing I'm sure of one hundred percent — you and I will always be friends."

Always. Again he'd said *always*. He'd never leave her. He'd always be her friend.

"Really?" she asked, her voice husky.

"Really," he said. "We'll be friends forever."

She liked that. "Friends forever," she repeated.

"Yes."

The crane is descending again. It scoops up another load of broken rocks and rubble and dumps it all somewhere that Eve can't see. Then the crane is back. It rises again into the air, and at its full height pauses for a long moment. Like royalty (King David perhaps?) expecting to be acknowledged and admired before deigning to descend again. She stares at this machine, entranced. It's starting to feel to her like a living creature. Now not a king, but a dinosaur, the way its long, graceful neck is bending down again — down, down it comes — to the ground, to the lowly height of a human. Eve keeps watching this crane, and it begins to remind her of Jake. He so much bigger than her; she so small he had to bend down to meet her eyes. Like an adult crouching down to talk to a child.

Oh, come *on*, she thinks impatiently as she walks away from the construction site. That's ridiculous. I may have thought that way back then, but I was wrong. I'm as big as Jake. I'm as big as anyone.

10. SONG OF THE STEPS: *SHIR HAMA'ALOT*

THE LIGHT IS STARTING TO FADE from the sky. Eve, strolling again along King David Street, passes a bus shelter with a large poster plastered to it advertising the *Niggun* conference, including the opening banquet tomorrow night. Flashing through her in the same instant: euphoria ("I'll see him again! I'll see him again!" with the notes going up to the top of the keyboard) and fear ("I'll see, him, again. I'll see, him, again," with the notes going lower and lower). The high note of a childlike enthusiasm — a piccolo — and the low note, a bell tolling doom. This is the two-note chord that Jake is for her. She tightens her lips and keeps on walking. I don't need to decide now about that conference, she thinks. I don't have to decide about it ever. I can just ignore it.

It's getting cold and Eve pulls her light jacket tighter around her. Then, turning right, she abruptly leaves King David Street and heads toward the Old City, with Jaffa Gate looming ahead of her half a kilometer away. A couple of minutes before reaching the gate, she stops and observes with interest and curiosity the block-long brick complex on her left. She realizes now that she is in Mamilla, in what used to be Jerusalem's No Man's Land. I'm in No Man's Land, she thinks wryly, which is where I should be, since I have No Man. She notices several chinks in what appears to be a long, solid brick wall. The blue signs at these openings are apparently entrances into an indoor parking lot. Right: Recently the municipality of Jerusalem turned this area into an upscale shopping mall complete with on-site parking, and now she is eager to see for herself this latest addition to the city. She heard this mall cost a fortune to build — evidently there was some scandal behind it. Well, everything that gets built in Jerusalem has a scandal, or at least a story, behind it. Conflict is built into these stones.

She starts climbing the dozens of steps that lead up to the swanky new shops and cafés. But before completing even the first dozen, she stops, panting and clutching the railing, and sits down near the banister on the left to rest. Jet lag. And a couple of sleepless nights before leaving on this trip. Facing her now and off to the left, she sees Gai Ben Hinnom, a valley (*Yea, though I walk in the valley of the shadow of death...*), and near it, the Sultan's Pool, an ancient site used nowadays as an open-air theatre. Thirty years ago (*thirty years!*) she saw Arik Einstein perform here to a crowd of twenty thousand. And a couple of years ago she and Reut came here for the Jerusalem Film Festival's opening gala, a fun and festive evening attended by many people she knew from the old days, and ending with live jazz by a talented young local quartet, while red, green, silver, and gold fireworks exploded above the walls of the Old City. Now she surveys the empty site in the fast-fading light, and beyond it west Jerusalem with its familiar landmarks: the King David Hotel, the YMCA across the street from it, Montefiore's windmill, and further on, the old train station and the long road leading to Bethlehem. She avoids looking at the separation wall. Instead she gazes at the darkening sloping hill (one of the seven that Jerusalem is built on), breast-like in its roundness.

I love you, she thinks.

The hill is silent, but seems to be listening to her.

I've never loved anyone more in my life.

And then: But you don't love me anymore, do you? You don't care if I'm alive or dead.

The hill says nothing.

Well, I don't love you, either.

This startles her. Because even though she has been saying this line for years, she realizes now that it's true. She doesn't love Jake anymore. She's still fucked-up over him, but she could live without him if she had to. She could.

Anyway, he'll be dying soon. He's old now. He turned seventy on May 10th.

The steps she is sitting on have so far been completely unpopulated, but suddenly they are full of people. A flock of children is charging upward in a long blurry wave, the parents lazily trailing behind, chatting in pairs. Then two lovers come strolling up the steps, holding hands. And then everyone's gone, and the steps are once again deserted.

That's what I don't understand, she thinks, looking pleadingly at Jerusalem, as if this place can give her an answer. How can you be alive one minute and dead the next? Like Brian, one minute pouring himself a glass of orange juice, and seconds later, the pitcher's in pieces all over the floor, and he's lying there in the middle of the glass and the orange juice, his body twitching and his face grey — and when the medics arrive a few minutes later, he's already dead. And the same thing with Mommy. Holding my hand at the top of a flight of steps (steps just like these) as we're about to descend. "Be careful, Eve. Hold my hand tight. Don't let go." But I did let go. (Or was it Mommy who let go?) And Mommy went tumbling down the steps, and at the bottom, she was dead. In less than ten seconds. That's the way life is. One minute you're alive and the next you're not. One minute Jake is next to me, alive and warm, and we're breathing all our breaths together, and he loves me, body, mind and soul. Then without warning he's gone, never to be seen again.

Dead. Because that's what dead is. Never seeing that person again.

Dead. She bangs her head against the banister.

Dead. (Bang.)

Dead. (Bang.)
Dead. (Bang.)

She stops banging her head. She's surprised. Ah, so this is what this is all about! Not love, not being dumped by a man, but Death. The great black vulture-vampire with its black cape and huge webbed wings — the way she pictured Death at three, after Mommy died. She almost laughs with relief. So this is one clue to the mystery of the past five and a half years. Well, at least she's not shallow. Losing all these years of her life over a man would be pathetic. But death — now *that's* respectable, she thinks with a rueful smile. That's something worth being tormented over. This puts me on par with the greatest philosophers, musicians, and poets of all time.

Just three lousy sentences and Jake was gone. That's all there was to Jake's goodbye note. Two short sentences (do, do), and one long one (dooooooooo), like two eighth notes and a whole note. Or a foghorn ending on a long, sad sigh. She knows this three-sentence email from Jake by heart. Its cold music has played itself over and over inside her for over five years. Both the notes and the silences: what was in that letter and what wasn't. For instance, there was no regret in it at all. No I-love-you (or even I-once-loved-you) or I'll-miss-you. No you've-meant-something-to-me or it-will-be-hard-for-me-without-you. Not one kind word, either about her or to her. Nothing. Only

It's over. Don't ever call or write to me again.

Those were the first two sentences.

Then came the long one: *I can't believe that because of you I've been playing fast and loose with my marriage — that I've risked losing Fran, who is the most important person in the world to me, and without whom I have nothing.*

She hugs herself, shivering on the steps. He couldn't just end it. He had to pour acid into the wound. He had to say he loved Fran and not her. When she first got this email, she screamed. She screamed for hours, until her voice was gone.

Luckily this email came on a weekday morning, when Michael and Ethan were both at school. When they came home that afternoon, she pretended to have laryngitis and a migraine, and she lay on her bed with the door shut and the lights off, one arm flung over her eyes, sobbing. She sobbed for most of the next twelve months. She did what she had to for her boys, but nothing really mattered to her. Nothing. The world was empty. Life was pointless. The only thing that could make it all right again would be a letter from Jake. So she checked her email every five minutes. Hundreds of times a day. Thousands of times a week.

Sitting on the cold steps now, she pulls her knees tight against her chest. I'm not like that anymore, she thinks. I'm better now. No more weeping in my bed, no more writhing with longing, impotent rage, and self-loathing. She looks out now over the landscape. Night has fallen, and except for a dim street lamp fifty yards away, and further off a few twinkles of light, blackness — as palpable as the coarse black sackcloth worn in mourning — covers everything. *I'm so afraid.* She huddles against the banister, in the shadows where no one can see her. A fifty-five-year-old woman, sobbing in public on the stairs.

11. MAMILLA

THUMP. THUMP. THUMP. Eve turns, wiping her cheeks. Missing her by mere inches are two grey-haired people of about seventy (*Jake's age*), sprinting up the steps, laughing and calling out to each other in what sounds like Swedish. Watching them, she feels inadequate: she is fifteen years younger and couldn't even make it up the stairs. She grasps the banister, pulls herself to her feet, and continues trudging upwards. Meanwhile she is thinking: Jake's not the crazy one; she is. Even if Jake *were* a psychopath — even if he were mad as a hatter (or mad as a hater; that's the real madness, isn't it: hating?) — still he isn't as fucked-up now as she is. He's not suffering. He's not obsessed, paralyzed in his life, like her. He got off scot-free. Free as a bird in the sky (while she is trapped in a cage). There he goes, contentedly living his life, untraumatized by their brief affair, and same as always, brilliantly productive and successful. Jurying all the major Jewish music competitions, and some non-Jewish ones, too, popping out one prize-winning book after another, and lecturing on the international circuit on Jewish Sacred Music. (As if he even knows the meaning of the word *sacred*. He said three weeks before leaving her that the bond between them was the most sacred thing he'd ever known. But what does that matter to him now?) There's Jake, bopping along, carefree. And here I am: working at half-mast, in a state of perpetual grieving, with the essence of me — all my creative juice — as sour and bitter as a lemon's. I'm the sick one. I'm the crazy one. Wasting all this time, waiting for Jake to come back. Even though I know he never will.

She has just reached the top of the steps, and she stands there, surprised. Up here, all darkness has been banished. Outside this mall, the valleys of Jerusalem are pitch black, but here everything is bright and festive. The dark sky has been replaced by long strings of light bulbs stretching overhead, illuminating the lengthy promenade of pale Jerusalem stone. She wanders, slightly dazed, between the dozens of shops on her left and right. The display windows glow: the finest and most expensive jewellery, clothing, and designer home furnishings are present-ed in a vast array of colours, shapes, and materials. Laughing throngs surround her, gently bumping into her, pressing up against her, sweeping her forward, including her as if they're all one body in the same warm ocean. She is no longer alone or lonely; she's part of this lively, exuberant mass. It feels like a street fair here, with blue and white balloons bobbing ev-erywhere, silk banners of crimson, purple, orange, and yellow flapping and snapping in the wind, and huge snowflakes made of crepe paper dangling above everyone's heads like a faux Canadian sky. She laughs. Everything here is innocent and good, and it's delightful, as she walks along, to feel all the life in her body, the blood flowing through her veins. A purple banner swirls and twirls and she imagines what it would be like, if she could catch it, to rub her face in that silk, and feel its textured softness against her bare skin.

Now she reaches the halfway point of the promenade, its central circle, filled with a huge *chanukiah*. Right, she thinks, Chanukah starts tonight. December 24th. Which is also Christmas Eve. She keeps strolling along. How could she have forgotten, she wonders with an astonished grin, about this real world outside her mind? That muddy swamp of a mind with its crazy dark obsession. She pauses in front of a jewellery store to admire a diamond in the window. It is beautiful and glimmering, and insistent somehow on its own hard realness. Yes, this is what's real. Not kisses from five and a half years ago. Not degradations by father-figure dead men. But this. All this. This world as beautiful and hard as a diamond.

She continues on through the promenade, almost in a state of ecstasy, even though normally she dislikes both shopping and shopping malls. But here everything is so alive and re-splendent. At least part of it, she knows, is because she is here, she is in Israel. On her left, streaming out of an open door, comes some Israeli "back to our roots" music, which she immediately recognizes as the poetry of Ibn Gvirol set to hard rock. She finds this Israeli roots phenomenon fascinating and even important, but she doesn't actually like the music. Neither did Jake, she recalls, but then pushes the thought of him away. The window of the store with the music pour-ing out of it isn't a music store displaying music scores or instruments; it's filled with hand-crafted smocks made out of different materials patched together: cloth, plastic, metal, wood, dried flowers, and paper. They're less smocks than wearable collages. The largest one dominating the window has a base of bruise-blue fabric, and onto this are glued some pressed, dead daffodils and laminated photos of people in twos or threes. The arms of the smock are stretched out dramat-ically and pinned to a backdrop, like a crucifixion, perhaps to appeal subliminally to Christian tourists. The store next door to this one (as if in response) sells Judaica: *chanukiot*, *mezuzot*, *seder* plates, *kipot*, *tallitot*, and silver candlesticks, some of it tacky, some of it not. Two stores down, there's a confectionery selling pyramids of chocolates wrapped in red, purple, gold, and silver foil, long flat racks of Godiva and Schmerling chocolates, and round pink coconut-coated marzipan balls that look erotic to her, reminding her vaguely of men's pink hair-covered balls. For half a minute she stands in front of this window, gazing at the candy longingly like a child. Then smelling something so marvellous that it makes her salivate and turn around, she watches some shwarma roasting slowly on a vertical spit. The smell is heavenly, but the hands and fingernails of the man selling it are black with dirt and the shwarma's rubbery yellow fat is revolting. She crosses the promenade, enters a café, and at the front counter orders a cream cake and a cocoa made with a melted bar of Belgian chocolate. Then, while waiting for her name to be called, she takes a seat by the window overlooking a view of Jerusalem.

I never should have told him about Julia, she thinks. If I hadn't told Jake about Julia, he'd still be loving me now. How stupid could I be? You don't tell someone who's just fallen in love with you that for a significant part of your life you've been hated. Hated and degraded from age twelve on. No one, knowing that, could keep on loving you. No matter how nice they act right after you tell them. Where there's smoke, there's fire, people think. If someone hated you, there must be a good reason.

She hadn't wanted to tell Jake about Julia. She had told only a handful of people in her life, but he insisted.

"We can't have any secrets from each other, we have to tell each other everything," he'd said. So she did. And also she told him because she could see that he wanted to see her wounds. His eyes had glinted a few days earlier — he'd almost seemed to take a sick pleasure in it — when she told him about Mr. Monson, her high school teacher. The one who'd discovered her musical talent, told her she had a great and important gift, sweet-talked her into falling in love with him, started looking at her with glowing, hungry, wolf-like eyes, and then grabbed her that time in his office, fondled her breast, and licked the inside of her ear.

Jake *was* nice to her right after she told him about Julia. She asked him anxiously when she was finished, "Do you look down on me now?"

"Look down on you?" he asked, looking surprised. "Why would I do that?" He was sitting naked on his side of the bed, his back against a pillow and his legs straight out in front of him, and she sat near him, naked and cross-legged, covered up to the waist by a thin blanket. "*You* didn't do anything wrong in that situation," he said. "You weren't the crazy one."

"Still," she said, looking down at the blanket.

"No," Jake said firmly. "Look at me." She did. "I don't see you negatively at all, Eve. If anything, I admire you. How strong and brave you are. I can't believe you went through what you did and still somehow came out of it normal. And not just normal — a wonderful person. Anyone else would have ended up in a nuthouse."

"Oh, I don't know," she said.

"I do."

She didn't say anything.

"I'll tell you how I really see you and your past, if you want," he said.

She looked up at him. He was gazing at her steadily, with admiration and affection. "How?" she asked.

"You're not unscathed," he said. "But you're victorious."

She stared at him. What he'd said was perfect. He recognized her wounds (her "scath"), but also her strength, and he gave the greater weight to this strength and "the triumph of her spirit" than to her woundedness. By acknowledging both sides of her this way, he showed that he accepted, and loved, all of her as she was. Not just one part of her, as most people did. Grateful, she was about to reach up and touch his cheek, when his face clouded over with anger.

"I hate Julia," he growled.

She was surprised. "But you don't even know her."

"I know she hurt you, and that's enough for me. If you hate her, I'll hate her, too."

Jake, as he said these last four words, looked hopefully at her, as if he had just offered her a gift — the gift of his hatred

— and she, gazing back into his eager face, was touched by his loyalty and love. Yet it also seemed odd to her, even a little troubling, how ready he was to hate a total stranger.

*

Eve hears her name being called over the loudspeaker. Leaving her jacket behind to hold her seat, she approaches the counter and pays for her cake and cocoa. Waiting for her change (which takes a while: they've run out of coins), she thinks: That was sweet, how at first he admired me for what I'd lived through. But ultimately that's why he rejected me. He'd have kept on loving me if he thought I was whole, if he thought I was normal. Normal meaning not hated (and if you're hated, you're therefore hateable), and normal also meaning not having (because of that hate) an enormous, gaping wound right in the centre of you the size of the Afro-Syrian rift. If I hadn't told him about Julia, he'd still be loving me now.

The guy behind the cash still hasn't returned with her change. "He'll be back in a moment," says a pretty young woman with two high ponytails, and Eve nods. Meanwhile thinking: There's another reason, too, that Jake stopped loving her. It's because of the time she got off the toilet and left on the seat a little shmear of shit. Jake saw it and didn't make a face. (Like Julia always used to: Julia grimaced in response to anything to do with Eve's body functions. "Dirty," Julia would tell her. Or, "Disgusting.") But now Jake didn't grimace. He just wiped off the shit. Then he scrubbed his hands with hot water and soap for what felt to her like an hour, while she, excruciatingly embarrassed, and feeling dirty, disgusting, and unlovable, stood in the doorway, cringing, and repeating over and over, "I'm sorry. I'm sorry."

She holds out her open hand to the guy behind the cash and the cold coins clink into her palm. Then carefully, slowly she begins carrying the cake and cocoa back to her seat. Don't be ridiculous, she thinks as she weaves her way between the crowded tables. He sent you away not because of your adolescence or your poo, but because his marriage was falling apart over your relationship.

"A man has a right to save his marriage," said Jake, switching into the third person as he always did, to Eve's annoyance, when he felt defensive. She manoeuvers around a stroller blocking the middle of the aisle. Yes, it's true — she tries to be fair — one does have that right. It's even true that for a short while he fought with Fran to stay her friend.

"I'm fighting but I'm losing," he said to her on the phone, somewhere toward the end.

"If you love me, you'll fight until you win," she said. (She can't believe now the naïveté of that.)

"It's precisely because I do love you, and love you so much, that I'm losing," he said. "Fran can tell I still love you and don't feel toward you just as a friend. If I loved you less, it wouldn't be so difficult to retain our friendship."

She didn't say anything, and he continued, "Try and understand what it's like for me. It's twelve weeks since you left Israel, and I still can't make love to my own wife. I have to shut my eyes and pretend it's you. And if I open them, instead of seeing Fran's face, I see yours hovering between me and her. This can't go on. My marriage is falling apart. I'm going to have to do something drastic."

"*Drastic,*" she scoffed. "What do you mean by 'drastic'?"
He didn't answer.

He couldn't say it, she thinks now. He couldn't even warn me. She is standing impatiently, balancing her wobbly tray of cake and cocoa, while in front of her a man helps a woman into her coat. Jake tried to tell her, but then he faltered. He didn't have the guts to say he was about to do the one thing he'd sworn to her repeatedly he'd never do. The one absolutely impossible thing, so beyond the pale that she had never even seriously considered he might do it. End their relationship totally. Cut off all contact.

Amputate her from his life, like she was gangrene.

She is waiting now, increasingly irritated, while the woman in the coat slowly ties on her scarf and adjusts her hat. Glancing around the room, Eve notices a good-looking man sitting by himself next to the window, two tables down from hers. He is observing the view, smoking a cigarette and blowing it out at Jerusalem. Too young for me, she thinks, but he's definitely my type. Long hair, intellectual-looking. Long, slender fingers. Pianist's fingers. She smiles: How superficial, how banal, falling for clichés like that. But still — her gaze lingers on him — he does look like an interesting man. He is thinking about something deep, she can tell. Then she chuckles. Yeah, right, he must be deep if he's Israeli. She always falls for Israeli men; she knows that's at least part of why she fell for Jake. If she were in Toronto now, she wouldn't even look twice at this guy by the window. Much less imagine playing music on him, playing music up and down his arms.

The man at the window turns and looks at her. She blushes and nearly drops her tray. The cocoa sloshes and the cake slides to one side, and by the time she has regained her balance and composure, the man's looking out the window again, puffing on his cigarette, exhaling smoke. *Where there's smoke, there's fire.*

She sets down the cake and cocoa on her table and settles into her seat. The cake is rich-looking and magnificent: three layers of trembling nearly-white cream. She has an impulse to bend down, bury her face in it, and devour from the inside that cool, sweet cream. Instead she leans down and breathes in the steaming cocoa with the froth licking the inside edges of the cup. The heat from it flushes her face. Then the gentle, bubbly froth tickles her tongue and lips and then instantly disappears. The cocoa is delicious: the hot melted Belgian chocolate is first-rate. But the cake, when she tastes it, is a disappointment. Almost entirely without flavour; just pretty to look at. She pushes it away.

The loudspeaker calls out: "Shalom." To her surprise, the guy from two tables down gets up, goes to the counter, and brings back a cup of coffee. *So his name is Shalom*; she would have guessed it was something more like Nadav, the name of her therapist, whom she was in love with for the two years she went to him. She looks away as Shalom passes her table so he won't see her watching him. He sits down in his seat and lights another cigarette that he smokes with his coffee. Maybe I could bum a cigarette from him, she thinks. See what it feels like to smoke again. Or what it's like to pick someone up for the first time since Jake.

She stares out the window into the darkness. *I love you*, she tells Jerusalem. She muses over its hills and its beauty, its wounds and its wars, its courage and its frailty. And then she pictures its traffic jams, its open, overflowing stinking garbage bins, and its stern ultra-Orthodox men dressed from head to toe in black. When she finally turns back from the window to the brightness of the well-lit café, it's just in time to see Shalom's back as he walks out. *Peace has departed.* She finishes her cocoa, and then — just for the hell of it, just to be a little bit bad — bums a cigarette off the woman at the next table. She hasn't smoked since she was sixteen and she thought back then that it made her look tough. Now she inhales leisurely and exhales leisurely, enjoying being sixteen again, and pseudo-tough, and sexy. She finishes her cig, stubs it out, and gazes for a bit longer into the night.

12. THE CONFERENCE

JAKE IS NOT AT THE OPENING BANQUET on Tuesday night. He's not at the conference at three-fifteen on Wednesday, either, when Eve arrives at the Van Leer after finishing her music therapy seminar for the day. He's not coming, she thinks with surprise. He's really not coming. For the last two nights the possibility of seeing him again has so excited her (not just emotionally, but also sexually) that she barely slept. So now she is disappointed. But then, drowning this out is a tsunami of relief. *He's not here. I'm safe.* She looks around the elegant lobby, sees the people calmly milling around, and notes the sophisticated professionalism of the staff behind the reception desk. It's just the normal world now. Not that other larger-than-life thing. This she can handle.

Now she starts enjoying the conference. For the next five hours the panels, the mini-concerts, the informal socializing, and the conversations at the breaks all engage her intellectually and emotionally, and distract her from her gloomy obsession. Miranda, beginning last night, has been amazingly warm and generous to her, introducing her to everyone ("This is Eve Bercovitch, a talented composer from back home"), and tonight at nine o'clock she even sneaks Eve into the "Presenters Only" reception. This private event takes place on the second floor of the Van Leer, in the swirling spacious lobby with waiters circulating among the guests with platters of hors d'oeuvres and red or white wine, and a lively, noisy crowd of fifty people clustered in twos, threes, fours, and fives. These clusters change constantly as Eve watches: they group and re-group in an ev-er-shifting pattern, like the silver magnetic marbles in one of Ethan's games. Eve, though often shy in this kind of situation, feels comfortable here, even happy. It's been years since she laughed so much in one day. What a delight this conference is. What a joy and comfort to be surrounded by all these Jewish musicians, assembled from every corner of the world, like an in-gathering of the exiles. She had no idea a conference could be like this. It's as if she's been wandering lost and half-dead in the middle of a desert and stumbled upon an oasis. This is the community she has been longing for without even realizing it. Not knowing what she needed until it appeared before her out of nowhere. For the first time since she can remember, she doesn't feel lonely.

I don't need Jake, she thinks. I don't need Jake to give me access to this world (or to any world, in fact). I can open the gate by myself.

She spots Miranda. Eve crosses the crowded room, smiling at people on the way, and clinks her glass against Miranda's. They laugh. Miranda's drinking red wine, Eve sees, but she is sticking with 7-Up. She doesn't want a repeat of the conference where she met Jake, when she got drunk out of boredom at the opening banquet, and just as everyone was leaving, went up to Jake — to the great Jacob Gladstone — and introduced herself. And after a couple of minutes of blathering on about the creative process, told him, "I need to be naked when I compose." Which made him blush. Which made her laugh. But the next morning she blushed, too, to the roots of her hair, and then realized with chagrin that she had to spend the next two hours on a panel with this man, and wouldn't be able to avoid him.

Miranda, still laughing, now clinks her glass against Eve's. She is standing with her back to the dessert table, and Eve spies, beyond Miranda's slim body, coffee urns, stacks of cups and saucers, cakes, and little pastries spaced out evenly on top of a white tablecloth. Standing next to Miranda is Alicia, a composer from Italy whom Miranda introduced her to last night. Eve and Alicia greet each other again now, and almost immediately Alicia resumes the rant she was apparently in the middle of when Eve came over. Alicia's angry about the last interview of the day, the one that ended just before this reception began. Nathan Singelman "in conversation with" Hector Levi, the grand old man of South American Jewish music, whom Eve (feeling embarrassed by her own ignorance) had never heard of till today. The two men, one old, one younger, sat in comfortable armchairs on the stage, in-between them a small round table with two bottles of water on it. Nathan was so deferential, even sucky, to Hector Levi, that Eve at first wanted to vomit and then was just embarrassed for him.

"I'm so sick of that cliché," Alicia sputters in an Italian accent. "'I am not a Jewish musician; I am just a musician. Musicians, indeed music itself, cannot be fettered by religion or nationality.' For heaven's sake. I didn't need to come all the way to a conference in Israel to be told that Jews are not only Jewish; we are also human. I knew that already."

Eve had a similar reaction to this remark of Hector Levi's. And to his follow-up comment that he had no wish to relegate his music to "a Jewish ghetto." As if it puts you in a ghetto to have a special interest in the music of your own people. But as a matter of principle, she refuses to judge the "Jewish identity" decisions of Holocaust survivors like Hector. For people like that, "ghetto" is not just a metaphor. Hector actually lived in one. Also she is silent because, thanks to Miranda, she knows the real reason that Alicia has it in for Hector Levi: he trashed her last composition, a choral suite for Purim, in the most recent issue of *Niggun*.

"Perhaps," Miranda says soothingly to Alicia. "But Hector's viewpoint is quite a common one. Even here at this conference, a fair number of people share it."

Forever the diplomat. Eve smiles to herself, but charitably. "I need coffee," she mutters, and with a two-finger wave, slides away toward the cloth-covered table. The decaf coffee gurgles out fast from the tall silver urn — much faster than she expected — and before she can stop it, it's sloshed wildly beyond her cup and saucer and is staining, in an ever-expanding brown pool, the pristine white linen. Mortified, she wants to mop up the mess, but it's hopeless: by the time she has found a paper napkin, the damage is done. Furtively she glances around, hoping that nobody saw. But no such luck. Hector Levi is standing at her right elbow, smiling down at her.

"It did that to me at lunchtime," he says.

"Really?" She looks up at him gratefully. "That's kind of you to say."

Hector's eyes are nothing like Jake's. They're brown, not blue, and the face they sit in is round, leathery, and nut-brown, not long and pale. But Hector's hair, like Jake's, is white, wavy, and a bit long over the ears. *The hair of an intellectual* is how Eve thinks of this type of hair, and up until a year or two ago, anytime she saw "intellectual" white hair — on the street, in a movie theatre, anywhere — she would experience a physical jolt as if she had touched a live wire. *It's Jake!* her body would cry out for a second, until realizing it wasn't. Now though, with Hector, this hair causes only a faint buzz of recognition: a low-current vibration like an obedient electric razor's. Yet this buzz has intelligence. It is telling her: No. *No.* Don't do this again.

"Well," Hector is smiling, "we Luddites have to stick to-gether."

Eve laughs.

"Tell me about yourself," says Hector. "I know almost ev-eryone here, but I've never seen you before."

Eve lowers her eyes. For the second time in one minute, she is embarrassed in front of this man. First there was the coffee, and now he has identified her as an impostor, which she is.

He could see in an instant that she doesn't belong here. (That she's not good enough to belong here.) That she isn't truly part of this in-crowd.

"It's my first time at a conference in Israel," she mumbles, blushing, gazing down at the tablecloth. The brown stain is still spreading, though more slowly now. It reminds her of watery poo defiling clean white underwear.

"Well, then, welcome!" Hector says heartily. "I only hope you're not too bored."

"Bored?" She looks up at him with relief. "No, it's fascinating! I'm having a terrific time."

They chat for a few more minutes, interrupted now and then by various people greeting or waving at Hector. Then Nathan Singelman saunters over. Eve has never seen him up close before. He's a plain-looking man with a pockmarked face, and not as tall as he looked on stage. Shaking his hand as Hector introduces them, she thinks, so this is the guy who never answered my email from four months ago. Since seeing him for the first time up on the podium at last night's banquet, she has been vacillating about whether or not to approach him at this conference, remind him of her letter, and ask for his help. So far she hasn't dared. But now the prospect seems more promising. Nathan obviously didn't recognize her name just now, but he is greeting her with politeness — no, more than that: respect. Because he sees me as associated with Hector, she thinks. All of a sudden, thanks to that, I have status and credibility.

Now someone else joins their little group. A thin, tense, olive-skinned woman who resembles a dried-out twig. This woman, while kissing Hector and Nathan on both cheeks and curtly nodding to Eve, chatters non-stop about her latest opera, which is currently being performed in Paris. The men listen courteously as she brags on and on about her various triumphs. Eventually Hector interrupts her to introduce her to Eve. But when Eve hears this woman's name, she almost laughs out loud. Rebecca Milner? The Rossi Prize winner from four and a half years ago, whom Jake praised so highly and ardently that she lost a whole night's sleep? Imagine being jealous of this twig! She now chuckles to herself, shaking Rebecca's thin hand, being careful not to crush the brittle sparrow bones. After this handshake, Rebecca turns away, addresses herself solely to the men, and ignores Eve completely.

Ah, so she's *that* sort of woman. With quiet amusement Eve watches Rebecca frantically do her song-and-dance, trying to impress Nathan and Hector. Nathan seems to be enjoying this. He actually expands physically, his chest puffing out like a robin redbreast's and his height increasing, the longer Rebecca keeps on. Now Rebecca is asking Nathan and Hector a question for the first time. She asks it in a high-pitched, querulous voice, acting like an admiring student eager to learn. Where do they think the real centre of the Jewish music world is today? Is it in America or Israel?

"Israel?" sneers Nathan. "Absolutely not! Oh, sure—" he gestures dismissively with one hand, "some of the folks here are producing some interesting work. And of course this trend of Jewish roots music is quite intriguing. But the real centre of Jewish music in the world now is definitely in America. It's been this way for decades, and will continue to be for the foreseeable future. America is the centre of the Jewish world, and I don't mean only in music. Anything of real interest Jewishly nowadays comes out of New York."

Eve's mouth has literally fallen open. She is stunned by Nathan's American arrogance, and the insult not only to her and Hector, but to Israel. Of course, to Nathan the United States is the centre of the world (for Jewish matters, and for everything). It's the centre of gravity holding the whole planet together. But she, being Canadian, doesn't worship the States. And she loves Israel and takes seriously Israeli music and musicians. So Nathan's smug superciliousness offends her to the core.

"Excuse me," she says, and walks away. A minute later, she glances back over her shoulder. Neither Nathan nor Rebecca seem to have noticed her departure. But Hector's eyes have followed her, smiling, and she thinks that she sees him wink.

*

At one end of the reception area, there's a long, narrow table displaying books and CDs, as well as some flyers and business cards. Eve gravitates, in spite of herself, toward Jake's latest book, *"Dear Papa": The Letters of Salamone Rossi To His Father, 1586-1610.* The book he was writing when they were together, that he told her about as they lay naked in bed. She picks up the heavy green book. So this is what Jake has been doing for the past five and a half years, instead of writing letters to her. She stands there, fighting the impulse to open the book to the inside back cover where she knows his photo will be. The last time she held in her hands a book of Jake's, it was around three years ago. She was cleaning out her basement, sorting through broken crockery, non-functioning toasters and irons, odds and ends of cutlery, as well as carpets, knick-knacks, old books and records, and outgrown clothing and toys. In the toy box, she had just come across two old puzzles of Ethan's: one was a knot challenge that she briefly tried to do and couldn't, and the other one was two linked metal rings that you were supposed to take apart and then put back together. She couldn't do that one, either. She stood there frowning as she jingled these joined metal rings, thinking that these rings were like her and Jake: she would never be able to separate them, and it was hopeless to even try. In these sorts of things, she thought, no amount of brain power or honest effort was going to help. Ultimately these were magic tricks, and only through magic could a solution be found.

A few minutes later, she went over to the pile of old books, and there right in front of her was Jake's book from two years earlier, *What's Sacred About Jewish Sacred Music?* This book, with its glossy, pale blue dust jacket, had a photo of him on the inside back cover that she had stroked lovingly (and even impulsively kissed a few times) in the days between meeting him at the conference in Toronto and re-connecting with him one month later in Israel. Stumbling across this book now in her basement, she wished there were some way to get rid of Jake — to erase him from her mind, and her life — once and for all. She was still dreaming about him at night, and daydreaming about him frequently during the day, and the harder she tried to push him out of her thoughts, the more insistently present he was. Now here he was again in this photo. Insouciant. Cheerful. Unsuffering (unlike her). She gazed at Jake's familiar, arrogant smile, and those intelligent, but also mocking, blue eyes that said to her now, "What did you expect, Eve? We had an affair. And then it ended (affairs always do). What's the big deal?"

She gazed into those cool, ironic eyes.

"I'm sorry," she said, "but I think you're going to have to die."

He didn't react.

She removed the dust jacket from Jake's book and tore its glossy paper in half. Then into fourths. Then eighths. Then sixteenths. She scanned the room, searching for something, and then she spotted the *yartzeit* candle for her father flickering on the windowsill on the opposite wall. She strode over to it and dropped onto the flame one of the fragments of the dust jacket. She stared, fascinated, as the shiny paper caught, curled at the edges, and with an acrid smell and a sizzle, disappeared. Now she fed another piece of the dust jacket to the *yartzeit* flame, this one containing two of the words from the book title: "*What's Sacred.*" When these were gone, she added another fragment of the paper to the fire. Then another. And another...

There was something beautiful, almost sacred, about this flame, this mini-bonfire ritual, and joy surged up in her. Especially when she got to the last piece of paper: one slightly larger than the others that she had been saving for the end. Carefully she inserted it into the *yartzeit* candle, and watched entranced. The paper didn't catch right away — it seemed to be hesitating, waiting for something. Then Jake's hair was on fire. His white hair was a leaping orange. And then his hair was gone, consumed, and then his forehead, his high brow. Then his eyebrow disappeared, and his eye socket, and his eye. Then the other eye. Next his cheek caught fire and burned, and his nose, and last but not least, his mouth. That mouth she loved. Gone. Burnt away. Gone forever.

Now there was nothing left at all of Jake's face. Just a wisp of white smoke, curling up in the air.

*

She stands in front of the display table at the conference, staring blankly. That afternoon in her basement three years ago is more vivid to her than anything in her present surroundings. Gradually, though, the sounds and sights around her (voices, bright fluorescent lights, the ringing of the cash register, the piles of colourful books) penetrate her consciousness and bring her back to the present. Dazed, she places Jake's heavy green book back down on the table and wanders down the spiralling ramp into the main lobby. Then out the great front doors of the Van Leer into the cool dark night. How silly, she thinks as she walks, to imagine that one can burn away love. Or exorcise obsession in a sort of voodoo ceremony. Her symbolic murder of Jake had no real effect. Sure, there was an immediate sense of catharsis, a few hours of joy, exhilaration, and an almost delirious feeling of liberation. (Like the song from *The Wizard of Oz*: *Ding dong, the wicked witch is dead.*) But by the next morning the Jake she had squashed down was back, grinning at her like a triumphant jack-in-the-box. It's hopeless, she thought with despair. I'll never escape from Jake. I'll never get over this. Never ever ever.

She now clomps down the long deserted street in the darkness. It surprises her that the street is so empty at this hour. It feels lonely, and even a bit frightening, this almost solid blackness paired with silence. To break this silence, she says, "This street is empty."

Then: "Dark, and deep."

"But I have promises to keep."

"And miles to go before I sleep. And miles to go before I sleep."

Then the street is silent again. But it turns out that she isn't alone. Now she hears from somewhere above her, maybe in a tree, a bird singing. *Hee-hee. Hee-hee.* Hee hee suggests laughter, but the tune is wistful. It's comprised of just two notes which she recognizes right away as high B followed by high A. The bird is singing the A for about the length of a quarter note, and the A for three times as long. *B, A… B, A…* Walking along, she listens to the bird song and reminisces. The first letter Jake ever wrote to her was about bird song. (Not "bird song at morning," meaning pillow talk, but really about the singing of birds.) As soon as she arrived home in Toronto after her thirteen days with Jake in Israel, she ran to her computer and found what she had hoped for: an email from him. She read it so many times she still remembers it by heart.

> *By now you're back in Toronto, and I already miss you terribly. I woke up an hour ago, and I've been lying in bed listening to the birds singing outside my window. Their music is probably just as beautiful now as it was yesterday morning when you lay in my arms and we listened to them together. But now they all sound doleful. "Where is Eve?" they're singing now. "Where's my Eve gone?"*

Eve herself feels doleful now as she plods down the unlit street. But the bird accompanying her sounds cheerful: "Hee-hee. Hee-hee…"

"Hee-hee," Eve sings, imitating the bird. Then she does this again, but this time she is singing the tune back to the bird, as if answering it. Now it answers her back. "Hee-hee. Hee-hee." She smiles. I could make some music out of this, she thinks. She can picture the beginning: she would open with those two notes — high B and A — and then build some variations on these. Advancing down the dark street, she hums a little to herself. She can hear it now: this music is starting in her. In the way, as fragile as gossamer, that a piece of music always starts in her. The moment of conception that feels to her like a deep inner tickle. Now her footsteps, as if of their own free will, speed up. Faster. And faster. She is hurrying down the street now. Then breaking into a run. To get back to her hotel room as fast as she can, to write this music down.

PART II
DEVELOPMENT

13. I COME FROM A FAMILY

THE NEXT MORNING SHE ARRIVES tired and cranky to her music therapy seminar because last night she was up till four a.m. composing her new piece, *Bird Song*. Today is Thursday, the second to last day of this seminar and also of the Jewish music conference, and of her traipsing back and forth between them. Since Tuesday she has been spending from nine to three at the seminar and then from three to nine at the conference. Back and forth, she thinks, between music therapy and music, between healing and art, between the social, interpersonal world and the inner one where she creates. This polarity exists in her life in Canada, too, she knows, but here it feels more acute. The Van Leer Institute is located just a few blocks from the Israeli Music Therapy Institute, so she has only five minutes when walking over there to make the transition between worlds.

Today she sits at the square seminar table, bored almost to tears. She is finding this five-day course much duller than the ones in previous years. Maybe it's the contrast to the conference: there the intellectual level is so much higher and the discussions infinitely more interesting. Or maybe the problem is this particular crop of students, or the teacher. Whatever the reason, she is deadly bored. She looks at her watch: two o'clock. Another hour to go. She wishes she could be at the conference instead. A Turkish Jewish feminist, Esther Alhadeff, at this very moment is beginning to perform the new *T'filat Tal* she wrote for oud and alto recorder, and afterwards she is going to be interviewed by Jacquie Halfon, whose essays on music Eve admires. It'll all be over by the time she arrives at ten past three. Meanwhile here at the front of the room stands Hava, asking them all to self-disclose about what kinds of clients they find the hardest to work with, and why they think this is. Eve sees where this is leading (into a discussion of their families of origin) and she wants no part of this. As far as she's concerned, this class has already got from her its pound of flesh closest to the heart, and she owes them nothing more.

The woman from the southern U.S., Elizabeth (by now Eve knows everyone's names), raises her hand.

"I don't like working with angry, hostile, or rejecting clients," she volunteers with her southern drawl. Like duh, thinks Eve; who does?, while Hava tries to link Elizabeth's statement to the family she grew up in (especially to the possibility of anger, hostility, and/or rejection on the part of her mother). *Fuck, how banal. And how intrusive. I'm not opening my mouth.*

But Hava doesn't ask her to. After this one example from Elizabeth, she "invites" the class to write a short composition.

"It's just for you," Hava assures them all. "No one else will see it. But it's a useful tool to help you understand how un-resolved family of origin issues might be affecting your work as a music therapist." Encouragingly Hava tells them to write something that describes where they come from. What their family was like. Maybe they could start with the sentence, *I come from a family...* "Try not to take your pen off the page," Hava advises them. "Don't think. Just write." She turns over the sand dial in front of her. "You have half an hour, but you can go a bit longer, if you wish. When you're done, just leave quietly. We'll see you tomorrow."

Eve scowls resentfully down at her notepad. She already knows what type of family she comes from. And she's not in grade four that she should have to be writing compositions during class time. But obviously she has no choice. Hava is watching them all with her beady bird-like eyes; Eve can't very well just sit here with her hands folded. Grudgingly she picks up her pen. But I'm not writing about Daddy's family, or Daddy, she thinks. I'll take the easy way out and write about the "healthy" side of our family: Mommy's.

"*I come from a family*," she writes. And suddenly, to her surprise, she hears these words being sung to the music she wrote last night and this morning. Her pen keeps moving on the page, and all the words come riding in on the winds of this music.

⤜ *I Come From A Family* ⤛

I come from a family that loves very deeply. We love so deeply we think that if you love someone, you have to pretty much die when they do. Literally, if possible. When my mother's father died, her mother (my Baba) said that now with Zayda gone, she didn't want to live anymore, and within the month she, too, was dead. One level down in true love, but still acceptable, was my Aunt Jean. When my mother's brother Philip died, Aunt Jean never remarried, even though at Uncle Philip's death she was only thirty-three. She never even dated another man. And to our family this seemed completely normal. How *could* she remarry? we thought. If she did, it would mean she hadn't really loved Uncle Philip.

When Mommy died I was three, when Baba and Zayda died I was five, and when Uncle Philip died I was seven, so by the end of grade two I had learned the cardinal rule about loving: When someone you love dies, you throw yourself, as best you can, onto their funeral pyre. Anything less means it wasn't real love.

My mother's two surviving siblings, Uncle Stan and Aunt Molly, obediently exemplified this rule. Mommy's brother and sister, still in their thirties when they lost both parents and two siblings, got sad and stayed sad. They continued with their duties — Uncle Stan still went to work every day and was a dependable husband and father, and Aunt Molly kept house and kept her husband and brought up her children — but neither of them ever laughed again. Not a real laugh. Not an open, happy laugh, just because you're glad to be alive. After Uncle Philip died, all Uncle Stan was capable of was a fake hollow laugh that he'd pull out, like a handkerchief from his pocket, whenever a laugh was socially required. Once when I was eight, I asked Uncle Stan where his real laugh had disappeared to, why I hadn't heard it in a long time. Uncle Stan wasn't offended by the question, but it surprised him because the answer seemed to him so obvious.

"Laugh?" he replied, his dark bushy eyebrows raised in wonderment. "How could I laugh? How could I ever fully enjoy life again, after your mother and Philip and my parents died? When, in a sense, my whole world had died?"

From this I understood that one must never let go of memories or of the past. You should never stop loving someone just because they're dead. You have to keep on thinking about them and remembering all the things they said and did, or else their soul won't find peace in heaven. Even ten, twenty, or forty years after you last saw them, you should still love them, and even all that time later if their name is mentioned, it should hurt you to hear it. Sadness should come into your eyes and stay there awhile.

I knew how to bring this look into Uncle Stan's or Aunt Molly's eyes even at the age of eight. It wasn't deliberately cruel or entirely frivolous on my part; I did really want to know about my mother. What she was like, things she had said and done. But I also knew that if I wanted their attention, all I had to do was say, "Tell me about my mother," and they'd immediately stop what they were doing. Aunt Molly's hands would freeze mid-air in the middle of drying her hands on her green-checked apron; Uncle Stan would lay down his newspaper or book. (I asked this of Uncle Stan more often than Aunt Molly since I saw him more: his house was nearer to ours and he had kids close to my age to play with.) Uncle Stan's face would instantly change, and his eyes would mist over.

"Aah, Betsy..." he'd say, and sigh. And then he'd be gone, staring in front of himself, remembering. I could get him to remember out loud if I was patient and encouraged him by asking questions. He'd reminisce about the good old days, about the happy childhood they'd shared when they were all still together. He'd tell me stories about my mother, but also, if I asked, about Uncle Philip and Baba and Zayda. Apparently my mother and Uncle Philip were pranksters, being the youngest ones, and remembering something funny that my mother or Uncle Philip once did, Uncle Stan would start to laugh. But then his face would grimace with pain. "Ach," he'd say, and he'd pat my cheek and stand up. "What a waste." And he'd walk away.

So in the family I come from, this is what it means to love someone. You never stop loving them. You never stop missing them. You never stop crying. Uncle Stan taught me this implicitly, but Aunt Molly was explicit. She conveyed the family credo through the stories and anecdotes she told me over the years, sitting at her kitchen table. There was the husband of one of her old schoolmates, for instance, a guy named Casey Bauman (I remember his name even now), who, ten days after his mother's funeral, was seen out on the links playing golf.

"He obviously didn't love his mother," said Aunt Molly, shaking her head. "A cold-hearted man."

There were dozens of such stories in her repertoire, about things people had done a week, a month, a year, or two years (sometimes even longer) after the death of a family member or loved one. Aunt Molly concluded each of these stories by saying smugly and with pride, "Our family is special. Other people 'get over' things. They 'move on.' But they don't love the way we do. Our love is deep. When we love, we really love."

Then she'd look at me tenderly. She'd stroke my cheek. And she'd say with satisfaction, "You, Eve, are one of us."

14. BETWEEN TWO WORLDS

EVE NODS CURTLY TO HAVA on the way out of the classroom. Outside the wind slaps her face; it's blowing wildly and there's something gritty and sharp swirling in it. A Middle Eastern sandstorm. She lowers her head, butting it like a bull against the wind, and starts the walk over to the Van Leer, her thoughts whirling in a sandstorm of questions. Does she really believe what she just wrote down? Is it true that, coming from her mother's side of the family, she's never allowed to stop thinking about, or grieving for, the people she has lost — that she is expected to weep for them forever? It sounds to her a bit far-fetched, even melodramatic, as she stomps along, her eyes half-shut against the sand. She has always thought of her mother's side of the family as the "healthy" one — and certainly it was compared to her father's — so she resists the idea now that all these warm and loving relatives were, in fact, pathologically obsessed with grief. Yet, at the same time, she knows that everything she wrote was true, and that looking at it objectively, the beliefs of her mother's family were a little crazy. She shivers and hugs herself as she tramps down Chopin Street. Well, not *that* crazy, she tells herself. There are worse things than remembering the dead people you've loved. It's a sign of respect to remember them. It's part of Jewish tradition, and most other traditions, too. Why is it sick to want to remember Mommy, Uncle Philip, Baba, and Zayda?

And Jake? asks a taunting voice. Do you have to remember him, too, till the day you die?

Eve knows this voice. It belongs to one of the witches who sometimes come to visit her. There are three of them and they come to her either individually or as a group. This one's come alone, but two weeks ago, all three of them visited her on the afternoon she bought her plane ticket online for this trip. As she printed it off on her computer, she was telling herself that although love affairs are often banal, friendships are not. And that this is what redeemed her relationship with Jake from banality. They were friends.

Friends, said the three witches in one voice. This one voice, these three witches speaking as a collective, are her chorus — her Greek/Jewish chorus, the one that appeared one day, unbidden, in her love-and-hate song cycle. She imagines these three witches, like Macbeth's, stirring a black, steaming cauldron. *Double bubble, toil and trouble...*

Friends shmends, they said scornfully to her that afternoon. Or sang it: she heard three ascending notes for "friends" (E, F, F#) and four descending ones for "shmends" (A, G, D#, D).

We *were* friends, she protested. He said we were. He said we'd stay friends forever.

Nothing is forever, said the chorus.

But he promised, she said. Then she felt stupid: she sounded like a whiny six-year-old, and the witches were cackling uproariously as if she had said something incredibly funny. They had three separate voices now, not one: they laughed at her in three different registers. Rivka, Rachel, and Leah, she named them now: the names of three of the four biblical matriarchs.

The witches finished cackling. One of them said: A guy'll promise anything to get a woman into bed.

When the cock gets hard, the brain goes soft, said another.

It wasn't like that, Eve insisted. Jake and I were *friends.*

At this the chorus cackled loud and long, in a series of high-pitched descending scales. There was wave upon wave of laughter. Then in an instant they were gone, as if deciding that Eve was too foolish to waste any more time on. But for hours afterwards their cackling echoed in her ears.

Now just one witch is visiting her. Eve sighs before answering her question: And Jake? Do you have to remember him, too, till the day you die?

If I stop remembering Jake, Eve explains, then I'm no better than he is. We promised we'd love each other always, and I'll keep that promise, even if he doesn't.

You promised him that? laughs the witch. Till death do you part? And she crows with delight.

Stop it, says Eve. Stop it.

The crowing stops. Soberly the witch says, You don't have to mourn forever, Eve. Not for him. Not for the others, either.

Of course I do, says Eve impatiently. No one but me ever thinks of them anymore. The two older generations are gone and none of my cousins care. If I stop remembering Baba and Zayda and everyone, what's going to happen to them?

What do you think will happen, Eve?

They'll die.

They're already dead.

No, they're not. If you remember people, that keeps them alive.

Metaphorically speaking.

Not just metaphorically.

So you think they're still really alive?

Yes, in a sense. In their souls.

In their souls?

I mean, obviously I know they're really dead. I just mean that remembering them can keep them a little bit alive.

A little bit alive? Is that like being a little bit pregnant?

Eve doesn't answer.

Who told you this, Eve? And how old were you at the time?

Aunt Molly. I was three or four, maybe five. It was sometime after Mommy died. Aunt Molly said that if I was a good girl and thought about Mommy a lot, I could keep her memory alive. She said that whenever someone remembers a dead person, it's like in that moment the dead person is alive again.

So you could make her alive, bring her to life, by thinking about her?

Yes.

And did you bring her back to life?

A flash of pain runs through Eve. Not enough, she answers. I didn't think about her non-stop. Sometimes I got distracted. I recall one time I was about to start a game of Blockhead with my friends, and I realized I wouldn't be able to think of Mommy while I was playing, because Blockhead requires all your concentration. So for the hour while I played that game, she had to stay dead, waiting for me to come back.

You played with your friends. You had fun.

Yes.

And that's why your mother stayed dead?

Yes. But it's not as stupid as you're making it sound.

It's not stupid for a three- to five-year-old to believe that. But it is if you're fifty-five.

I wasn't a good rememberer. At a certain point I forgot what she sounded like and looked like. With Brian, too. I can't remember his face or his voice now. It's terrible.

Did you try thinking about Brian constantly, like you did with your mother and with Jake?

No, I didn't have time. Ethan was always pulling on my arm. Mummy this, Mummy that... And Michael needed me, too. He wasn't like Ethan; he just stood there quietly, very quiet and still, looking out at me through Brian's amber eyes. But he needed me, too.

So there wasn't time...

No. I just kept going. Grieving was a luxury I couldn't afford. In fact I tried not to think about Brian. I tried not to remember.

Her forehead is cold now and nearly numb from being whipped by the wind and sand. But as she turns left onto David Marcus Street, the change in direction eliminates the wind and there is instant calm and quiet. She raises her chin from where it was pressing into the top of her coat and surveys the length of the street ahead of her. At the end of this block she'll turn left, and a quarter of a block later she'll be at the "King Lear" (as she accidentally called the Van Leer yesterday, talking on the phone to Reut).

Unlike with Brian, says the witch, with Jake you have all the time in the world to grieve. You can mourn him every day till the day you die. And you should. After all, only shallow people "get over" things and "move on." If you ever "got over" Jake, it would mean you never really loved him.

I'm a loyal person, Eve answers stiffly. I keep my word. Not like Jake.

I see. So to prove you're better than Jake (and maybe also to please your dead Aunt Molly), you'll flush another five and a half years of your life down the toilet. (Or maybe ten and a half, or fifteen.)

It's not a waste of time to love somebody.

It is if they don't love you back.

Jake still loves me, cries Eve. I know he does. Not in the usual sense, maybe, but in a certain special way.

The witch cackles. Right. In that same special way that the dead are really alive.

Eve is silent.

Anyway, says the witch, even if he did love you, romantic love is grossly overrated. One can do very well without it. But since you seem to think you need it, why not love Darryl?

Darryl? The milquetoast music therapist back home who has a crush on me?

He's a good man, and he's in love with you. What? Can you only love someone who's married or who you'll never see again?

Shut up. Go away.

I was just leaving.

And with a poof! and a cackle, she is gone.

Eve turns left at the end of David Marcus. In three or four

minutes she'll be back at the conference, surrounded by people, light, and pleasure. I can't wait, she thinks. Enough of inner demons and witches, dead people and death. Mommy wouldn't have wanted that for me. She would turn in her grave if she knew about this cult of mourning I was brought up with, that her family started in her honour. Eve's mother, from everything Eve recalls, was a happy, social, life-loving person, an accomplished violinist, known to sing at the top of her lungs at parties, and someone who loved to laugh. Eve can see her laughing now. She's standing with her head thrown back and her mouth wide open while a waterfall of clear, tinkling notes cascade from her thin yet sensual, sardonic, lipsticked lips. This isn't a "real" memory, Eve knows ("real" meaning a memory drawn from "real life"). This image of her mother, like most of Eve's "memories" of her, are derived either from old family photos or the home movies that Uncle Stan filmed way back when. From these two sources, combined with the dozens of stories she has been told about her mother, Eve has formed a composite collage of her. Something that, like a wire mannequin — just the bare bones structure of a person — Eve could use to hang her dreams on and her grief. The way the Jews exiled to Babylonia hung their violins on weeping willows.

The earliest photo of her mother that she has ever seen is an old black-and-white picture from when Mommy was about eight. She is standing with Baba and Zayda and her three siblings, apparently at the wedding feast of some relative. Mommy is wearing a plain white dress with a matching bow in her hair and is looking gravely at the camera. The latest photo of her that Eve has seen looks like a more spontaneous shot. Mommy is seated on Baba and Zayda's verandah next to Daddy, wearing her horn-rimmed movie-star sunglasses, and a cigarette dangles rakishly from her good-humoured lips.

Eve sets foot onto the long, curving path leading to the dignified front doors of the Van Leer. *Remembering Is The Key To Redemption* — that's what they taught us in Hebrew

15. THE CONFERENCE (AGAIN)

EVE, OPENING THE DOOR TO THE Van Leer, is greeted instantly by warmth, bright lights, and the subdued voices of the competent staff behind the front desk. She glances at today's schedule posted in the front lobby and then at her watch. She has missed hearing Esther Alhadeff's *T'filat Tal*, but because she finished her class composition quickly, she can make the last twenty minutes of Aldaheff's interview with Jacquie Halfon. Eve slips into a vacant seat in the front row of the auditorium, and then turns around to wave — unobtrusively, she hopes — to Miranda, Alicia, and a few other people, who all smile back or wave. Halfon is a good interviewer: astute, well-informed, and respectful of her subject without being too dazzled by her to probe or challenge her. Alhadeff, for her part, is thoughtful, reflective, and unpretentious, and Eve finds the interview enjoyable and stimulating.

When it's over, she heads downstairs for "Intersections and Interchanges Between Jewish and Christian Sacred Music." The first sacred music she ever heard was Christian: the hymns and Christmas carols that all Canadian public school students forty-eight years ago had to learn — "Abide With Me," "Silent Night," "O Come All Ye Faithful" — and she has loved them ever since. She feels embarrassed about this occasionally, though, as if this love makes her, in some way, less of a *bona fide* Jew, or anyway less of a *bona fide* composer of Jewish music. But that's ridiculous, she tells herself now as she makes her way to this session. She is especially eager to hear André Hendler, the second speaker. Hendler, an up-and-coming young Beethoven scholar from Paris, will be tracing the impact of one of Beethoven's pieces (the *molto adagio* movement of his String Quartet in A minor — the long, exquisite, and profound "Sacred Song of Thanksgiving to the Deity from a Convalescent in the Lydian Mode," which Eve loves) on the subsequent sacred music of both the Jewish and Christian traditions. This session is just one of three offered for this one-hour time slot, but the relatively small basement room, when Eve arrives, is packed as if everyone from the whole conference is there. One of the organizers, a woman named Tsipi, is running in and out, shlepping extra chairs, and Eve, after a few minutes of waiting, gets the last one. After her, everyone has to stand against the back wall, and these people — lined up like this in front of that blank white backdrop — look to her like they're awaiting a firing squad.

At the front of the room, three people (two unidentifiable because they're looking down at their notes) are seated at a long table. A fourth person up at the front is already standing at the podium, as if too eager for his turn to wait for it sitting. Eve, with a jolt, recognizes Bernie Sachs, or B.S., as she nicknamed him once. She can't stand this man. He came to lecture at her *shul* about ten years ago; there had been a *shabbaton* in honour of *Shabbat Shira*, and they'd brought him in as Scholar-in-Residence for the weekend. The woman who'd arranged the whole program, Rona Mandelcorn, was well-meaning and hard-working, but neither sophisticated nor particularly bright, and on Friday night, after his talk, she had asked B.S., in front of the whole congregation, the first question. She asked in a tremulous voice whether sacred music could help to make you a better person, or maybe even a better Jew. B.S. squashed her like a fly.

"Self-improvement, ethics, morals," he spat out contemptuously, as though he hated each of these words. "Such concepts are completely irrelevant and out of place in a discussion of sacred music. Music, thank God, has no reparative or redemptive responsibility when it comes to the inadequacies of human beings."

His tone suggested clearly that he also had no responsibility for those of Rona Mandelcorn. The woman paled, withered, and shrank visibly in her seat. For the rest of that weekend, Eve gave B.S. a wide berth. She had to attend his final session (a lecture over Sunday brunch), though, because the *shul* choir, which she was in, was performing then, a finale to conclude the whole weekend. B.S.'s lecture was on the concept of *hesed*, lovingkindness, in the Jewish mystical tradition, and how this was reflected in Hasidic music during the nineteenth and twentieth centuries. For some reason, B.S.'s sister was there: a mousy, frightened-looking woman who opened her mouth only once to make a comment, and was immediately slapped down by her brother. She looked like she might burst into tears, but didn't. This particularly shocked Eve because for every other second of his lecture that morning, B.S. spoke extremely gently and softly, in a sweetly ethereal "spiritual" tone of voice. The contrast was so jarring that ever since then Eve has associated that sort of "sweet, spiritual" tone of voice in a man with inner savagery.

Now here is B.S. himself, leaning on folded arms on the podium, looking down with a smug smile on the late arrivals straggling into the room, who then line up along the back wall. After a few minutes, he is joined by Mariella Cardozo, Nathan Singelman's assistant. Mariella introduces B.S. glowingly and at length, raving about his new book on Hasidic music. She then explains to the audience that she is introducing the introducer, and he in turn will introduce the two panelists for this session. But B.S., once he has the mike, won't let go of it. According to the program, which Eve soon checks, his "introductory remarks" were supposed to take five minutes; instead he reads from his new book for over twenty-five. Meanwhile Eve keeps looking impatiently at her watch. Why doesn't Mariella stop him? Why doesn't she or somebody else say something? Not until forty minutes into this one-hour session (which started ten minutes late) does B.S. finally sit down. Eve is furious. Calm down, she tells herself. What difference does it make? But she very much wants to hear André, and she is outraged by B.S.'s latest act of abuse. It's theft, she thinks: you've stolen time from the other presenters.

The next speaker (not André) stands up, and Eve recognizes Shlomo Cadjman. The man in the music library back then who Jake said looked like he'd had his cookie stolen away. She tells Cadjman in her mind: There are now twenty minutes left. You can have ten, and that will leave ten for André. But Stolen Cookie takes ten, then fifteen, then seventeen minutes. As he finally wraps up, Mariella is whispering something into André's ear, who then, with a shrug and good-natured laugh, comes up to the podium. In a charming French accent, he explains that with only three minutes left till the break, he will not be able to give the paper he prepared, but instead will offer just some brief remarks. He speaks eloquently and his remarks are pithy, but what can anyone say in just three minutes? It's almost worse than nothing at all. It's like being teased in sex: getting turned on and then having it taken away.

Eve, full of indignation, stands up. She is immediately swept forward on the human wave surging out of the room and up the stairs, and then getting spilled out, like Jonah from the whale, into the lobby. She stands there for a minute, confused, disoriented. She has the odd but distinct sensation that Jake is somewhere nearby. That he has come to this conference just for the final evening, to show his face, and that in a second or two, this face, gaunt and sardonic, topped by wavy white hair, will appear bobbing above the crowd. Her stomach flips over and fearfully, expectantly, hopefully, she scans the room. But Jake isn't here. He's not here, she thinks glumly. He really isn't coming. I'm not going to see him on this trip, and probably not anywhere ever again.

She heads toward the bathroom. Maybe Fran will be there. Countless times she has pictured encountering Fran in a ladies' room somewhere in Israel, their eyes meeting in the bathroom mirror as they both look up into it at the same time, while washing their hands. But on the way, Eve passes a silver pay phone and stops and gazes at it. I could call him, she thinks. I could call him and hang up. Or call him and not hang up. Just call up and talk. One human being to another. Why not? People call each other all the time. It's not illegal to call someone and say hi.

She now has such a powerful desire to hear Jake's voice — that deep, resonant voice with the English accent — that she has to physically, sharply, turn her back on these phones. As she does this, she notices she is panting slightly. What's happening to me? she wonders. I thought I was beyond this now.

Then she sees how she must look, standing here by herself, staring blankly. A silent island in the midst of a swirling, noisy, political sea.

"Stop staring, Eve, you look like a retard," Julia would say whenever Eve was deep in thought. As if one's eyes should only be turned outward, never inward, because that's a sign of mental illness or social failure. Eve searches the room now for someone to talk to. The cluster closest to her is Nathan Singelman chatting with Esther Alhadeff and Jacquie Halfon. She hesitates for a moment, then starts toward them. But a second later, before Esther and Jacquie have seen her coming, they turn away, smiling, from Nathan and leave him standing alone. Eve almost turns back. But then she thinks, Now's my chance, and she strides toward Nathan. He smiles at her as she approaches.

"Hi," he says.

"Hi."

"How are you enjoying the conference?"

"It's great, thank you. You've all done a fantastic job. How about you? I hope you are not too busy working to enjoy the fruits of your labour."

Nathan chuckles. "I'm pretty busy, but also having a good time. I was just at Nella Mikhoel's session and she was amazing."

Nella Mikhoel. "She always is," Eve manages to say. "I went to 'Intersections Between Jewish and Christian.'"

"Oh, how was that?"

She shrugs. "I very much wanted to hear André Hendler, but someone went overtime, so he was left with only three minutes at the end."

Nathan nods vaguely, indifferently, obviously not sharing her sense of injustice. In fact, she is not sure if he even heard her; he is scanning the room now as if seeking someone more interesting to talk to. Quickly she speaks before he can leave her: "I wrote to you a few months ago. I'm not sure if you got my email."

Nathan's eyes return to her and there's a slight flicker of interest in them now. "What was it about?"

"I wrote an oratorio called *Hallelujah*. A previous composition of mine, *Kaddish Concerto*, won a prize, and I think this new piece is just as good, or better. But I'm having difficulty getting it performed. I hoped you might have some suggestions."

In a matter of instants Nathan's face has shut tight. All interest and friendliness have vanished and his eyes have a caged look. "It's a hard time to get new work performed," he says, "unless you're already well-established."

"I know," she says.

"With all the cutbacks..." he adds.

She nods. Standing her ground.

"All I can suggest," Nathan says impatiently, "is patience. Bide your time. Hang in there till the climate improves. Sooner or later it's bound to."

She tries again. "I understand that *Niggun* is offering some grants to subsidize the performance of new works."

"Yes," says Nathan, looking like he'd rather be anywhere else in the world than here with her. "We've just made our selections for our first year of grants, but you can try for next year. I should caution you, though. We had three hundred applications competing for only two grants."

He has managed to make her feel, in under two minutes, utterly worthless and hopeless, and there's no point in humiliating herself further. But for a few seconds she gazes at Nathan, thinking, you wouldn't be talking to me this way if you knew about my relationship to Jake. You think I'm a nobody. But on that hierarchy you so respect, I'm not below you, but above. Jacob Gladstone, whom you admire, once was my lover and I was his best friend and confidante. We were equals and he respected me. Whereas you, to him, were just a meal ticket. And a second-rate composer lacking either talent or courage.

"Nice talking to you," says Nathan. He bounds off, reminding her of a rabbit. Out of curiosity her eyes follow him, and in less than half a minute, Nathan is laughing with Nella Mikhoel and B.S., his wide hands splayed across each of their backs. How do people like this get power and fame? she asks herself. She gazes at Nella Mikhoel, the grande dame of Jewish music, wearing her trademark red blazer and chunky bauble necklace and bracelets. She remembers Nella reflecting bitterly on the same question many years ago, before she was at all well-known: "Fame and talent have only an incidental relationship to each other," she said to Eve then.

The two of them were at some sort of family event, maybe a wedding or bar mitzvah, because one of Brian's uncles was related to Nella through marriage. Eve has never forgotten Nella's comment, and in a way it comforts her now. But she feels no desire to go up to her and say hello. Nella always kisses her when she sees her and cries out with joy as if greeting a long-lost friend, but she has never answered any of her emails about *Hallelujah*. Also, Nella knows Jake. They have a warm friendship spanning decades, they and their spouses socialize whenever Nella and Arthur visit Israel, and Eve knows that if she and Nella start talking, she'll have an overwhelming desire to tell Nella about her and Jake, or at least find some pretext to bring up his name.

Nathan and B.S. guffaw so loudly that Eve can hear them from where she stands. She flinches. These guys like to think of themselves as musicians, but in the art and commerce equation they are really all about commerce, and they embody all the vulgarity and arrogance that goes with that. *Hevel havalim,* vanity of vanities, she thinks contemptuously. Yet at the same time she knows that she is not actually any better than them. If she were successful now, and part of the Nathan, Nella and B.S. club, then she would perceive all this very differently. She would believe, as she did when she was awarded that prize seven years ago, that the recognition she received was her rightful due, the pure product of her talent and effort, and nothing to do with politics or corruption. And if she ever received a government grant or was adopted by a patron like Beethoven's Razumovsky, she might even dedicate some of her music to her benefactor, grateful that the oil of wealth could fuel the hungry soul of art.

Now, with the lights flashing to indicate the end of the break, a calmness falls over her, like the soft, slow descent of snowflakes on a silent winter's night. Success is just a random thing. It doesn't say anything about her that she's not (yet?) successful. It doesn't mean she's scum. It just means she's not successful. And as for Nathan Singelman, and B.S., and all the other B.S.'ers around, well, people like this have always existed and always will. It is simply, as Congreve said, "the way of the world."

*

An attractive young woman in a navy blue suit like a flight attendant's is trying now to herd Eve and everyone else back into the auditorium. She urges haste, but pointlessly: they are all blocked from entering by the bottleneck at the door. So Eve chats, proud of her Hebrew, with two Israeli composers, a married couple whom she met yesterday, and once inside, she sits with them two-thirds of the way up the slope. On the stage at the front, a woman in a tight bun and a tight, tailored pant suit waits for silence. When she has it, she introduces herself as Rivka Marcus, one of the directors of the Van Leer Institute. Then, at her invitation, Nathan joins her on the stage, and she starts making a speech. Eve tunes out. Instead she plays over in her mind the main theme from *Bird Song*, and contemplates a problem she is facing with the overall structure of this composition. Suddenly everyone is looking at her. The people in the rows below her — two-thirds of the auditorium — have turned around in their seats and are craning their necks to see her. She is flustered and embarrassed. What do they want from her? What did she miss while she was off daydreaming? Then her neighbours, the married composers, also turn to look behind them, and Eve sees that it's not her everyone's peering at; it's Hector Levi, sitting immediately behind her. Now Hector is rising from his seat and making his way with slow dignity down to the podium. When he gets there, he stands between Nathan Singelman and Rivka Marcus, and Rivka announces,

"The Inaugural Award for Lifetime Achievement in Jewish music, established last month by the Van Leer Institute together with *Niggun* magazine, goes to Mr. Hector Levi. Mazal tov, Mr. Levi!"

Hector doesn't look the least bit surprised; he must have been notified beforehand. Graciously he accepts the gold-plated statue that looks, from Eve's distance, like a golden calf. But no. Now that he is holding it up she can see it's a lyre.

"A David's harp," explains Rivka Marcus. "So you'll never forget Jerusalem."

Hector thanks the Van Leer and kisses Rivka on both cheeks, making her blush. Then he smiles, warmly shakes Nathan's hand, thanks both Nathan and *Niggun*, and calls *Niggun* "the

most important journal of Jewish music in the world today."
Hector speaks only briefly, but is erudite, humorous, and full
of old world charm. On the way back to his seat, hands reach
out to him and he shakes them with one or both of his hands.
But when Eve extends hers, Hector, with a pretend scowl, says,
"A handshake? No," and leaning over the Israeli composers,
kisses her on the cheek. Then he whispers, "I need to talk to
you. Sit with me at supper?"

Eve nods, smiling, feeling flattered. But then her smile fades.
Oh no, she thinks. Not again.

Now at the front of the room, Mariella Cardozo is standing
with a *chanukiah*, waiting. The room gets quiet and Mariella
lights the fourth candle of Chanukah. Then a choir of Israeli
schoolchildren, clad in blue and white, burst into song. With
shining faces, they sing three traditional Chanukah songs,
and then, joined on stage by two dozen adults, also in blue
and white, and a string quartet, a flute, a keyboard, a snare
drum, and a gong, they begin performing Uri Lvovy's *A Great
Miracle Happened Here*. Jake, Eve knows, arranged Lvovy's
great earlier masterwork, *Redemption* (originally written for
a full orchestra) for an ensemble. Jake's new arrangement was
so successful that nowadays this is the version most often
performed, and only a few people (musicians in-the-know)
realize this isn't the original. Jake confided to Eve one day in
bed that Lvovy isn't as great a composer as everyone thinks:
Jake had to fix up all sorts of mistakes while doing his new
arrangement, and if it weren't for these improvements, Lvovy
would never have achieved his current reputation. Eve was
astounded by the arrogance and silliness of this claim, but
didn't challenge it.

Now she listens to *A Great Miracle Happened Here*. It is
splendid music, done justice to by the fine voices and instrumen-
talists, and enhanced by the rosy cheeks and earnestness of the
children. She shuts her eyes and lets herself be carried away by
the music, and also by the story it tells about the desecration of

the Temple and the miracle of the inextinguishability of the oil needed for the *menorah*. Which seems to her a metaphor for the miraculousness, inextinguishability, and redemptive power of music. She relaxes now, cradled by the music, swaddled in it, feeling safe. Safe enough to travel inward. And as she travels, entering deeper and deeper into the heart of the music, into its vortex, what she meets there is Jake's smirking face.

I'm not a whore, she tells him.

And then he disappears.

I'm not a whore, she thinks. Even if he made me feel like one. Even if he referred to me that way, laughing strangely. She and Jake were talking on the phone, it was six weeks after she returned to Canada, and he told her what he told her ostensibly out of honesty (they'd promised to tell each other everything and not hold anything back). But he said this laughing, which lent it a certain brutality: "Fran says she can't compete with your young flesh."

"My what?"

"Your young flesh," he said with a smile she could hear.

She was mortified. "What did you say?"

Jake laughed again. "I said she was probably right."

What? she thought, going silent on the phone. You didn't even object? You didn't tell her that I'm not just "young flesh" to you, but your friend? How could you let your wife talk about me that way?

But that wasn't all. "That's not even the worst of it," added Jake, sounding cheerful, apparently enjoying himself.

"What do you mean?"

"She called you other names, as well."

"Like what?"

"You don't want to know."

"Yes, I do. Tell me."

There was the briefest pause. "She called you a slut," he said. And then, after another pause, "And a whore."

She couldn't breathe. A slut? A *whore*?

"She also said if I love you so much," he continued, "why don't I go live somewhere with my *pi'legesh*?"

Pi'legesh. A concubine, she thought. And I'm a slut. And a whore.

"Are you upset?" Jake was asking empathically. "I didn't mean to upset or worry you."

She didn't answer. She was still thinking, *a slut. A concubine. A whore.*

"I didn't want to tell you," he said. "But you insisted."

Somehow the conversation continued. It shifted organically from one topic to another, as always happened with them. But she doesn't remember a word of what came after this. Just that by the time they hung up, Jake had spun the whole conversation — like spinning cotton candy out of sour sugar — so that Fran's insults of her were nothing but a detail in another one of his half-mocking anecdotes about his problems with Fran.

But from that point on, she recalls, his perception of her began to change. (The music swirls around her now: "Let's count our heroes and our acts of heroism," sings the choir.) It was like Jake had started to share Fran's perspective on her and he began relating to her in a more and more limited way. He became less interested in her thoughts, her composing, her ideas about music, what was happening in her life, or her feelings. One day, she was worried sick because Ethan, then twelve, had a high fever for the third day in a row, and Jake not only didn't care; he didn't even pretend to. All he wanted to talk about was himself. The crisis in his marriage and — not the least of it — his impotence with Fran ever since he met Eve. (Sub-text: Evil Eve who was destroying his marriage. Even though his marriage and sex life, he'd told her, had both been lousy for years before she came along.)

The other thing Jake wanted from her that day was a blow job over the phone. She had, as he requested, introduced him to oral sex when they were together in Israel, and to phone sex once she returned to Toronto. Now Jake, putting the two things together, wanted phone sex with a focus on oral sex every time they got on the phone. She'd get him moaning and groaning from across the ocean halfway around the world. And this didn't bother her. She loved him, and if two people love each other, she reasoned, then nothing they do is dirty or wrong.

But later on, as Jake became cooler and more selfish, the things they were doing did start to feel dirty and wrong. And she herself started feeling dirty and wrong. Like a lascivious old man was just using her for what he couldn't get from his wife. The same way a hotel, if you're lacking a toothbrush, will oblige you by providing a cheap, disposable, temporary replacement, so for the time being you'll have everything you need. She, in a way, was this toothbrush.

How revolting, she thinks, and she feels the hundreds of musical notes in the air swarming around her like sperm. While all this was going on back then, she couldn't understand what was happening between her and Jake. She didn't grasp how he had split things up, so that Fran was the madonna (virtuous, maternal, and asexual) and Eve the whore (erotic, powerful, and bad). All she knew was that Jake was withdrawing from her, and she had to hold on to him however she could. Any relationship with him, however minimal, was better than none at all. So if Jake was interested now in only one instrument in the orchestra, and the music for that instrument had to be written only in one key, and even within that key he wanted to hear only one tune — the tune of sex —- then this was the music she would play for him. She didn't find it hard to ignite Jake's old body. When they were together in person, her just being naked near him was enough to bring his body back to life. He was so excited by her that a single kiss was all it took to delight him, and re-light him like a *chanukiah*.

But she remembers one time in their hotel room when they tried doing it standing up. They were both naked, and her warm body, not young but not yet old either, was pressed up against Jake's old, bony, desiccated one. When she grabbed his buttocks, instead of them feeling alive and responsive, like she was used to with Brian, they fell into her hands, sagging like empty sacks. Physically revolting her, making her almost gag. But then her love for him overruled that. She still wanted him — not his old body, but *him*. When she kissed him, she forgot all about the loose flesh on his old man's bum. Young Flesh, Old Flesh, she thinks — who cares? I just loved him. That unhappy, music-filled, love-hungry, sad, old man.

*

Eve is jarred by the silence all around her. It's from a pause in the music, a break between movements. She glances down at her program. There are two sections to *A Great Miracle Happened Here*. They've just finished "The Miracle of the Oil" and in a moment will be starting "The Miracle of Light." The children in the choir fidget and shuffle their feet, and in the audience there are a few coughs, some whispers, and a rustling of programs. The conductor raises her baton. Then they begin again. The children sing: "A great miracle happened here…"

Eve listens. It's magnificent music. But by the twelfth bar her mind has begun to drift again. She wasn't a whore. Even if Fran called her that. Or spun all that bullshit about her "young flesh," and later on about her being Jake's "younger woman." His young chickie. Young chickie? She was fifty years old when she and Jake met! And the age difference between them was fourteen years — not nothing, but certainly not the twenty-five, thirty, or forty year stretch between the stereotypical "older man" and "younger woman": the sixty-four-year-old man and his forty-, thirty-, or twenty-five-year-old chick. Fran just said this to preserve her own self-respect and her self-delusion that Eve was nothing to Jake except flesh. Fresh young flesh. Not his friend. Not his love. Even though Jake had told Fran she was.

To Eve now it makes perfect sense that Fran would do this. Along with the other things she did. Like warning Jake that the erotic passion he felt for Eve would soon fade and wither like grass — in a matter of months, or a couple of years at the most — and definitely wouldn't last another thirty-eight years, just as theirs hadn't. (An argument that seemed to sway Jake.) Another thing that Fran did was cook for Jake all of his favourite foods on his sixty-fifth birthday, which fell one month after Fran first learned about his "affair." She lined up all these foods on their dining room table, and for some reason, this deeply moved Jake. "The way to a man's heart is through his stomach" seems to be true, Eve thought when Jake told her about this. And then he asked her if, by the way, she was a good cook, too. He was thrilled when she said she was ("very good, in fact"). Though afterwards, thinking about it, she found this question bizarre. She wasn't applying for a job as Jake's housekeeper-cook, or even as his homemaker-wife.

No, she doesn't really blame Fran. The string instruments now join the choir, and the flute and gong, too. She would have done the same sorts of things herself if Brian had come home one day in love with another woman. She'd have used every weapon in her arsenal to try and keep her man. Fran was only trying to save her marriage. Eve feels a little guilty toward Fran. She never meant to harm another woman, a "sister." Maybe we'll meet someday, she thinks, and I can apologize to her, woman to woman. Perhaps we'll bump into each other in a bathroom or a restaurant, or at a film festival or a concert like this one. She has pictured all these scenarios, and more. She has also dreamt about Fran from time to time. She can never remember much about these dreams afterwards, but in one of them at least, Fran was crying.

No, she doesn't blame Fran for what happened. It's Jake she blames. It's Jake she can't forgive, for believing Fran. For not staying faithful to what he knew to be true about Eve. He knew she was a good person. Worthy of respect. Worthy of love. Yet he accepted Fran's depiction of her as worthless scum. This is what torments her. This is what she can't get over. That Jake, one of the most powerful, original intellects in the international music world, couldn't hold onto his own opinion, onto his own mind, when confronted by his wife's. He sold out both himself and Eve.

"It's one thing to sell me out, but don't sell out yourself," Eve said to him on the phone, when he was still negotiating with Fran over staying friends ("just friends") with Eve. "It's one thing for her to say you don't have the right, while married, to have a lover — that's fair enough — but you do have the right to have a friend. Ever since you got married, Fran's never let you have a single friend, female or male. She's made sure you've never had anyone but her. This is your chance, Jake, to change that pattern. Don't sell yourself out."

But he did. He handed himself over to Fran, and he handed Eve over, too.

Weak men, she thinks, wiping her eyes with a tissue and blowing her nose. Wimps. Slaves to their wives. Fran, Julia, it's all the same. Of course Daddy had a right to get re-married. But not to someone who hated me on sight.

Six months after Julia married Daddy, Eve, aged twelve and sitting cross-legged on her bed, overheard them talking about her when they thought she was outside in the back yard.

"You're a smart man, Henry," Julia was saying, "but when it comes to Eve, you're as blind as a bat. I know you're very attached to her; it's been just the two of you for the past nine years. But you're not seeing her clearly."

"Julia, my dear—"

"No, let me finish. When it comes to Eve, you're too soft. I understand, as you keep saying, that you've been 'both father and mother' to her all these years. But I'm more objective. With you she's as sweet as sugar. But why wouldn't she be? She's got you wrapped around her little finger. You can't see it, but everyone else can. She's manipulative and spoiled; you've spoiled her all these years. I know you did your best, Henry, but the hard truth of it is that your darling girl, your precious Eve, is a spoiled brat. Disobedient, rude, bitchy. You don't hear how she talks to me when you're not home. She needs to be taught some manners and some discipline, and as soon as possible. And she'll never learn these things living in this house with you. I'm a woman, I know better than you what a girl this age needs. I'm only thinking of what's best for Eve and her development as she goes into adolescence. Now I've done a little research, and it turns out that there's a first-rate boarding school only four hours from here..."

Eve sat on her bed with her mouth hanging open in shock. That bitch, she thought. I've never been rude to her. She's the one who screams at me and pinches and slaps. I've never done a thing to her.

Boarding school? *Boarding school?*

Now Daddy was protesting. But over the next two months, as Julia kept after him about this relentlessly and with increasing ferocity, his protests became progressively more feeble and impotent. And the next thing Eve knew, she was on a bus with a single suitcase by her side, on her way to boarding school. All her entreaties had been in vain.

"Please don't send me away, Daddy. Please. I'll be good. I promise. Just don't leave me. Please don't send me away."

*

Eve feels two taps on her shoulder. Startled, she turns around. Hector's leaning forward, his hand reaching over her right shoulder, offering her a white cloth handkerchief.

"It's beautiful, isn't it?" he whispers, his eyes damp, glistening.

It takes her a moment to understand that he means the music, and that he thinks that's why she is crying. She accepts the handkerchief, whispering, "Yes. Thanks." Then she feels awkward. She is not going to blow snot into Hector Levi's clean white handkerchief and then hand it back to him. Nor is she going to take it back with her to Canada so she can wash it properly in her machine there, and then mail it back to him in Buenos Aires.

"Actually, I'm fine," she whispers, pointing to her pack of tissues and handing him back his hankie.

"Are you sure?"

"Yes. But thank you, anyway."

Hector pats her on the shoulder paternally before settling back into his seat.

The choir is singing now, something rhythmic — up, down, up, down — like the rocking of a cradle. And something about Hector's hand on her shoulder like that — paternally (or was it paternalistically?) — reminds her now of her father. He, too, used to pat her shoulder, and carry white cloth handkerchiefs and offer them to weeping women. Daddy-Hector. And before this there was Daddy-Jake. She can remember the precise moment when Jake and Daddy first became linked in her mind. It was during that initial conversation with Jake in the music library. She and Jake were having the same type of talk about music and philosophy that she and her father used to have. In fact, it was so similar that at one point, when Jake made some passing reference to Truth, she responded automatically, "Aah, but what *is* truth?" in precisely the same philosophical tone that her father always used when asking that question. It felt at that moment like her father was inhabiting her, like she had become him, instead of herself. Which, in a way, means that Jake fell in love not with her, but with her father. And since he and Daddy had so much in common, that was nearly like Jake falling in love with himself. Narcissus gazing into the water.

And here it is, happening all over again. Linking Hector and Daddy. It's like a chain. Like some paternal torch being passed from hand to hand. From Daddy to Jake. From Jake to Hector. A paternal, electric-Electra torch being passed from hand to hand. She recalls how Daddy "passed her over" to Jake. Daddy had come to that conference back then to hear her speak. He was always trying to make things up to her, plus this was the sort of public gesture of filial affection he went in for, telling people he'd come to hear "his little girl." The day after that, she visited Daddy at his home. (*His* home; she had never thought of it as hers since the day they kicked her out to go to boarding school.) Her father didn't say a word about her presentation at the conference, even though it was a smashing success and there was a real buzz about it, as he must have known. But when she told him that she and Jake had had a long talk after the panel, and that he'd looked at her music and said that she had "great talent" and "the potential to be world-class," then Daddy was impressed. He sat in a winged chair — winged like a chariot, she'd thought, looking at it — just like the one she used to curl up in with him, to listen to music when she was three. Seated on the sofa opposite him now, she felt again like a three-year-old, because still, forty-seven years later, she craved his approval, and felt gratified now to get it. Even though, as she very well knew, this approval was only coming to her because someone else — someone famous, an accomplished powerful male, much like Daddy — had praised her music. Only for that reason did Daddy now see it, and by extension her, as perhaps having some value.

Her father, being a music lover, had of course heard of Jake before hearing him talk on the panel that day. He even had one of his books in his living room, and he stood up and took it off the shelf when Eve mentioned his name. He was impressed by Jake. And this struck her forcefully because never before had he been impressed by any of her men. Not even Brian. Especially not Brian, who wouldn't laugh at his little putdown "jokes" about Eve. Now she could feel his fascination with Jake, his respect for him. And sitting in the airplane on her way to Israel a month later, she felt she was flying there with her father's blessing.

Silence in the auditorium. The concert is over. Clapping erupts and someone howls "Bravo!" The clapping goes on for quite a while, along with more "Bravos," standing ovations, and repeated bows. Eve doesn't respond when the Israeli man on her right murmurs, "A tour de force." Clapping absent-mindedly, she is remembering something odd about that visit to Daddy's house. Even though by then he must have already been sick, riddled through with the disease that killed him only six months later (which was also one month after Jake left her), he still looked perfectly well on that particular afternoon, and she had no idea he was ill. Gazing at him holding a tumbler of whisky in his hand, she couldn't help noticing with surprise that he looked younger than Jake. At seventy-five, her father had grey hair but a face that was remarkably unlined. Everyone said he didn't look a day over sixty-five, maybe even over sixty, and they weren't just flattering him (though people often did). He truly did look young for his age. He was fit and trim and walked briskly and purposefully, and the overall feeling you got from him was of someone full of youthful energy: someone with places to go and things to do. Whereas Jake had deep, long, vertical lines in his face, furrows like rows ploughed in the earth, ready for planting. And although Jake wasn't heavy or slow-moving, he totally lacked the sense of physical vigour that Daddy radiated until just two months before the end. If you looked at Jake, at that lined face and white hair, you'd think: *old man.*

Everyone's standing up. The din of voices and laughter, and the jostling of bodies against Eve's as she and a hundred and twenty other people file out of the auditorium, jolt her back to the present. On the way toward the dining room, Hector is mobbed by congratulators and well-wishers and she can't get anywhere near him. She grabs one of the tables for two, reserves it with her jacket on one of the two chairs, and at the buffet is careful not to take too much of anything. This last supper seems to be quite a skimpy affair.

"Cutbacks," Miranda mutters to her as, next to each other in the line at the buffet table, they survey the modest spread. Then Miranda spots, on the far side of the room, the gang from London she arranged to have supper with, and waving at them, hurries off. Now Eve sits down and soon Hector finds and joins her. She wolfs down everything on her plate — there's variety if not quantity: a bit of cold turkey, some salad, a small slice of warm chicken breast and a few florets of broccoli — and, thirsty, she downs a goblet of white wine like it's water. Meanwhile, across from her at the table, a steady stream of people has been coming over to greet Hector or pay their obeisance. It's *déja vu*. Not just of the conference years ago with Jake, but of her entire childhood with her father. It feels now like she has spent her whole life alongside one Great Man or another as his young female, whether as his daughter or lover.

Now Hector turns away from the young man he has been conversing with in Spanish, and says to her, "Excuse me, my dear. I'll just be a moment longer."

Probably he is intending to be courteous and solicitous, to convey respect and consideration for her. But somehow this feels to her like a declaration of ownership. (If not current, then imminent: *Eve belongs to me*, or *Eve will soon be mine*.) Even so, Eve, digging into the rather dry layered lemon cake that a waiter just brought around (her fork clinking repeatedly against her plate: ting, ting, ting) can't help but feel attracted to Hector. To his warmth and bushy eyebrows, his old-world charm and gallantry, and his "my dears." Finally the line of admirers is almost gone. To Eve's delight, Hector now banishes the last visitor-supplicant, the awful, simpering Rebecca Milner, by saying, "You'll have to excuse me now, my dear. Eve and I have some business to discuss."

The business Hector wants to discuss is his upcoming trip to Toronto in a little over a month, to give a lecture. He has never been there before, and wonders what she would suggest he do on his one spare afternoon and evening. Perhaps, if she has time that day, she can show him some of the sights. Or even if not, he hopes they will at least see each other when he is in Toronto.

He attracts Eve. She can feel it in her blood, in her bones. She can't help it. But at the same time she is laughing to herself. So *this* is how it's done. Jake five and a half years ago was just picking her up at a conference. That's all that was. How naive she'd been! She had thought he was genuinely impressed by her ideas and her music. When really it was just a pick-up. No different fundamentally than being hit on when walking down the street or in a bar. It's merely a little more sophisticated and intellectual in style. Instead of "Haven't we met somewhere before?" you talk about music or Judaism or the soul. Just as Hector will probably start doing in a moment. Eve is laughing not just inside now, and Hector, interpreting this to mean that she is enjoying him, leans closer and touches her on the arm. His touch is heavy, and his fingers crude and red like the sausages on his plate. But Eve doesn't mind his fingers on her arm. She's laughing. She finds the whole thing funny. Funny-sad, maybe, but funny. Now she can get rid of Jake if she wants. If she needs another ubermensch in her life, some father-lover, she can trade Jake in, like an old car, for Hector. And after Hector she can always find someone else: another fatherly type, another old man, the chain going on and on forever. Or anyway until this chain, encircling her neck like a Medea-poisoned necklace, chokes her to death.

Still laughing, she has tears in her eyes. What kind of a stupid game has she been playing all these years? And how much longer is she going to keep on playing it?

Hector lays his hand on hers. She is still laughing. In a few days she'll be back in Toronto and she'll probably never see this guy again. But now Hector surprises her. Kindly, gently, he asks about her music. At first, not believing he cares, she answers glibly. But no, he does care. Or anyway, he won't accept her glibness. He persists, he presses her for answers, he seems genuinely interested, he asks her question after question until she breaks down and pours out her heart about her poor *Hallelujah*, which — like Cinderella-*Cenerentola* at the beginning — is good and beautiful but unloved and rejected; and why won't anyone perform it, and why won't anyone help her get it performed? He is drying her tears with his handkerchief, his good, clean, white hankie, and saying, "I'll help you, I'll help you, I will." He says if he likes it (and he can't imagine he won't), he'll connect her to a producer he knows and he'll get *Hallelujah* performed in London and New York.

"Don't worry, I'll help you," he whispers into her hair, as she throws her arms around him.

PART III
RECAPITULATION

16. KIBBUTZ

THE NEXT MORNING, FRIDAY, Eve finishes up at the seminar and the conference (the final half-day for both). Then she hops a bus up north. It's a two-and-a-half hour ride and looking out the window at the changing Israeli landscape (from mountainous desert to flat plain, then to rolling hills and valleys), she worries about still not having an ending, or even a title, for her love-and-hate cycle. She has barely given this any thought over the past five days, and in only three more she'll be back home, and just one week after that is the deadline for the annual Jewish music competition that she wants to submit her cycle to. This contest feels like her only chance to get her cycle performed and also to get her name "out there." And equally – maybe more — important, there's a bag of money attached to this prize: $10,000, which would buy her some time away from her music therapy practice so she could compose full-time for almost six months. How I'd love to win that prize money, she thinks, gazing out the window at a lone farmhouse, four cows eating grass with their heads bowed as if they're praying, and a neglected-looking broken tree. I need to find an ending for this cycle (this cycle that keeps going round and round). Time is running out.

At three o'clock she reaches her cousin's kibbutz. The kibbutz is glorious this time of year: it's the rainy season and everything is green, moist, fragrant, and swelling with life. The main crop here is avocados, which Eve visits as soon as she has dumped her canvas bag on the porch of her cousin's little three-room bungalow. They're not expecting her till four; she is sure they won't mind if she goes for a walk now. In the orchard the ripe avocados hang heavily from the trees. They're a deep, dark green, their leaves (the same colour) are shiny and dripping wet from the recent rain, and the orchard smells like life itself. Recalling the story about the four rabbis who entered an orchard and had a mystical experience there, Eve — wearing her cousin's rubber boots, borrowed from his front porch — sloshes along the muddy paths feeling happy and alive. For the next half hour, there are no thoughts in her head as she tramps her way through the avocado grove. She is all avocado fruit and rustling leaves and strong rough tree trunks and the smell of the wet earth and the fresh damp air and the forest's deep magical silence. Co-existing with this silence, not disturbing it at all, there's the boom, boom of her footsteps and the snapping of branches and the scurrying of small animals in the underbrush and the chirping of birds high up in the trees, while along the forest floor, the late afternoon sun has silkscreened a dappled pattern onto the shadows. In the midst of all this, she feels such joy, such ecstasy, that at one point, noticing it, she is embarrassed. I'm like a foolish child, she thinks, happy for no reason. ("Wipe that foolish smile off your face," Julia used to say, "before I wipe it off for you.") But now in this orchard Eve knows that it's not foolish to be happy, and that there are many good reasons for happiness, especially here in this enchanting, enchanted place. So as she continues along, she is grinning and laughing, and dancing little dances when she sees she is alone on the path, and now and again humming snatches of this and that. There are no big thoughts or ideas here in this orchard. No words or worries. Just the same, when Eve emerges a half-hour later from the dark grove into the clear light of the late afternoon, she knows some things somehow that she didn't know before.

She knows, for instance, that Jake was a really sick man. Never mind the label — psychopath, sociopath, it doesn't matter. The fact is he was, and is, a deeply disturbed person. As dark as the shadows in an avocado grove. No. Darker.

The other thing she now knows is how sick she herself has been for the past five and a half years. I've had Post-Traumatic Stress Disorder, she thinks with surprise. The reason that she hasn't been able to get over what happened with Jake isn't, as she has supposed all these years, because what they had together was so good; on the contrary, it was because it was so bad. So degrading, maybe even abusive, in the last seven weeks of the relationship. Once Jake gave up his own voice and took on Fran's, from that point on he made Eve feel hated. Disgusting. Contemptible.

Post-Traumatic Stress Disorder. She grimaces as she crosses a field lit up by the thin rays of late afternoon sun. Her version of PTSD is milder, obviously, than that of people who have been kidnapped or psychologically abused over a long time, but she has been experiencing, for these past five years, all the same symptoms, including one of the hallmarks of PTSD: flashbacks. Like that time Michael was helping her in the kitchen after supper one evening (she was hand-washing delicate items that couldn't go into the dishwasher, and he was drying them), and he asked her, "Mom, what's wrong?"

She was standing at the sink, frozen in mid-motion, holding a plate a few inches above the dishwater, with suds all over her hands. She had just remembered reading for the first time the email from Jake where he broke it off, and how she screamed and screamed and screamed. And now with Michael next to her, she stood transfixed at her kitchen sink, lost in the past. Back then memories like this attacked her often. Almost constantly at first, over a thousand times each month for the first year or two, because at that stage everything, all roads, led to Jake. Everything she thought, everything she felt. The way streams and rivers automatically flow to the sea.

Repeatedly, all day long, she was interrupted by memories of incidents that had happened with Jake (some positive, some negative). Gradually these memory attacks became less frequent, though it still happens once in a while. Like little electric shocks or mini lightning bolts. On that particular evening with Michael, it took some time till she realized he was speaking to her. When she finally became aware of him, she saw that he looked frightened, and she heard him asking her, "Mom, what is it?"

"Nothing, honey," she answered after a few moments, touching him reassuringly on the arm. "I just remembered something."

But those weren't just "memories," she recognizes now, even though that's how she has always thought of them. They were flashbacks. Just like the flashbacks experienced by some of the clients in her music therapy practice. She has had clients over the years who, either in Canada or in the countries they came from, survived various traumas: fires, physical or sexual abuse, earthquakes, terrorist attacks, torture in dungeons. What they endured is obviously on a completely different scale from what she went through with Jake. Yet undeniably she has many of the same symptoms. *Why?* she asks herself urgently. What is it about what happened with Jake that was so profoundly traumatic? She doesn't want to see herself as a "traumatized" person or as "a survivor" — especially not "survivor," which to her is just another word (the currently fashionable word) for "victim." Yet in spite of this, as she trudges through the field outside the orchard, she can recognize, even if reluctantly, that something happened to her with Jake that was genuinely traumatizing. So here's one little clue to the Big Mystery, she thinks. The mystery of why I lost more than five years of my life over what was, on the face of it, a simple affair.

It was not a simple affair.

This is what Eve learned from the avocados. From the birds on the kibbutz, she learns something else. Walking back toward her cousin's house, she crosses a long meadow covered in yellow flowers and hears a bird's song she's never heard before. *ABC. ABC. ABC?* she thinks. This bird sings an alphabet song!

ABC, it sings. *ABC*.

A couple of minutes later, strolling along, on her right she hears:

GGGG high D, GGGG high D.

In a tree off to the left, another bird replies: *DC#. DC#.*

GGGG high D, GGGG high D.

DC#. DC#.

GGGG high D, GGGG high D.

DC#. DC#.

GGGG high D, GGGG high D.

Now silence.

Then loudly, sharply, urgently, as if it's crying out, Where are you?:

GGGG high D, GGGG high D.

A pause. Then a faint, far off answer: *DC#. DC#.*

Silence.

GGGG high D, GGGG high D. But more softly now, more warbly.

An answering call comes to it from much further away.

As she is standing there listening to this, a cheerful-looking red and yellow bird swoops down from somewhere and flies all around her vigorously, loudly flapping its wings. Then it hovers for a while, still flapping, above her head. (She hopes it doesn't shit on her.) And from all this bird music and from the proximity of this friendly, humorous visiting bird, she realizes that her *Bird Song*, the piece she started composing two days ago, is completely lacking in joy. It's not an utterly worthless piece, but it's plodding and dull, and in some places dead. And she doesn't feel dull or dead anymore. So she grabs a pen and notebook from her back pocket and starts jotting things down. A minute later, scribbling furiously, she sinks down, cross-legged, onto the squishy, marshy grasses and flowers, and writes happiness and joy into her music.

Last but not least, Eve learns something new from the flowers. After fifteen minutes of composing, she stands up and is rubbing off the mud and grass from the seat of her pants, when she glances down at the ground and notices the depression that she has left there. She has inadvertently sat on, and crushed, a few yellow flowers. She always apologizes to the bugs she kills in her house or the flowers she plucks from her garden, and now automatically says, "I'm sorry," to the flowers she just crushed. Then she sees how weird this is. Surely she, like everyone else in the world, has a right to sit in a field and accidentally crush a few flowers without feeling like a murderer. This earth is her home, too, as much as any bug or flower's. She has a right to be here, and to live here without apology or shame. She recalls the words of her mother's old aunt Mildred, sounding and looking like a witch, right after the funeral. "How can you laugh and sing now, you terrible girl? We just put your mother into the ground two hours ago. How dare you sing!"

I'm allowed to be happy, Eve answers her now. And yes, I dare to sing.

Grinning a huge grin, and bellowing out GGGG *high* D as if she's Pavarotti, she enters her cousin's house.

17. FRIDAY NIGHT

EVE IS GREETED EFFUSIVELY by her cousin and his wife. She is embraced, fed tea and cake, questioned, listened to, laughed with, and enjoyed. It's been eighteen months since she was last here (she doesn't travel north every time she is in Israel), so they have some catching up to do. Most exciting at their end is the news that their daughter, the graceful and outspoken Shira, is engaged. Just yesterday she and her fiancé made the announcement, and within half an hour of Eve's arrival, this little bungalow is full of people and joy. Shira and her shy young man, Yuval, sit on the couch holding hands while friends and neighbours drop in to congratulate them. Eve's cousin Barry is, generally speaking, outgoing and gregarious, but now he is ebullient and positively glows as he offers around trays of cake and wine, pressing his guests to eat and drink. On his way back to the kitchen at one point to refill the cake tray, he passes his wife Leah coming out with some glasses, and surprises her with a kiss on the cheek.

"You see?" he declares jovially to his guests. "It's not just young people who are in love!" A couple of men his age laugh, and then joke back and forth with him a bit. Eve watches all this with pleasure. She loves Barry ("Baruch" he calls himself now, but she'll never be able to think of him as anything but Barry), and feels he deserves all this joy and *naches*. And even though she doesn't know any of his three children well, she has always liked what she has seen of Shira.

"To the bride and groom!" Eve cries in Hebrew, raising her glass of wine toward the young couple. Everyone there, crowded together in the small room, those sharing chairs or perching on tables or standing, raise their glasses (or their teacups, or *rogelech*, or whatever they're holding in their hands), and echo: "To the bride and groom!"

A couple of hours later the party breaks up as people head over in small clusters to the communal dining room for Friday night dinner. Eve is relieved to see that, despite the privatization of the country's kibbutzim in recent years, Barry's kibbutz still provides a communal meal on Friday nights. She finds it interesting, though, since this isn't a religious kibbutz; in fact, it's an anti-religious one.

"Even so," Barry says to her when she mentions this, as they take an after-dinner stroll, just the two of them, around the kibbutz, "Friday night is Friday night."

A short walk from the dining room, Barry shows her the latest development on his kibbutz: extensions being built on the bungalows of the three longest-standing members. (Barry and Leah's turn, he says, will come in two and a half years.) Eve and Barry, ambling along the clean white kibbutz paths, discuss the effects on the whole community of this latest example of the trend toward privatization, as well as the implications of the imminent "restructuring" (a euphemism for privatization) of the kibbutz's avocado business. Barry, cheerful and optimistic by temperament, is more upbeat about all this than Eve. She feels gloomy about the unravelling of the traditional kibbutz way of life and the death of this unique socialist experiment in collective enterprise. Not that any of this is really a surprise to her. She has watched this creeping, creepy privatization of the kibbutzim nation-wide over the past fifteen years. Barry's kibbutz, though, is one of the last in the area to fold to the capitalist ethic, and so it feels to her like something major and symbolic has happened since she was here last. Then again, she thinks as she and Barry tramp along, what right do I have to expect this group of people to continue a lifestyle that is no longer economically viable for them? Why should they have to live out my romantic ideals and dreams? I'm not living here. Barry and his family, and everyone else on this kibbutz, is entitled to a larger house if they want one, and all the same material comforts I enjoy in Toronto. She sighs. She knows all this is true. Just the same, the whole thing saddens her.

But Barry cheers her up. Barry always does. He remembers that she likes the petting zoo on the kibbutz, a project started ten years ago by Leah's brother's wife to teach the kindergarteners about small animals and their habits. So now he leads her in that direction. On the way they pass a couple dozen people returning home from Friday night dinner in the dining room, a few of them (city guests probably) dressed in the traditional Sabbath white. Barry smiles or waves at everyone, greeting one or two by name. At the petting zoo, which has only twelve species of animal, the monkeys whoop and screech and the squirrels run on the wheels in their cages. As Eve watches the monkeys, one of them flings itself against the bars closest to her and peers out at her. A minute later a goat licks her timid hand with its rough pink tongue and she laughs. Then, getting a pungent whiff, she says, "He needs a bath!" and Barry laughs, too. His laugh is boisterous and big and he has a big beard to match (once black, now greying), which makes him look like Theodore Bikel in *Fiddler*.

The air is gentler up here than in Jerusalem, with none of the biting-into-your-bones coldness and wind Eve has endured for the past few days. Here there is only a mild coolness, and being near the sea, a soft humidity. As a result there are flowers and fruit trees everywhere. Continuing on their stroll along the lit-up paths (the lamps came on as soon as it got dark), she and Barry pass magenta bougainvillea cascading over the balconies and walls of the rec hall and children's houses, and splashing with colour many of the white concrete bungalows.

In front of these, on small front lawns, lush fruit trees tower proudly: plum, apple, lime, and loquat, and also her favourite, the heavenly-smelling orange tree with its lily-like white blossoms. In addition, she spots flowers in many sizes, varieties and colours (pink, purple, red, yellow, and orange) cheerfully lining the two sides of the path she and Barry are walking on. Now Barry stops and shows her a small garden. It's a circle filled entirely with white flowers, but of ten different species. Barry explains that this garden was planted just a few months ago in memory of two boys from the kibbutz who were killed in the second Lebanon war. Since one of Barry's hobbies is learning about the wildflowers of Israel, he knows both the English and Hebrew names of every flower in this garden, and now, with evident self-satisfaction, he points to each one and tells Eve its English name: "Mad Apple. Stinkwort. Winter Crocus. Angel's Trumpet. Star of Bethlehem. Nightshade. Shepherd's Needle. Greater Bindweed. Narcissus."

Narcissus! Jake's flower.

"Speedwell."

Godspeed to you two boys. And flights of angels sing thee to thy rest.

She and Barry mosey companionably on. A dog, chasing a cat up and down the path they're on, is barking loudly with frustration, and nimbly weaves around them, at one point darting in and out between Eve's legs. She nearly trips but steadies herself, laughing. Then, after a minute or two of sauntering on in pleasant silence, she says to Barry (thinking this might interest him since his mother and hers were first cousins):

"À propos of memorializing loved ones who have died..." And she tells him about *I Come From A Family*. Barry laughs uproariously.

"That is so true!" he cries out, still laughing. "Our family is crazy. Wonderful but crazy! They love to mourn. That's one thing I love about Israel: it's exactly the opposite. God knows we always have enough to mourn about here. But (or maybe not but; maybe that's why) people here grab every opportunity to rejoice."

She nods. What he says about Israelis is true. Now they've reached the dairy cow sheds and chicken coops, and here they pause, gazing at the cows. Leaning on a fence, she inhales their good, natural smell and listens to the night-time silence broken only by the occasional moo or clucking of chickens. From somewhere not far off she vaguely senses the presence of the cool avocado groves and the rhythmic waves of the sea. Everything here feels alive and peaceful. Quietly she begins to hum. An old Israeli folk dance tune from her first days in the youth movement. Barry joins in. They smile at each other and then sing the whole way back to his house, despite a disapproving frown from an old man, Barry's neighbour from two doors over. Back at Barry and Leah's, Eve chats with Leah while Barry pops next door to help someone with a broken hot water heater. Then he, Leah, and Eve sit out on the porch, chatting, laughing, singing, drinking tea, and nibbling on plums, home-baked cookies, and the chocolate-covered cashews Eve brought. Barry seems happy, she thinks. And with good reason. Kibbutz may no longer be the idyll it once was, but it's still a good life. And Leah, calm, quiet, practical, and warm, is the perfect counterbalance to Barry's enthusiastic boisterousness. Now their youngest child, Gil, still in high school, drops by to borrow Barry's video camera, and the flow of affection between him and his parents is palpable. This family seems happy and at peace.

After Gil leaves, Eve, Leah, and Barry sit for a while, absorbing the deep silence around them. There is no sound here of cars or planes or machinery, just the soundless music of the hills and forests and the ploughed and unploughed land. Then Leah stands up and says she is turning in. Barry rises, too, and they all kiss and say good night.

Eve smiles contentedly as she gets ready for bed. And for the ten thousandth time since leaving Israel thirty years ago, she thinks: Maybe I should move back here. I feel safe in this country. I feel at home.

Then: Don't go there. Don't start that all over again.

And she doesn't.

She sits on the edge of the bed she'll sleep in (which belongs to Barry and Leah's middle child, Isaac, who's now in the army), and checks her email on her Blackberry. Mixed in with a lot of junk is an email from Hector. It's short, just a few sentences long, but it's warm, appreciative, and mildly suggestive (just suggestive, not seductive, or anyway not crudely or embarrassingly so). Just perfect.

Eve, my dear, what a delight to meet you this week! You were the highlight of this conference for me. I eagerly look forward to seeing Hallelujah *and also to seeing you again* very soon. *Affectionately, your new friend, Hector*

Smiling, she turns off her Blackberry and curls up under the home-made quilt, crocheted by Leah one square at a time and then sewn together. But just as she is dozing off, sinking into oblivion in the final minute before sleep, something happens to her that happens to her every few months. She sees faces. Faces of people she doesn't know. They come toward her, one at a time, look her right in the eye for a few long moments, and then make room for the next person. It's like a slide show, with one face after another filling the whole screen. Some nights just two or three people visit her; other times it can be up to fifteen, their faces flashing quickly before her like in a lightning round. Right now she is looking into the rough, lined, suntanned face of an old Greek man, a labourer or farmer of some kind, and his eyes gazing into hers are wise, full of life experience, and extraordinarily alive. Next comes a black woman from Africa with a red and yellow striped head scarf, holding a plump, naked baby. Then there are six or seven more faces, one after another: men, women, and children she has never seen before (unless perhaps she passed them in a crowded street or sub-way). It's a parade of people she doesn't know, just part of the mass of unknown humanity. Yet they don't feel unknown to her. It feels like she knows them all. Each and every one of them, and intimately, too, as if in a former life they were her family or friends.

Sometimes she gets confused by this, so much so that she is not sure who she is anymore. Some nights it feels like she is all of these people she is looking at. Even in the daytime occasionally, she'll be in the middle of doing something, like walking from the living room to the dining room, and instead of seeing herself doing this, she pictures that it's someone else. Instead of her own face, the face of the walker belongs to one of her sons, maybe, or her father, or mother. Or even to one of the strangers she sees at night.

Now lying under Leah's cosy quilt, she notices that the mouths on some of the faces she is looking at are moving. They seem to be speaking to her, trying to tell her something important, something urgent. But she can't tell what. She can't hear what they're saying, try as she might. Their mouths silently open and close, open and close, like fishes'. And then she falls asleep.

18. SATURDAY TILL 3

SATURDAY MORNING IS LOVELY and relaxing. Eve, Barry, and Leah go for a leisurely walk that skirts the avocado orchard and ends at the kibbutz pool overlooking the mountains. Eve goes in for a quick dip, then sits around the pool chatting with Barry, Leah, Shira, Yuval, and Yuval's parents. Back at Barry and Leah's, the three of them share a pleasant simple lunch (quiche, a variety of salads, and a fruit pie), and then Barry and Leah disappear for a nap — a euphemism, Eve knows, for Shabbat afternoon sex. Obligingly she leaves the bungalow and sits with a music therapy book in Barry and Leah's backyard. Or anyway the narrow, untended, thistle-ridden patch behind their house, with a view only of a neighbour's back wall, dominated by a protruding, rusty air conditioning unit. Not in the mood to read, she contemplates this wall.

Do you love me? she asks. She knows by this time that she isn't any longer asking this of Jake. But whoever it is she's asking it of, she needs to ask it at least a few times each day.

Do you love me? she asks, gazing at the air conditioner. Do you?

Of course you don't.

Will you hold me, though? Just a little?

No. Of course you won't.

Shit. As soon as she thinks she is okay, or anyway "better" than she was — the minute she is sure all that craziness is behind her — zing! it's back again, flicking her in the face like a rubber band. And this right now is ridiculous: sitting on a cracked plastic chair in this ugly, depressing spot, rather than on Barry and Leah's front porch, just because being alone there might bring back some memories. This is truly crazy.

She gets up, tramps around to the front of the house, and on Barry and Leah's porch settles into the loveseat swing that sometimes swings and sometimes doesn't. She gives it a try: no luck this time. Eve closes her eyes for a minute or two. Only then does she dare to open them and raise them to the little footpath that links Barry and Leah's bungalow to the main path running through the kibbutz. Now she can see Jake walking up this little path toward her. Because this is where she sat, on this porch, and in this exact loveseat, five and a half years ago, waiting for him to arrive. And on that day he did. It was a Saturday afternoon just like this one, only warmer because it was spring, and she had spent a relaxing twenty-four hours with Barry and his family, similar to the ones just now, except that Barry's mother, Varda, was still alive then. The last of her generation on Eve's mother's side, Varda had been diagnosed a couple of months before with cancer, but was already fading fast, so at Barry's invitation, Eve had come here to see her one last time. By that Saturday, though, Eve had met Jake three times in Jerusalem and was in love, and would have much preferred to be with him, rather than her relatives. But seeing Varda had really been the *raison d'être* for this trip to Israel — without Varda's illness, she reasoned, she wouldn't be getting to know Jake at all — and anyway, she knew he'd be here soon to give her a lift back to Jerusalem.

On that particular Saturday, this porch was crammed with relatives and neighbours. Barry, Leah, Isaac, and Varda were there, as well as a cousin of Barry's on his father's side who was visiting with his family, as was Leah's sister. There were some neighbours and friends, too, a few of them lolling about on the outer sides of the banisters. Everyone was sipping cold red or green syrupy drinks as they chatted, gossiped, laughed, and fanned themselves in the unseasonably warm spring weather. Eve was trying to be polite to Leah's sister, who kept asking her questions about music therapy, but Eve was too excited and nervous over Jake's imminent arrival to answer in a focused way, and she kept glancing at the front path, which then, as now, had a broken brick about halfway down, and an unhappy-looking shrub on one side. Eve was stammering out another indifferent reply to Leah's sister when, all of a sudden, here was Jake striding up the path. Jake with his lovely long legs ("Daddy long-legs," she thought), and a smile at her that was so broad and happy, it was on the verge of turning into a laugh. She smiled back, but looked quickly down. They had agreed the day before on the phone that they would act as casual as possible in front of her relatives.

"Like colleagues," she said. Which is how Jake had asked her to act whenever they were out in public together. He was concerned about his reputation. They'd practised on the phone:

"Good afternoon, Ms. Bercovitch."

"Good afternoon, Mr. Gladstone," before bursting out laughing. Now she watched as Jake, striding up the path, struggled to conceal his joy at seeing her again, and she found this very touching, and felt tender toward him.

"Ready to go?" he asked her brightly, when he reached the bottom of the steps leading up to the porch.

By this time all the conversations had stopped and everyone was openly observing her and Jake.

"Yes," she answered self-consciously, feeling like the two of them were performers in a play in front of an audience. She could feel how much he wanted to just whisk her away and not have to deal with her relatives. But she also knew this wasn't possible. "First, though," she added, "come say hello for a minute." To her relatives and their neighbours she said, "This is my colleague, Jacob Gladstone."

Jake came up the steps. "Nice to meet you all," he said to

the whole group in Hebrew. They answered him back, he and Barry shook hands, and Jake smiled at everyone politely, but his eyes kept coming back to her. She could sense like a physical force how badly he wanted to be alone with her, how he wanted, needed, to have her all to himself, so he could hold her and kiss her and touch her. So she rose from the loveseat, explained that Jake was in a rush, thanked Barry and Leah for their hospitality, and kissed them goodbye. They kissed her back and then hugged her affectionately. Jake drank this up with his eyes, watching this scene proudly, almost proprietorially, as if Eve were his, and how loved she was somehow reflected well on him. He descended the steps halfway, waiting there for her, and soon she followed. Then she cried, "Oh!" and spun around and ran back up to the porch. Off to the right, a little away from everyone else, sat an old woman with white hair.

"This is Barry's mother," Eve said to Jake. "My mother's cousin Varda." And she beckoned to him.

Jake came up to one step below the top, leaned toward Varda with a smile, said "Nice to meet you" in Hebrew, and shook her hand. Standing, as he was, one step down from the porch, he had to bow slightly forward when he did this, and this made him look gallant to Eve, as if he were a nobleman at court, bowing to kiss the hand of a dowager. But as charming as he appeared to Eve, Varda looked unimpressed, and didn't return his smile.

"Your mother's cousin didn't like me," Jake whispered to Eve when they were a reasonable distance away from the house. "Do you think she guessed about us?"

"I don't know," she said. "She's always been a smart woman, but now that she's sick, she's not all there. She 'goes in and out,' as they say. She may not even know who you are."

"I don't know who I am, either," he smiled. "Am I still Mr. Gladstone, or can I now be Jake again?"

She chuckled. "Not till we get to the car. We'll be there in just a minute or two."

They were walking along a dusty trail that led to the parking lot, situated near the cow sheds. As they approached the car, there was a pungent bovine smell.

"Don't open the window till we're off the kibbutz," she advised. "The smell clings."

Inside the car, they smiled at each other and held hands for a moment. Then they drove off the kibbutz.

It's still so clear, she thinks now with surprise, sitting on the flower-patterned loveseat. That whole scene is as vivid to her as what she ate for lunch today. But that's okay, this doesn't bother her. These are happy memories. Not the ones that torment her. Dreamily she recalls what happened next.

They drove toward Daliat El Carmel, where they'd agreed to visit for a few hours before driving southward back to Jerusalem. Jake had suggested this two days earlier, when Eve spoke wistfully about not having been to this charming Druze village in over twenty-five years. At first, in the car driving there, everything felt normal to her. But soon, after they'd been riding for a little while on the highway, she started feeling like she was in a dream or having a *déja vu*. This scene felt very familiar. She was sitting in the passenger's seat of a car, a little girl next to a big strong man who was driving. She felt young with Jake, but also safe, as if she had known him all her life, and knew he would take care of her. As they drove along the coastal highway, she gazed at him, entranced. At his profile (his fine Roman nose and slightly upturned lips — those lips that reminded her of something but she didn't know what), and his powerful hands on the steering wheel. Jake, feeling her gaze upon him, didn't take his eyes off the road, but his right eye slid toward her, and he smiled. She smiled for a moment, too, but after that went back to staring, transfixed, at him. She felt like she was three years old. And over the next few minutes, there started in her a loneliness, a longing, and an aching to be close to him. It grew, and when it was unbearable, she said, "Jake?"

"Yes?" he answered, still watching the road.

For a few moments, she didn't reply. She didn't know how to put into words what she meant. She didn't really have anything to say; she just wanted to be connected to him. Close like they'd been on Thursday night on her bed. She didn't want to be alone while he gazed straight ahead at the road, instead of at her. She cast around for words like a fisherman casting a net wide on the water. And she found what she needed: the single word that, even if you have nothing to say, you can use to make contact with another human being.

"Hi," she said.

She was gazing steadily at Jake. For a second he looked confused. But only for a second. Then tenderness came into his eyes. He drove for a bit, looking lovingly at the road, and then he turned and looked at her.

"Hi," he answered softly.

He'd understood. He'd completely understood. There was silence again in the car now, but this time it was different: a good silence where they were connected and she wasn't alone. For a little longer she kept watching Jake drive. He drove, under her gaze, skilfully and masterfully, with strong, certain hands. And past his fine profile, she saw the bright blue sea.

Twenty minutes later, though, it happened again. They were cruising along the highway, and she was looking at Jake, but he wasn't looking back at her, and she felt invisible. It's not his fault, she told herself. He's driving. He has to keep his eyes on the road. But still she couldn't bear it, this feeling of being ignored, and superfluous, as he kept gazing straight ahead, apparently oblivious of her. She needed him to look at her, to see her.

"Can you pull over?" she blurted out.

He glanced at her worriedly. "What's wrong? Are you sick?"

"Just pull over. Please."

"I can't. There's no shoulder…"

"Please." I need to touch you, she thought. I need to feel

connected, and close to you, again. "I need to touch you," she said.

Jake blushed. "I'd like you to touch me, too," he said. "But we can't. I'm driving."

"Please?" She heard herself sound like a petulant little girl. "Just a little."

Jake blushed more deeply. She found it touching how innocent he was. How real, and close to his true feelings. "I don't want to lose control," he said.

"Of the car or yourself?"

"Either," he smiled.

"Oh, all right," she said, with petulance part mock, part real. "I won't do anything while you're driving." And she stuck her bare feet up on the dashboard.

He glanced at her feet.

"You don't mind, do you?" she asked.

"Of course not. But you are unique."

"What do you mean?"

"You have your own way of doing everything. Even how you sit in a car."

"Well, I'm glad you like me."

"I don't like you," he said. "I love you."

"The two aren't mutually exclusive."

"No," he laughed. "Lucky for me."

"Lucky for me, too," she said, and reached out to touch his knee, but then stopped her hand a couple of inches above it. "Better not," she said.

"Better not," he agreed.

They drove for a bit in silence. Then she asked,

"How long till we're there?"

He glanced at the clock on the dashboard. "Twenty minutes, maybe. Less if the traffic's good."

"Well then, let's talk," she said. "About something intellectual, not anything romantic. So we don't end up in a ditch."

"Good idea." Then: "I know, tell me about the music therapy

research you did. Ever since you mentioned it, I've been meaning to ask about it, but other topics keep getting in the way."

"Sure. If you're really interested."

"I am."

So for the next fifteen minutes, she described the research project on women with borderline personality disorders that she did for her Master's. She spoke passionately about it, feeling confident and strong. She was a competent adult now, an intellectual and a professional, no longer the vulnerable little girl of a few minutes before, hungry for Jake's approval. After she finished, he said that although he didn't usually hold much with psychology ("it's just a bunch of labels, and people poking around trying to ferret out your weaknesses"), he'd found her research interesting.

"I enjoyed that a lot," he said. "Hearing about your intellectual life — your work and your ideas. I learn new things from you."

"I learn things from you, too."

"Yes, but what I mean is, I like this part of our relationship. I like being with Ms. Bercovitch The Researcher. Of course, I like all the different aspects of you. But it's a real gift that on top of everything else that exists between us, we have this intellectual bond. I find it very exciting. I don't have this ... rapport..." — his speech slowed down; he was treading carefully, she could see — "with very many women."

Ah, she thought. Here it is again. What's missing between him and Fran. They can't connect intellectually. He can't talk to her about ideas.

"Neither do I," she said. "With men, I mean. Most of the men I know are threatened by my mind."

He looked surprised. "You, a threat? But you're such a..." — he groped for words — "a sweetie pie!"

She laughed. "Maybe so. Just the same, a lot of men find me intellectually intimidating."

He glanced at her, and after a moment said, "Yes, I can see

that. One of the first things I noticed about you was your mind. But that, for me, was part of the attraction. I saw at that conference how you always operate at two, or more, levels at the same time, leaping back and forth all the time between the big and the small. Very few people can do this. For instance, you related how the cold cuts at lunch were arranged on the platter (they were in concentric circles) to the internal structure of Schoenberg's *Moses und Aaron*. You dazzled me. I remember thinking in that music library: I have to get to know this woman. I have to get inside this mind."

Pleased, she said, "This is very rare for me, too. To be able to connect with someone not just on one or two levels, but on all of them. Including intellectually. To know that everything I say is understood. Not just bits and pieces of it, but all of it. Everything."

"Yes," he said hoarsely. "That's it, exactly."

She had an impulse to lean over and give Jake a kiss, but restrained herself. *Best not to start that all over again.* Once more there was silence in the car. Jake was watching the road and she gazed out the window at the view. In the last fifteen minutes it had changed dramatically. Now the sea was crashing and thrashing, white foam exploded repeatedly on the shore, and up above the sky was overcast. She felt suddenly lonely again.

"The next two nights," she said, "you're busy, right?"

"Yes, tomorrow I have a board meeting at the Institute, and Monday night is Yael's birthday. I'm taking her and Dina out for supper." He sighed. "They're thirty-five and thirty-three years old — a little bit old, don't you think, for Abba to still be taking them out on their birthdays? Neither of them is married yet, and I don't know why. They're both quite attractive..."

Attractive! she thought. That's got nothing to do with why women get married. Lots of ugly women marry and there are attractive ones who don't. It's something internal.

"But on Tuesday night," he said, "I'm coming to Jerusalem as we planned. And we'll be together every night until Saturday night when you leave."

"I know. That's great," she said, but listlessly. She didn't want to talk, or even think, about leaving Israel, which meant leaving Jake, in just seven days. She changed the topic.

"Tell me more about your daughters. What are they like?"

Jake frowned, shot a sharp look at her, and sighed. Then he began to talk. It was the first time he'd told her anything substantive about his family and even what he told her now was quite cryptic. He spoke for only a couple of minutes. But she, with her clinical training, read quickly between the lines. As soon as she heard the phrase "eating disorder," her stomach sank, and she thought, Oh no, I'm fucked. She knew all about eating disorders — she'd had to study them for one of her courses — and she knew that wherever there was a family with an anorexic or bulimic girl, it was never just her problem; the problem belonged to the whole family. The girl was just the symptom, the visible part of her family's pathology, like the ten percent of an iceberg that protrudes above the water. And if there was something seriously wrong, something profoundly troubled, twisted, and dark in a family, this was because there was sickness in the marital system, and therefore in both of the marital partners who had created it. In other words, there was something deeply wrong with Jake.

Eve, sitting next to Jake as he drove down the highway describing Dina and her problems, started to feel queasy and disoriented. All sorts of alarm bells were going off in her mind, telling her that she was in over her head, she had swum out way too far into the ocean, and that now she was in great emotional danger. As the car bounced along, she looked straight ahead at the highway: it seemed to be disappearing in front of her, getting devoured piece by piece as they travelled over it. She tried to take in all the new information she was hearing from Jake, and to grasp the implications of this for the two of them, and for her. But she couldn't. It was all too much. She pushed away, almost with a physical push, what she half-sensed. Because she knew in her heart it was too late. She was already in love with him. In love with him up to her eyeballs. And there was no way she could extricate herself now. She and Jake were one, and whatever the future held in store, she had cast her lot with him.

He was saying now, looking slightly sheepish, "Fran keeps telling me that I've hurt Dina badly over the years, and that I should be nicer to her and try to like her more. But what can I do? If I'm honest with myself — and honest I must be — I have to admit that I just don't like her. I never have. I mean, how can you like a child who, for the first nine years of her life, once, twice, sometimes three times a day for an hour, gets down on the floor and punches it and kicks it and screams and howls? She all but destroyed our family, and severely strained my relationship with Fran. How am I supposed to like, much less love, someone like that?"

His lip was curled upward in contempt and revulsion for his daughter. Eve looked away. Gazing straight ahead through the windshield, she could see Dina as a little girl: the red tear-streaked face, the pounding fists and feet and howls of rage. She could feel Dina's misery and frustration and felt sorry for her. But she could also see this situation from Jake's point of view. In the silence now in the car, it seemed that he was waiting for her to say something. She turned to look at him, at his tense, slightly flushed face, and said gently, "It's hard. This must have been very hard for you."

"Yes, it was." He turned and looked at her gratefully. "I knew you'd understand."

"Yes," she said. "I do."

"You understand everything," he said.

"Well… Not everything."

"Yes, everything. Everything that matters. You certainly understand me."

"Yes," she said thoughtfully. "I think I do." Then for one second a flash of fear ran through her, but almost immediately it was gone. I'm not in danger, she told herself. This couldn't happen to me. He loves me. He never loved Dina. I won't ever see that side of him. The dark side of the moon.

*

Daliat, up on the top of the mountain, was hopping. This was the busiest day of the week for tourists because of the Saturday market. People were shouting, laughing, and bargaining, donkeys were braying, dogs were barking, and the warm air smelled of animal and human sweat mixed with spices and roasting meat. Everywhere Eve turned she saw something else: colourful dresses hanging from high-up hooks, piles of rolled-up carpets, woven baskets, housewares, and tables laden with dry goods, knick-knacks, oils, cheeses, pastries, and anything else the heart could desire. But all she desired was Jake's mouth. She wanted to kiss him. To throw her arms around him and kiss that mouth, that long, thin, sensitive mouth. She wanted to feel it pressed hard against her own and then opening so they could be tongue against tongue, their two tongues intertwined like the two strands of DNA in one person. She needed to be connected to his body.

He was surveying with pleasure the vibrant, noisy, cheerful scene around them. He turned to her and asked, "What do you want to do? Would you like to eat something? Or just walk around?"

"Kiss," she said.

He looked confused. "What...?"

"Kiss," she repeated.

He laughed. "Well, so would I, Eve. Very much. But how can we? We're in public."

Yesterday on the phone, he'd told her that he'd been astounded and appalled at his behaviour five nights before. He was referring to their first time meeting in Israel, when they'd strolled down the main street near her hotel and then randomly selected a nondescript café to have coffee in. They had a long and enjoyable talk there, touching on many topics, like in the music library, and then Jake had said out of the blue, "I haven't been able to stop thinking about you ever since we met. I've been married for thirty-eight years, and in all that time I've never once been unfaithful. But since meeting you, all I can think about is getting to know you and making love to you."

Eve, who had thought about nothing but Jake since the conference, looked down at the slightly greasy table. So she hadn't been imagining the whole thing. He'd felt it, too, this thing between them. She raised her eyes. Across the square table Jake, waiting for her answer, looked anxious, even vulnerable, like a boy.

"Me, too," she said. "I thought about that, too."

"Really?" His face lit up.

She nodded.

Jake grinned, a beautiful, radiant grin. But then she felt embarrassed and looked down again at the table. Suddenly there was silence between them, and the silence grew, becoming awkward. He seemed to be waiting for her to speak, but she couldn't think of anything to say. Finally, she looked up at him. His eyes, watching her, were both worried and hopeful.

"Well, then," she'd said, "are you going to kiss me?"

Jake half-rose out of his chair. "Now?" he asked, leaning forward, as if she had meant he should kiss her at that very moment, bending across a not-very-clean arborite table in a café. She frowned and waved her hand, saying, "No, no. Not in public," while he, slowly nodding disappointedly, sat back down.

It was in reference to this interaction that Jake had made his comment the day before on the phone. The idea that he'd been ready to kiss her right then and there if she had let him — in front of the café window, in full view of whoever happened to be passing by in the street (and all this less than a mile from the institute he'd founded, and less than a ten-minute drive from the home where he lived with his wife) — had astounded and appalled him.

"We'll have to be much more careful in future," he said. "I have a reputation to protect."

Now the two of them stood at the entrance to the lively, clamorous market. Jake pointed to his left, toward stalls selling bright fabrics, multicoloured spools of thread, and souvenirs, and said, "We could go this way. Or that." He pointed to the right, toward pyramids of plums and melons, and a butcher's shop with its strung-up blood-stained carcasses.

With a grimace, she looked away. Then, without answering him, she began scanning the rest of the market, as if searching for something.

Jake watched her curiously. "What is it?" he asked.

She kept searching, and then stopped. "There," she said, pointing at something far ahead and a little off to the left. It was a thin, vertical line running like a vein of dark ore through the bright bustling market. "We could go there. That alley doesn't look as crowded as here. No one would see us."

Jake blushed and gave a slight laugh that sounded like a bark. "Eve…"

"Please?" She looked up at him longingly. She couldn't bear this feeling of of separateness from him. Nothing but physical contact, his mouth pressed against hers, could assuage this ache in her. "I need to," she said. "Just one."

Jake's face was a mixture of astonishment and delight, and she could see he was flattered by the intensity of her desire for him. Looking slightly dazed, he followed her passively through the chaotic market as she led the way toward the distant alley. But once there, it turned out that this alley wasn't all that different from the place they'd left behind. True, there were fewer people here, but still there were some; it wasn't truly secluded. She then tried a second alley one street over, but this one proved the same as the first.

"Oh, well," she said with a resigned shrug. "I guess that's that."

She and Jake, who still looked a little dazed and amazed by this, walked around for a while in the heat, moving from one stall to the next. She fingered a pretty bead necklace and stroked a hand-embroidered tablecloth, but listlessly. She was tired and also bored. Then Jake said he was hungry, and she realized she was, too. She had had a light breakfast, just a plum and a roll, and nothing since; she had been too nervous to eat as she waited on the kibbutz for him. So now he guided her back to the main part of the market to a restaurant he knew. He'd been there twice before with a friend, and when they walked in, the Druze family that ran the place welcomed them so warmly, Jake was sure they recognized him. Eve and Jake were the only customers in the restaurant, and as soon as they were seated, an old man in traditional Druze dress brought them menus and the man's granddaughter, slim and with black eyes, served them cold water and large, paper-thin pitas. Eve studied the menu, and asked Jake to explain a couple of unfamiliar items. He did this delicately, she noticed, not at all patronizingly. But when he offered to order for both of them, she gratefully agreed.

The food took a long time to arrive, but when it did, it was delicious. They ate hungrily from the platters of fragrant, steaming food. All the while they were watched by the whole family. This family, Jake knew from his friend, consisted of the old man and his granddaughter, the granddaughter's mother (a plump woman in her forties who'd come out of the kitchen to help serve the food), and someone's little boy. (Whose? wondered Eve. The daughter's? Or maybe the granddaughter's?) This little boy stared at her steadily with his thumb in his mouth the whole time she was eating. The family seemed hospitable and friendly, and politely stood a little distance off in the small restaurant, but even so, Eve felt self-conscious under this close attention. The way they watched her, it felt almost like they were chaperones, constraining her from touching Jake. She felt she couldn't touch him at all. Not even a quick caress on the hand. Not to mention touching him on his face or lips, which she longed to do. Or climbing onto his lap, throwing her arms around his neck, encircling his waist with her legs, and giving him a deep, passionate kiss on the mouth. Nothing like this was possible now. All she could do was eat in silence. *The Silence of the Lamb*. The silence of the rice with pine nuts. And of the chickpeas. And the chicken. And the bulgur. And the tomato and cucumber salad. And the olives. The little boy's big black eyes (like black olives or black-eyed peas) watched them from the corner.

As soon as they finished eating, she said to Jake, "Can we go now?"

"Don't you want dessert?" he asked, surprised. "They have mint tea, which might be refreshing in this heat. And they make a good baklava."

She liked baklava. "Okay," she said, and they had dessert. A wordless dessert, just like the rest of this meal, where the only contact between them was when they'd occasionally look up from their food at each other and smile. Sipping mint tea and sampling the baklava, she felt as speechless, as dumb, as an ox. The only language she could understand now was the language of the body: touching Jake or being touched by him. Nothing else felt real. She wished she hadn't agreed to extend the meal for this dessert. The little triangles of baklava, dripping with warm honey, were oddly unsweet, soggy rather than crunchy, and the pistachios in them were stale.

Only now did she remember that she had promised to call Michael.

"Oh, fuck," she said. Jake grinned. He liked her swearing. During their conversation in the music library, she had evidently sworn a lot (though she hadn't even noticed), and he had mentioned this the first time they met in Israel, saying to her admiringly, "I like a woman who can swear like a man." Now she glanced at her watch: four-twenty. In Canada nine-twenty in the morning. Michael had basketball at nine-thirty. She had to call him now.

"I have to make a call," she said to Jake, leaping up and hurrying over to the doorway of the restaurant, where she turned her back to him, faced outward toward the market, and dialled. Michael answered right away; he'd been waiting for her call. They had a pleasant chat where he gave her an update on everything that had happened at home since their talk the day before. After Brian's death, she had tried hard not to burden ten-year-old Michael — not to make him "the man of the house." But Michael had always been, even back then, the reliable type, solid and dependable in contrast to Ethan, and she ended up counting on him in a certain way. Now Michael was reporting that the day before he had gotten back a math test and two term papers, and received two As and an A minus. He said that Ethan had been accepted the night before into the new jazz quartet he'd been trying out for, that Brian's sister had invited him and Ethan for supper the following evening, and that Irma, the family housekeeper who dropped in each day to check up on the boys, would be coming in later that day for the whole afternoon to do some spring cleaning. Eve asked Michael what they'd eaten the night before for supper.

"Chicken oregano," he said. One of the dinners she had prepared for them and frozen in plastic containers before leaving on her trip.

Everything at home sounded fine and perfectly normal. She listened to her oldest son talk about his chess club and his friends, and she responded to him, she thought, the way she usually did, but just the same this conversation felt different. There was a wall between them — a wall because of the secret she was keeping from him about Jake. She turned and glanced at Jake. He didn't notice since he, too, was now on the phone. He was leaning back in his chair, his long legs stretched out in front of him. This man, she thought, his body just a few feet away, was now the person in the world who was the most important, and the most real, to her.

"I love you," she said to Michael before hanging up, and she meant it. But she also said it out of habit, those three words that she couldn't yet say to Jake — couldn't-wouldn't until she was ready. These words hung in her, though; they sat inside of her, like plums ripening, until they were ready to be said.

As she arrived back at the table, Jake was just shutting the cellphone he had borrowed from the old man and was handing it back to him.

"So," he asked her, "who were you speaking to?" His blue eyes were warm yet demanding, drilling into her a little when he asked her this. She told him and he looked relieved, she thought.

"Once again we're in perfect sync," he said. "I just called my daughters to confirm our plans for Monday night. But I got asked where I was; the sounds of the market were audible in the background."

"What did you tell them?" she asked.

Jake leaned toward her, rested his chin on his hand, and said, "I said I am in Daliat el-Carmel eating baklava with a fascinating, beautiful woman whom I've fallen in love with."

She stared. "Really?"

He laughed. "Of course not. Though that's what I wanted to say. No; what I said was that I was in Daliat with a colleague visiting from Canada. Which isn't a lie. Even if it's not the whole truth."

Yes, she thought, picturing Michael. Lies of omission vs. lies of commission. Like the distinction on Yom Kippur between sins of omission and sins of commission. But one is held accountable for both.

"What did they say when you told them that?" she asked.

"What did *she* say, you mean. I only called Yael. I usually just call her and she passes on the message to Dina. Yael said, 'Have a good time, Abba.'"

Eve absorbed this for a moment, then asked, "And are you?"

"What do you think?"

They smiled at each other. Then, feeling shy, and aware once again of the Druze family watching them, she looked down at her plate. Slowly she swirled her finger around in the pool of honey that had leaked out of a baklava triangle. Because of her, Jake had lied to his daughters. She felt guilty, as if all the duplicity in the last fifteen minutes — not just hers, but Jake's — was somehow her fault. But at the same time she felt triumphant and elated. She must be very important to Jake if he'd lied to his daughters for her. In a way this meant he loved her even more than them. She was his favourite girl.

She put her finger in her mouth and slowly, thoughtfully, sucked off the honey. Jake watched her, with admiration, affection, and desire.

*

Eve gets up off the loveseat, stands, and stretches. Then she bends backwards with her hands on her waist. Who the hell was that? she wonders as she straightens up. Who was that regressed childlike woman back then?

That's not me now, she thinks, standing on the porch, gazing at the footpath. But back then it was. Behaving like I was mesmerized or on some sort of drug, letting myself be pulled along by Jake as if I was his pull toy. With him I was like a little girl with her Daddy. Talk about "splitting": He was big and strong and I was little and weak, and I believed if I stayed sufficiently little and weak and defenceless, he'd take care of me and I'd be safe. Crazy. And pathetic. How weird, too, competing with Jake's daughters, and being happy when it looked like he loved me more than them. Actually, I didn't just want Jake to love me more than his daughters. I wanted to *be* his daughter.

She starts walking, then running, down the footpath, away from Barry and Leah's bungalow, as if to escape this last thought. The horror of it fills her. Horror that feels like molten lead starting at the bottom of her stomach and then rising into her chest and throat and into her mouth. She hurried along the path toward the petting zoo. So this is another clue to the Big Mystery. Another explanation for why she experienced such trauma that it lopped off years from her life. Jake was her father. She fell in love with, and then slept with, her own father. Oh my God, she thinks. "Oh my God," she says aloud. She feels the horror of this, the taboo-breaking horror of it.

She can hear a whole Greek chorus of women crying out, "Horror! Horror!" in the background behind her, as if she were the protagonist in some Greek tragedy (*Eua and Iakobos*).

Oh, shut up, she tells herself, clucking her tongue. You're not in a Greek tragedy and Jake wasn't your father. Your father's name was Henry Bercovitch, and this man's was Jacob Gladstone. Or in Yiddish, Yaakov Glatshteyn, like the Yiddish poet — which you and Jake both found delightful. No, Daddy and Jake were two different men.

And anyway, she thinks, even if there was a little of that father stuff mixed in with my relationship with Jake, so what? What could be more natural, in a way, than a girl loving her father? It's in every psychology textbook on page three. Page three, age three. Electra 101. It's so universal a phenomenon that it's banal.

Reaching the zoo, she stands in front of the monkeys' cage, remembering Harlow's research on Rhesus monkeys, which led to Bowlby's theory about attachment and loss. She wonders if girl-monkeys and their father-monkeys have Electra-fied attachments. And what about mother-monkeys and their sons? No, she doubts monkeys have Oedipal/Electra relationships. And it seems to her now that in this relationship with Jake, she was lower — or anyway, definitely no higher — on the evolutionary scale than a monkey. I was, she thinks, as instinctive, drive-driven, and primitive as a hairy ape scratching its armpit.

She reaches upward into a tree, swipes from a low branch a lovely red apple, wipes it quickly on her shirt, and bites into it with a loud crunch. It's tart. And good. She realizes as she leaves the petting zoo and strolls along the main path that she is hungry. *I haven't eaten anything since breakfast. And all I had for breakfast was a plum and a roll.* Suddenly she is so confused she stops walking and stands in the middle of the path, looking perplexed. Which Saturday is she inside now? The one in Daliat or the other one? On the Saturday that Jake picked her up and drove her to Daliat, she didn't eat anything until the mid-afternoon at the restaurant there, except for breakfast (a plum and a roll). But on the other Saturday she had breakfast and then later also lunch: there was quiche and salads and a fruit pie — but when was that?

Now she comes to. The lunch of quiche and salads and fruit pie was an hour ago. Here, on this kibbutz. At Barry and Leah's house, five and a half years after she visited Daliat. The lunch of quiche and salads and fruit pie came after they'd been sitting with Shira and Yuval and others by the pool. Right. She takes a deep breath. She recalls now what she always tells her clients, the PTSD sufferers, when their inner life feels stronger, realer, to them than the outer one: *Find something real, something concrete in your environment, to ground you.*

She looks down at the white path beneath her feet and stretching out ahead of her. This path is real. She feels the cool, smooth apple in her hand and looks back at the tree it came from, swooshing lightly in the Shabbat afternoon quiet. She hears the birds singing in its branches: *Doo-doo-doo. Doo-doo-doo.* Bird song. She has written a piece of music called *Bird Song.* She can smell the sweetness of the pink and purple flowers lining both sides of the path. She crouches down and touches the slightly damp, pungent-fragrant soil of their flowerbeds. This is real, she thinks. This is reality.

She continues walking. A young woman passes her pulling a wagon, its wheels rattling loudly, and to Eve's surprise, inside the wagon lies a swaddled baby. She smiles at the baby and woman and a minute later passes a boy of about eleven with his parents and little sister. A towel is slung over the boy's skinny naked shoulder; they are obviously headed for the pool. This is reality, she thinks. Stay in the present tense. Be Here Now. And she laughs. *Be Here Now.* That spiritual self-help book was written by Baba Ram Dass, the famous Hindu guru, who was born Richard Alpert, a Jew. What a crazy world.

Quite a strong breeze is up now, and there's a hint of chill in the air. The sun will be setting soon, in an hour or two. But for now the sun is shining and everything is quiet and peaceful. She imagines everyone on this kibbutz either napping or having sex, or else listening to music in their bungalows, reading on their porches, or relaxing at the pool. Abruptly she stops walking. Here's the pay phone she used, five and a half years ago, to call Jake, sneaking away from her relatives before or after almost every meal. I could call Jake now, she thinks; it's almost an automatic reflex. *Nah, fuck it.* If she wants to call Jake before flying home on Monday, she still has two more days to do that. Why call now and ruin a happy day?

But she can't help herself. She can't just walk by this pay phone. This pay phone of all pay phones: the one into which she whispered with love to Jake. Her love must still be somewhere inside this phone. She walks up to it and touches its cold metal with two fingers. Then she touches the whiteboard nailed to the wall next to it, a message board in case someone's walking by and hears the phone ringing. A red marker rests on the little shelf protruding from the bottom of the whiteboard. She picks it up and writes in blood-red letters:

φίλος ἄφιλος.

"*Philos-aphilos*," she says. A term she and Jake discussed in a conversation they had about Greek philosophy, specifically about the Greeks' different classifications of love. *Philos-aphilos.* The Greek concept of love-in-hate.

19. JAKE'S HOUSE

BACK ON THE LOVESEAT, on Barry and Leah's porch, Eve shuts her eyes. Barry and Leah seem to be still sleeping, or doing whatever they're doing. She listens sleepily to the chirping of the cicadas in the silent, slowly wafting Shabbat air. Then time collapses and she returns to that other Shabbat, the one when she and Jake went to Daliat.

*

After Daliat, Jake didn't drive her straight back to her hotel in Jerusalem. Instead he took her to Tel Aviv to see his house. He suggested this on their way back to his car after their meal in the restaurant.

"I'd really like to show you where I live," he said. "I want you to see as much as possible about my life, because from now on you're going to be a part of it, in some form or another. So you should know everything about me. I don't want there to be anything about me you don't know. I don't want us to have any secrets from each other."

She agreed, touched by his eagerness to share his life with her. Jake's house, it turned out, was off a secluded road on the outer fringe of Tel Aviv, an area she had never been to before. As they approached his neighbourhood, she had only a vague idea of where they were geographically. On the final stretch to his house, winding slowly along a road through a forest, she thought, This place could be anywhere in the world. It feels like I am, at the same time, Everywhere and Nowhere.

Jake was proud of his house. As he parked in his driveway, he told her that he and Fran had built and designed the house themselves, attending lovingly to every detail. Leading Eve up the front path, he pointed out the lush garden on their right. There were yellow, pink, and red flowering bushes, delicate clusters of white blossoms, three fruit trees (two bearing fruit and one not), and everywhere in between, thick green plants bursting out of the ground. This garden, she thought, is the one that Jake was watering the first time I phoned him, right after I got to my hotel in Jerusalem six days ago. He didn't answer till the sixth ring because he was outside watering this garden.

"You were watering this garden," she now said, pointing, but Jake didn't seem to catch the allusion. He was hurrying, leading the way up the stone steps. When she reached the top of the stone porch, he gestured grandly toward the view, like a mini-Moses indicating the Promised Land.

The view was magnificent. Jake's house was on top of a hill, and from where she stood, Eve could see lesser hills and fields and orchards in various shades of green and gold stretching out before her all the way to the horizon.

"It's spectacular," she breathed. She was glowing and flushed, feeling the warmth of the afternoon sun on her face.

"Yes, isn't it?" said Jake with proprietary satisfaction, as if everything they were looking at belonged to him. Almost as if he had tilled all these fields himself. He ushered her through the front door and she found herself standing in the middle of a long rectangular living room. It was still bright outside, but here in this house, despite its large windows and high ceilings, it was quite dark, giving the impression of a cavern.

"Let there be light," said Jake, flicking a switch, and the room brightened slightly, but still there was a subdued, even mildly depressed, feel to the place. The walls were grey, dotted here and there with paintings and sketches, and the couch, well-designed and comfortable-looking, was also grey. The single spot of colour in the room, an easy chair covered in a geometric pattern of pastel pinks and greens, couldn't hope to counterbalance all the greyness. To Eve, everything here felt cool, elegant, sophisticated, and lonely.

Feeling the need to say something positive, though (she could feel Jake waiting), she said, "You have good taste."

He was obviously pleased. "Well," he said, "Fran gets most of the credit. She has a good eye. Of course, I helped, too."

She strolled around the long room, looking at everything, and Jake said with pride, "We hired an architect from Tuscany to design this house. To the best of my knowledge, this is the only authentic Tuscan house in Israel."

She didn't answer, knowing nothing about Tuscan architecture.

"You've been to Tuscany, of course," said Jake, as she walked around.

"No," she said, looking at one of the pictures on the walls. "I've been to Italy a few times, but never Tuscany."

"You haven't?" He seemed shocked. "Oh, then I must take you there. You'll love it. The museums, the castles, the vistas. Not to mention the most fabulous food and wine in the world."

She could picture being in Tuscany with Jake. The two of them, during the day, walking hand-in-hand through sun-drenched sunflower fields or cool fragrant vineyards, and at night drinking Chianti Classico and making love. She smiled at him. "Sounds like heaven."

As she ambled around the room in her thin sandals, she became aware of the hardness of the floor under her feet and also its coolness. The floors — in fact the whole house, she noticed — felt cool, almost cold, despite the heat outside.

"Maybe it's because of the Tuscan design that your house feels so cool," she suggested.

"Exactly!" cried Jake, launching enthusiastically into a detailed explanation of all the unique architectural and engineering features of his house. She only half-listened as he described how the positioning of the house in relation to the sun and the natural air currents in the area kept it cool in summer but warm in winter. She was feeling a bit dazed. I'm in Jake's house, she thought. This is where he lives. This is his home.

Jake stopped talking. "Sorry," he said. "Too much detail, I know. I get carried away when it comes to this house. I'll stop talking now and you can just have a look around."

She continued to wander around the room, feeling acutely self-conscious under his eyes. The same way she felt the first time she visited the office of Mr. Monson, her high school music teacher, who'd invited her there to chat about her "great talent and great future." That day in his office, already in love with him, she had pretended to admire his pictures and books, when really all she was aware of was his eyes on her and how much she wanted to impress him. Now here with Jake, she felt much the same. She wasn't seeing anything in this room; she saw only herself being seen. She was an object, not a subject with eyes of her own. But then one of the sketches on the wall above the couch caught her attention and she forgot her self-consciousness and took a step closer. It was a nude woman, as minimalist as you can get, just a few lines. Not the sort of thing she usually went in for, but this one was so fine and so evocative that she was quite taken with it. It also piqued her interest because, although it felt very New York in its sophistication, it was at the same time very Israeli.

"I like this one," she said to Jake, still gazing at the sketch.

"Ah, of course. It's…" And he mentioned a name that sounded something like Yukateli.

She had no idea who Yukateli was, or even if she had heard the name correctly. For all she knew, Jake had said "Ukelele." But she nodded as if she recognized the name and was impressed. He seemed glad to have impressed her.

She continued her slow pensive tour of the living room, and Jake watched as she stood in front of the mahogany bookcase, fingered the fine wood, and began examining the photos displayed there. He came over to her as she gazed at one particular picture that stood out from all the rest because it was larger and in a fancy silver frame. It was the photo of a woman about her age with an arm around each of two young women, one on either side. The one on the left was fair; the one on the right was dark, and her head was tilted toward the older woman's, almost leaning on it. All three women had their arms around each other, and to Eve there was something classically beautiful about these three attractive women all smiling and intertwined.

"That's Fran," he said, pointing to the woman in the middle. "And this," pointing to the blond one on the left, "is Yael. And," indicating the last one, "Dina."

Eve continued to study the picture. The two girls looked more or less as she had pictured them, but not Fran. Jake by this time had referred to Fran several times as having "put on quite a lot of weight over the years" and as now being "quite heavy," so Eve had imagined her as dumpy and unattractive. But here in this picture, she was anything but. Taken, Eve guessed, about fifteen years before, Fran wasn't overweight at all and in truth was very attractive. She had good clear skin and a lovely smile. But what made her not just attractive but beautiful was her eyes. They were a striking violet-blue and perfectly shaped, reminding Eve of Elizabeth Taylor's, and also of Mr. Monson's wife's. Eve gazed at Fran's gorgeous eyes.

"She's pretty," she said unwillingly.

"Well, of course she is," laughed Jake. "Do you think I'd marry a *miskayt*?"

"I guess not." She forced a smile. Then she added, "Your daughters are attractive, too. You're a good-looking family."

"Thanks," he said, pleased and proud. "This photograph was taken on Fran's fiftieth birthday. We were on our way out to a restaurant to celebrate."

Fifty, she thought. The same age I am now. She squinted a little longer at this family photo: A family, like any other, going out to celebrate a birthday. These people are real, she realized with a jolt. These women have skin like hers that, if she met them, she could touch. They're not just characters in a story about Jake's life.

He was crouching near the bottom of the bookcase. "And here are our photo albums. They go way back, to when the girls were very young." He pulled out one of these albums, stood up, and flipped it open. Eve, leaning over Jake's arm to get a better view, saw four little girls in cone-shaped party hats sitting around a table. The blond girl sitting at the head of it was looking gravely in front of her at a cake with flaming candles.

"This is Yael turning three," he said with affection.

She noticed Jake's right hand as it held the album open. A long, bony, beautiful hand. She resisted the impulse to bend down and kiss it.

"She's cute," she said.

"Yes, isn't she? I can show you some pictures from when she's older..." He began flipping through the album and then stopped. "But you don't want to look through all twenty-five of our picture albums, do you?"

She smiled.

"Of course you don't," he said. "It's just that I want you to know everything about me. About my house, my family, my work, everything all at once. I want to share with you everything that's ever happened to me."

"*L'at l'at. Shwaya shwaya.* There's time. We don't have to say everything today."

His face changed subtly, turning a little calmer and less frantic. "Yes, you're right."

They stood gazing at each other for a short while. Then Jake said, "Come. I'll show you the rest of the house."

He began the grand tour by explaining that all the rooms in this house extended outward from the living room like the spokes of a wheel. The first rooms he showed her, extending off to the left from where they stood, were the girls' bedrooms.

"Of course, they moved out long ago," he said. "But they still come home to visit pretty often, with or without their boyfriends, so these rooms get used."

Next to the girls' rooms was the master bedroom in its own little alcove with an ensuite bathroom. She stood beside Jake just outside the doorway to the bedroom and peeped in. A quilted afghan, Mennonite style, lay across the bed. She could feel him waiting for her to say something, but her throat and mouth felt like they'd been stuffed with cotton batten.

He said, "We can lie down here and take a rest, if you're tired."

"Here?" she asked, incredulous. She was shocked, even re-volted, at the suggestion that she lie with him on his marital bed, the one he slept in with Fran.

"Well, why not?" he said lightly. "It's my bed."

"Yeah, but it's also Fran's."

"Never mind then. Suit yourself," he said coolly with a shrug. He led Eve, who now felt confused, alienated, and even a little frightened, into the kitchen.

It was a splendid kitchen: bright, sunny, and very upscale and sophisticated. It looked like a model kitchen, something that would be featured in *Better Homes and Gardens*. *The New York Times Magazine Cookbook* was displayed on the counter in an attractive splash-protected book-holder, shiny copper pots and pans hung from hooks along the wall just like in the kitchens of professional cooks, and an assortment of utensils (spatulas, ladles, wisks — all the miscellaneous items that in Eve's kitchen were crammed messily into an overstuffed drawer) were here neatly contained in a charming stoneware crock decorated in a cheerful yellow, orange, and azure pattern with Italian words painted across it. Probably from Tuscany, she thought sourly. This kitchen irritated and depressed her with its stylishness and casual perfection. It made her feel not just a few years, but also a few steps, behind Jake and Fran. And yet at the same time a little superior to them. What sort of people need all this trendiness and fashionableness? Who cares what your kitchen looks like as long as you can cook in it? Her own kitchen at home was pleasant: it was cheerful, colourful, and even in its own way charming. But it wasn't an ad in a magazine.

Jake was showing her the new espresso machine he and Fran had recently bought. An Italian brand, she noticed: Giotto.

"It makes perfect coffee," he told her enthusiastically. "And I've got some great fresh beans. I picked them up yesterday specially for you." He took down a bag of coffee beans and a grinder from a shelf above the stove. "Can I make you a cup?"

She hated coffee. She hated the taste and it gave her headaches. But there stood Jake, coffee beans in hand, looking as eager as a boy of sixteen to please her.

"It sounds great," she said regretfully. "But I don't drink coffee."

"Oh, come on," he said. "It'll be the best coffee you ever had."

She felt terrible, almost guilty, disappointing him. "I'm sure it would be. But I really can't. It gives me migraines."

"Migraines?"

"Yeah. I can't have caffeine. I'm sorry."

Jake looked so desolate that she put a hand on his arm.

"Never mind," he said. He turned away and put the beans and grinder back on the shelf.

"I'd have some if I could."

"Don't be silly, it's fine." Now he turned back to Eve. "But isn't there anything I can give you instead? Some tea, maybe? Or a cold drink?"

She shrugged, grinned, and pointed up at the shelf. To the left of the coffee beans was a transparent jar full of chocolate chip cookies. His eyes followed her finger.

"You mean the cookies?"

Wordlessly she nodded. She felt young and childish now, and also a bit foolish to be wanting a cookie — such an immature request compared to a coffee, a mature "adult" one. But Jake didn't seem to mind. He just laughed, took down the cookie jar, and placed it on the wooden kitchen table. "For you," he said. "Have as many as you want."

"I love chocolate chip cookies," she said happily, sitting down in front of the jar, opening the vacuum-sealed lid, and greedily biting into a cookie. "I could never keep a jar of these in my house," she said. "They'd be gone in a day."

He laughed. "So we all have our little vices. Coffee, cookies…"

"Better than theft or murder," she said, her mouth full of cookie, and he chuckled. "Mmm, good," she said.

Jake watched her affectionately. Then he said, "Maybe if you're so hungry, I should start making supper. I bought some eggs and vegetables."

"That would be great," she said, reaching for a second cookie.

He took a few items from the fridge and started breaking eggs and dicing red pepper and onion. Then he frowned and turned to her, knife in hand. "I should have asked you: Do you like pepper and onion?"

"Yeah, sure. But I should have asked *you*: do you need any help? I can help chop, if you like."

"No, you just relax. You're my guest."

"Okay," she said, cheerfully munching away. Her father had sometimes cooked for her like this when she was a child before the advent of Julia. (That's how she thought about her life with her father: divided into before and after the advent of Julia.) Her father had made only simple things like eggs, pancakes, and grilled cheese, but those moments of sitting on a kitchen chair watching him cook for her were among the happiest memories of her childhood. Now she sat in this kitchen watching Jake cook while she nibbled on his cookies, and she felt contented, cared-for, and safe.

Then the phone rang.

Jake, with a slight jump, paused in his dicing and glanced at the kitchen clock. "Six o'clock. That's four o'clock in England. It's Fran calling from London."

"Oh," she said, startled.

He put down his knife. "I have to take it. She always calls at this time and she'll worry if I don't answer. I'll use the phone in my study upstairs. You don't mind?"

"No, of course not."

The phone rang for the fourth time. He stood in the doorway, poised to run upstairs.

"If you feel like reading, there's an article I wrote two days ago." He gestured toward a newspaper lying open on the opposite side of the kitchen table. "I won't be long."

"No rush," she said. She followed him into the living room, but already he was gone, bounding to the other end of the house, where a staircase wound upstairs to the loft he used as a den.

Back at the kitchen table, she read Jake's article. It was one of those fluff pieces he'd told her he sometimes wrote when there wasn't much going on in the Israeli music scene, and he had nothing to write about for his weekly column in a British Jewish newspaper. This particular piece was lyrical and almost content-free, an ode to the beauties of Israel at this time of year. The music of nature and all that. The rushing and gushing of Israel's rivers and streams, the flow of sap running through her tree trunks (he always referred to Israel in the feminine form), the buds on her branches bursting into bloom. She read the first paragraph, but wasn't able to concentrate. It felt peculiar being alone in this kitchen without Jake, while he talked to his wife on the phone upstairs. Eve, having seen her picture, knew now (unlike a month ago, a week ago, or even an hour ago) that Fran was real. Eve looked blindly down at the newspaper, thinking: Jake is married. Fran is his wife. They are married, just like Brian and I were married. As for this house, it isn't only Jake's; it's also Fran's. This kitchen is definitely hers. She probably picked out this table and this chair I'm sitting on. What am I even doing here? I feel like a trespasser.

She heard Jake calling her. He'd seen her last in the living room and now she wasn't there. "Eve?" he was calling. "Eve?" with a trace of panic in his voice. The same panic, she thought, as in the music library the month before, when she had gone to get her manuscript from the stacks and he thought she wasn't coming back. When she'd returned, relief had flooded his face. And now she saw it again and heard the same relief in his voice when he found her in the kitchen and said, "Oh! There you are!"

She was sitting with her head bent over the newspaper and didn't look up at him when he entered the kitchen. He came over, stood behind her, and silently put his hands on her shoulders. Without turning around, she asked, as if to the newspaper, "Do you still love me, even though you've just been talking to your wife?"

"What a question! Of course I do!"

She could hear his astonishment at her question. She turned around and looked up at him. She saw his white hair. The direct blueness in his eyes. The mix of tenderness and naked need and longing. And she believed him.

"Good," she said, satisfied, as if he'd given a satisfactory answer to a question about the weather. Then she asked, "How's Fran?"

"Okay," he said, moving over to where she could see him without twisting her head around. "Her mother's driving her crazy, as usual." Now he noticed his article open in front of her. "Did you read that?" he asked.

"Yeah, it was good. But you made a mistake in the title."

"What?" he cried, alarmed. "Where? Show me."

"Here," she said, pointing to the headline. "This article is all about how, with the advent of spring, everything becomes green and alive. The dryness and deadness of winter is past and the physical world is being reborn. The sap is flowing, the music is playing, everything is rushing and gushing and pulsing with the rhythm of life."

"Yeah, so?"

"Well, you've titled it 'The Music of Springtime Has Come to the Land of Israel.' But it's not about the land of Israel; it's about you. And its real title should be: 'The Music of A Second Springtime Has Come To Jacob Gladstone Since He Fell In Love with Eve Bercovitch.'"

"I see," said Jake and he smiled, but thinly. The anxiety of the moment before was still inside him.

"Plus," she continued, "Jacob's other name in the Bible was Israel. So saying rebirth has come to Israel means rebirth has come to you."

Now his face lost its strained tension. The danger was past. "Maybe you're right," he said. "Maybe that *is* what this column is about. But you gave me quite a scare there for a moment. I'm glad I didn't make a fool of myself in front of twenty thousand readers."

"Nah. No one but us could guess what this article's truly about."

"Our little secret."

"Yeah."

They smiled at each other.

"I guess I'll finish making the eggs now," said Jake.

"Okay."

He started turning toward the counter.

"No, don't," she said.

"What?" he asked, turning back.

She frowned. In order to do his chopping, he would have to turn his back to her again and then she'd lose contact with his eyes. And she'd feel alone.

"Never mind the eggs," she said, going to stand right in front of him, and looking up pleadingly into his face. He blushed. For a few seconds he peered off into the distance with the same expression on his face that she'd seen in the market at Daliat. A look of amazement and delight that this attractive younger woman could want him so much. It said,

She wants me! as if he couldn't quite believe his good luck. (Like he was still in high school, a lonely, nerdy guy, who somehow had been picked by the most popular girl in the class.) But it seemed to Eve that Jake's face just then also reflected the miracle of his second springtime, following "the dryness and deadness of winter." Fran, she understood from things Jake had said, hadn't wanted him sexually in years. Desire had left her almost twenty years before, shortly after menopause. And ever since then, sex between them was something always initiated by Jake, and only tolerated by Fran. Whenever she gave in to him (which was about half the time), that was what it felt like to him: she was giving in to him. Doing him a favour. Putting up with his smelly bodily urges and needs. Which always made him feel vaguely but deeply ashamed.

Now he gave a little half-laugh of surprised joy, and looked down at her beseeching eyes.

"Shall we go to my bed?" he asked.

She shook her head. "I can't. It's creepy."

"What's creepy about it? It's my bed. Fran's two thousand miles away."

He doesn't understand, she thought. But she persisted. "Isn't there any place here we could go that's just yours? That you don't share with Fran?"

He considered this for a second, then brightened up. "Yes, of course! My den. That's just mine. No one's allowed up there except me."

"Really?"

"Well, once in a while, every month or two, Fran drags the cleaning lady up there and they try to 'make order out of chaos.' Though I keep telling them not to. Every time they do that, it takes weeks till I find my stuff again."

Something else they have in common. "I'm the same way. I'm at home in my happy little mess."

"Exactly. *You* understand," he said warmly.

Now she felt more cheerful. "So it's only your place? No one goes there but you?"

"No one but me. And now you, if you want to."

"Sounds great," she said.

So the two of them left the kitchen, ignoring the diced peppers and onions sitting out on the cutting board and the smashed eggs in the bowl, and they began crossing the big living room toward the loft. Passing the bookcase on the right with the photos, her eye was caught by a black-and-white picture of a dark-haired intense young man, maybe fifteen or sixteen years old.

"Who's that?" she asked. "Is that you?"

Jake stopped walking and peered. "Yes, that's me in high school. My hair, as you can see, used to be dark brown, almost black. Darker than yours."

She studied the photograph. She couldn't recognize Jake in it, or anyway not the Jake she knew. The lips in the picture were thin like his, but much harder, and the eyes (though logically she knew they must have been the same blue as Jake's) here looked dark and impenetrable. They were two drawbridges closed against her, two locked doors.

"Tell me," Jake asked, "do you think you could love a boy like that?"

She glanced at him and then contemplated the picture for a while. She didn't like this face at all. It even scared her a little. But if this was Jake, or anyway a part of him, then she must find a way to love this boy. After all, she told herself, there's no one in the world who isn't lovable in *some* way.

"Yes," she replied unsteadily, feeling like a liar. "Yes, I could."

Jake looked satisfied. Then he led her across the living room, which felt to her as long as a river, and after traversing it to the other side, they climbed a rickety spiralling staircase.

20. JAKE'S DEN

EVE SITS ON THE FLOWERED LOVESEAT on Barry and Leah's front porch, remembering Jake's den. What a funny word, *den,* she muses. A lion's den. A den of iniquity. It probably was only about an hour that she spent in Jake's den that afternoon years ago. But she can't forget that hour; she has lived and relived it thousands of times since it happened. And it's still real to her. As real as this loveseat she is sitting on now. No. More real.

*

"Here's where I really live," he said when they got to the top of the winding stairs. His den was a skinny room with bookshelves lining the two long windowless walls, a rolled-up exercise mat in one corner (that he said he never used), and papers and music scores strewn everywhere — not just on the desk, but on the floor and on top of crates and hassocks. On the desk sat a computer, and next to it an old CD and diskette player peeked out from all the papers and clutter. The creative chaos of a brilliant man, she thought, looking around her, a bit awed. Here she felt that finally she was inside Jake's life. In the inner sanctum of it — not just in the courtyard of the Temple, but in the Holy of Holies. The place where the deepest part of his mind and soul sprang to life. He'd just said it himself: "Here's where I really live." And he'd never let anyone into this space up till now. She felt very honoured.

She stood facing a bookcase. "Here is where," he said, coming over to her, "*you* are," and he showed her where on the shelf he'd placed her *Kaddish Concerto*. Now she saw it: the copy she had given him on her first night in Israel, in that unimpressive café. She had swapped her music for his book on music (it seemed like a fair trade at the time). She was touched to see her *Kaddish Concerto* displayed on his bookshelf as part of his treasured collection of music scores. And flattered to find herself sandwiched, because of her last name, between Ahron Beer (the author of the oldest written version of *Kol Nidre*) and Leonard Bernstein. Several of Bernstein's scores were here, including *West Side Story*.

The previous week, as it happened, she had been thinking about "The Rumble" in *West Side Story*. Something about it had gnawed at her. The opening three notes reminded her of something, but she couldn't think what. Then she realized that these three notes sounded like a *shofar*. Bernstein was inspired by the *shofar!* she thought, whether he was conscious of this or not. Now she surveyed the other scores on the bookshelf. She was on the same shelf as Bach, Beethoven, Berlioz, Bloch, and Brahms. She was, it seemed, in Jake's classification system, now sitting among the greats. (Or anyway the Great Men.)

"This is amazing," she said, turning to Jake with a grin.

He grinned back. "I know. I'm very lucky to have this private space, just for me. Though it feels fine having you here, totally natural and ... right somehow. Which tells me something."

She wound her arms around his neck.

"Wait," he said. He pulled over the exercise mat from the corner, unrolled it, took her hand, and pulled her down with him onto the mat. He kissed her and started to touch her.

"Jake?"

"What?"

"About Tuesday night..."

They'd confirmed on the drive over here the plan they'd been hatching over the past few days. On Tuesday evening, three days from now, he would drive to Jerusalem, pick her up from the small family-owned hotel where she was staying, and take her to the King David Hotel, where they'd spend the night together. And then the three nights after that: all three of her remaining nights in Israel before she returned to Canada on Saturday just before midnight. Both of them were waiting anxiously for Tuesday night because this would be the first time they'd make love.

Now lying with Jake on his exercise mat, Eve said, "Maybe it's too much all at once. Making love when we've never even seen each other's bodies. Maybe we should look at each other naked now. Just to start getting used to each other."

"Sure," Jake said eagerly.

She stood up, turned her back modestly to him and undressed. When she turned around again, standing naked before him, he too was undressed but sitting on the exercise mat, his arms clasped around his knees. He looked at her but didn't say anything. She, feeling insecure because of his silence, asked: "Do you like my body?"

He studied her body up and down, coolly, appraisingly. Then he said in a flat factual tone, "Yes."

For a few moments she was deflated, disappointed, even hurt. He hadn't praised her body or rhapsodized about her beauty. But the truth was, she wasn't a pin-up girl, and she knew it. Her body was fine — it was healthy and slim, and there was nothing in particular wrong with it — but she (like her kitchen) wasn't something out of a magazine. She was real. So her first reaction of offended vanity passed quickly. She was even vaguely grateful to Jake for his honesty. Honesty, she felt, was stronger than the treacly sweetness of compliments; you could rely on it, lean against it as against the wall of a fort or a *kotel* if you were tired or weak.

"Do you like *mine*?" Jake was asking her, as he stood up on the green mat. She hadn't yet paid any attention to his body; she had been too preoccupied with her own. So now she looked him up and down and was shocked. He was hairless. Other than the hair on his head, there wasn't a single hair on his body. She had never seen anything like it. All the men she had ever been with had had at least some hair on their bodies, and the men in her family, on her father's side, were all very hairy. "Hairy apes," she and her cousin Karen used to jokingly call them when, on family outings to the beach as they were growing up, they'd stare with fascination and repulsion at the dark, matted chests of their fathers, the two brothers. But here was Jake, as hairless as a young boy starting school, or a woman who, beauty-obsessed, had waxed off every hair. There wasn't one lonely hair on his chest, arms, legs, or even crotch. She wanted simultaneously to laugh and to vomit.

But then, the way the mind flips things around when you're in love, Jake's abnormality went from seeming to her like a defect, to being something desirable, even a sign of his innate superiority. Other men are primitive animals, they're hairy gorillas, is what she felt at that moment; Jake, by contrast, is a more evolved version of the species. More spiritual and sensitive. A higher kind of Man.

"Yes," she answered him, without elaborating further, and he, catching the equivalence in her reply (he'd said just "yes," so she'd said just "yes") smiled.

"Come here, you," he said, taking her hand and pulling her down. The two of them slid back onto the exercise mat. They kissed for a bit and then he began stroking her naked body, going places he'd never gone before. She gently removed his hand.

"Oh, come on," he said. "Let's just do it now."

"No."

"Why not? It's just three more days. It doesn't make any difference."

"To me it does. Anyway, I still have my period."

"Still?"

Three days before, she had gotten her period and Jake had been astounded by this. Fran hadn't had hers for seventeen years, and he had nearly forgotten about women's capacity to create new life. So at first the idea of Eve having her period had charmed him and cast onto her some of the aura and mystique of a contemporary fertility goddess: a walking, talking Astarte or Asherah. But then he had started grumbling. This period of hers, delaying as it did their making love, became an annoyance, an impediment to his pleasure.

"You don't appear to mind at all," he growled at her now. "You seem almost glad you have your period and we can't make love."

There was some truth to this. She had always loved having her period, unlike every other female she knew, and now as usual she was enjoying the sense of magical power in her woman's body. "I want to as much as you do," she said. "But also I'm glad I have my period because I need a little more time. I told you, remember? I'm slow in these things."

"I remember."

She had said this to Jake after they left the café that first night she was in Israel. They'd walked the two blocks from the café to her hotel and as soon as they were inside her room, standing right in front of the closed door, he opened his arms wide and she stepped into them. She felt his arms close around her, and she buried her face in his chest and started to cry.

"What's wrong?" he asked, alarmed.

Shaking her head, she said, "I don't know," and kept on crying. But she knew what it was. This was the first time since Brian's death that she had really wanted anyone, and she was afraid. She cried a bit more. Then she dried her eyes and looked up at Jake, who was observing her anxiously.

"I'm sorry," she said.

"No need to apologize."

"I think I'm okay now."

"Are you sure?"

"Yeah."

"If you don't want to…"

"No, I do. Just…" She searched his eyes. "I'm slow in these things. Promise you won't rush or pressure me. I hate that."

"I won't rush or pressure you."

Now, six days later, Jake remembered that. "I understand. And it's fine. It's just that I want you so much. Are you sure that in three more days…?"

"Yes," she said, amused. "It'll be fine. I'm already on the third day."

"Phew. I'm not sure I could last much longer. I'll have waited nine days!"

"Wow!" she grinned. "Nine whole days! In the Bible, Jacob waited seven years for Rachel."

Jake chuckled. She rested her head on his chest and he wrapped his arms around her. A minute later she giggled, thinking of his article.

"'The music of nature,'" she said.

He winced. "I guess I seem a little ridiculous to you at times," he said uneasily.

She pulled back from him so she could look at him. "No, not ridiculous," she said. "I was just teasing."

"I know. But still… I've been trying to picture how I look to you. I must look so old. My skin has wrinkles, I have lines…" He traced a long, deep vertical line in his cheek with a long sad finger.

She was silent for a moment, searching for words. "Yes, you have lines," she said. "But that's not what I see when I look at you."

"What do you see then?"

She appeared surprised, as if the answer were self-evident. "I see *you*," she said.

For an instant he seemed puzzled; then he burst into laughter. "You marvellous girl," he said. He opened his arms wide, and she jumped into them.

*

Later, still entwined, she asked: "Is it because of that, though ... even a little?"

"Is what because of what?" He looked down at her.

"Your age. Do you think you fell in love with me because you're turning sixty-five next month?"

"What do you mean?" He seemed genuinely perplexed.

"You know, intimations of mortality and all that. Wanting to recapture your lost youth..."

Jake looked surprised. "No, that thought never crossed my mind." He considered this idea a bit longer. "No," he said. "I love you because I love you. That's all there is to it."

Then he added, "What is the age difference between us, anyway? I don't even remember."

"Fourteen years."

"Feh, that's nothing. A drop and a day."

She had never heard this expression and wondered if it was a Britishism. "A drop and a day?"

"A drop in the ocean and a day in a lifetime. I read that somewhere. In other words, nothing."

"Nothing," she echoed.

*

Five minutes later, he asked: "Who was your first?"

She was still lying naked in his arms and felt herself immediately stiffen. As if any mention of certain parts of her past automatically triggered temporary rigor mortis. Jake sensed the change in her and stroked her back gently, soothingly, twice.

"Peter," she said.

His eyes widened with curiosity. "Peter? Tell me about him."

She didn't know how to tell him about Peter because she didn't want to tell him yet about Julia. But she knew that if it hadn't been for Julia, she probably wouldn't have ended up sleeping with Peter and he wouldn't have been her first. It all happened, she recalled, because the summer she turned twenty-one, Julia decided that she didn't want her home for the holidays (as she had been for the previous two summers), so she didn't have anywhere to sleep. Though it also happened, she knew, because Peter loved her. He'd confessed this to her at the end of one of her roommate Charlene's many house parties. It was their last big bash at the end of the school year before they and everyone else dispersed for the summer, most of them going home to their parents'. Her and Charlene's apartment had already been rented out for May 1st, the next day, and she had just learned that afternoon that Julia wouldn't allow her to move back home. Daddy had caved in to her, as usual.

"Can't you stay with one of your friends?" he'd asked her pleadingly on the phone, as she stood in the hallway in the midst of cleaning for the party, holding a wet mop in a pail of dirty water. "You have so many friends. Can't one of them put you up for a couple of months?"

Peter had to get very drunk in order to declare his love for her. When he finally did, she was completely taken by surprise. She hadn't had the faintest inkling.

"Really?" she asked. "You're not joking?"

She had thought that for the past eight months he had been coming over every day to their apartment to see Charlene, not her. In the early fall, he'd slept with Charlene a couple of times (Charlene slept with anyone she liked, and she liked Peter), and over the course of the school year, he became a regular fixture in their apartment, and gradually a good friend of Eve's, a sort of older brother. The two of them hung out together comfortably while Peter ostensibly waited for Charlene to come home from classes or wherever she was. Once when he staggered over to their place rip-roaring drunk at three a.m. on a freezing cold night, and banged on the front window demanding to be let in, Eve dragged herself out of bed in her nightgown to let him in. But she had never thought of Peter and romantic love in the same sentence.

"Really? You're not joking?"

"I've never been more serious in my life," said Peter.

So she had to calmly explain to Peter that he couldn't possibly love her because she wasn't lovable. By this time she and Peter were both pretty drunk, and they got into an argument about whether or not Peter truly loved her. They nearly came to blows. Eve, who'd been guzzling all night from a five-dollar, five-gallon jug of Malbec, practically spat out to Peter that if she said it wasn't possible to love her, she should know: she knew herself a *little* better than he did. Actually, said Peter, No; he thought he could see her more clearly than she saw herself, and he quoted something from *The Little Prince* about people only being able to see clearly with a heart full of love. Fuck *The Little Prince*, said Eve. If her own father and stepmother couldn't stand her presence in their house even for a couple of months in the summer, then obviously she was disgusting and unlovable and a completely worthless fucking piece of shit who didn't deserve to live.

Peter put up a good fight. At one point Eve thought this was like one of her high school debates, with her arguing for Con, and Peter for Pro, the main resolution being "Resolved that Eve Bercovitch Is Possible To Love," plus a couple of other related resolutions, such as "Resolved that Eve Bercovitch Has The Right To Live." Peter, who was planning on becoming a lawyer, argued cleverly and valiantly, his chief argument being that of the universal right to life of every human being, based on the 1948 Universal Declaration of Human Rights. Her arguments were more emotionally-based and within an hour she was intellectually vanquished. Peter summarized his concluding remarks as follows: "You are a valuable human being with the same rights as every other person on this planet. You are also, if I may add, an exceptionally fine, and very lovable, individual. In sum, Eve Bercovitch: You are not nothing; you are something."

At the end of this night, at five in the morning, with the movers coming at eight and the new tenants due to arrive at noon, Eve and Peter walked over to his place and made love (Peter not realizing, till Eve told him two days later, that she had been a virgin). Then she stayed at Peter's till the end of the summer.

Eve didn't tell all this now to Jake. Just the main theme of the concerto, so to speak. But still he got the gist of the whole. She could tell by the way he looked at her. Then Jake asked,

"Did you love him?"

She paused. "Yes. I did. He was a terrific person. And he saved me, in a way. But it's funny I was still a virgin at twenty-one. That was very rare in my circle of friends."

Jake's eyes lit up. "Really?"

She recognized by this flash of interest that the generational difference between them had surfaced again. When he was twenty-one, almost all girls — or anyway the "good girls" — that age were still virgins. The sexual freedom she had casually alluded to was foreign to him. Exotic and even titillating.

"Yeah," she said, blushing a little. "My friends all laughed at me. Here I'd lived away from home in a downtown student apartment since I was seventeen, and four years later I was still a virgin. Everyone thought it was hilarious."

"Why were you then?" he asked. "Why hadn't you...?"

She was now sitting cross-legged on the exercise mat — she had shifted positions while talking about Peter — and Jake lay on his side leaning on one elbow. She shrugged and answered with a sardonic expression,

"I'd like to say it was all my fine character, but if I'm honest, it wasn't just that. The idea of having someone bigger and stronger lying on top of me and wanting something from me that maybe I wouldn't always want to give — to someone like me, that wasn't a desirable situation."

His eyes were empathic.

"Also..." she said. She looked at him carefully. He was listening closely to her. "I never believed that the real measure of me, or any woman's morality, was whether or not you're a virgin. But still ... I think it matters who you let inside your body. It's not nothing. It's something."

"Yes, it is," he said in an approving way. "Call me old-fashioned, but I'm glad you are the way you are, Eve. I'm glad you waited."

"Me, too. It's funny, though, about waiting," she said. "I feel like I've been waiting for you. For a very long time."

"Really?" he asked, surprised. Then after a moment: "I haven't been waiting. I guess because I never believed this could happen to me. I think I'd given up."

Eve lay down again. They kissed, and then held each other for a while in silence. They had agreed from the first day she arrived that they wouldn't talk at all about "After" (after her trip was over and she returned to Canada). They wanted to live these thirteen days together as fully as possible, rather than ruining them with agonizing and pointless planning. But now — maybe because it was their first time being naked together — she let herself fuzzily imagine, just this once, what it could be like for them in the years ahead. She saw herself living again (finally, after all these years) here in Israel. And being near Jake: meeting him once in a while, once a week maybe — this detail was hazy. But she would have Israel and she would also have the man she loved. Lying with Jake, naked and peaceful, she thought: What more could I ask for?

*

"I'm tired," murmured Jake a little while later.

"Me, too."

"Let's take a nap."

"Good idea. But I'm a bit cold."

Jake pulled a light blue summer blanket over them. Her cheek rested on his shoulder and his arm was draped over her. She felt her breathing getting slower and heavier, and as sleep approached, she rolled off him and curled up with her back to him facing the door. Just as she was dozing off, she heard,

"Eve, where did you go?"

"I'm here."

"Why did you go away? Are you angry?"

"Angry? No." Groggily she rolled back to face Jake. "Why would I be angry?"

"You moved away from me. Come sleep in my arms."

"I can't," she said. "I'll never fall asleep like that. I need to sleep alone."

He looked petulant. "Fran and I go to sleep in each other's arms, and the next morning we wake up in the exact same position we went to sleep in."

She didn't answer. All she wanted now was to sleep. She rolled away from Jake again, returning to her usual sleep position (slightly fetal), meanwhile feeling inadequate. She should be able to fall asleep with him the way Fran does: intertwined, enmeshed, their arms and legs all jumbled up together like one person's.

"Fran says we're a little symbiotic," he was saying now, as if this were something to be proud of.

Sounds like that to me, she thought but didn't say. As she drifted off into sleep, it seemed to her it must be terribly oppressive to not be allowed to move all night long from one position. How awful, she thought, to have no freedom, even in sleep.

*

She woke up twenty minutes later, remembered where she was, looked for Jake, and there he was, his affectionate blue eyes already gazing at her. They began talking and soon he was telling her about his marriage. It did sound symbiotic, especially the way he and Fran were always trying to control each other. Which makes sense, thought Eve: If you believe that your well-being depends completely on your spouse, you'd have to control them in order to keep yourself safe and your environment predictable. But of course nothing is perfectly predictable, and you can never fully control another person.

So in a symbiotic marriage like this, there is always a dark underside.

"Did you ever hit Fran?" she asked.

"Only once," Jake answered, quite naturally, and without any surprise, as if he'd been asked if he'd ever scuba dived. "I didn't actually hit her," he said; "I just gave her a push and she went into the wall. I was so frustrated. No matter what I did, it was never good enough."

She nodded. Not saying it was okay he'd hit her, just that she understood his frustration.

"I don't know much about psychology," he said. "That's your field, not mine. But I read somewhere once that what everyone is seeking is the love of their opposite-sex parent. The love they may not have gotten enough of as a child. For me, from my mother."

She was embarrassed for him at this simplistic understanding. "Well," she said kindly, "that was once the theory. The literature has developed a lot since then."

"Yes, but don't you agree that basically that's correct? That boys are looking for their mothers, and girls their fathers?"

"Well," she conceded, "*basically*. One does want that parent's love."

He said eagerly, "There's always this feeling with Fran that there's never enough love to go around. If she gives some of her love to one of the girls, then she's giving less to me. And with my mother it was the same thing. But with you... I feel with the way you love me, you have as much love as I'll ever need." He looked vulnerable now and about the same age as Michael or Ethan, fourteen or twelve.

"I do," she said. "I could be like your mother. And you be like my father."

He looked astonished. "You'd let me be your father?"

She smiled. "As long as you're a good one."

"I will be."

"You're also a brother to me," she said, "and a cousin. You're not just my lover and colleague and friend. You're everything."

"I know what you mean," he said hoarsely.

There was a brief silence. Then Jake said, "I want you to know something."

He was sitting now with his back against a pillow, the pale blue blanket covering him from the waist down. "I know we agreed not to talk about the future, but one thing I want you to know about me: I'm not a coward. I can get fearful or afraid at times, but I'm not cowardly. As a child I ran away from bullies, but I won't run out on you now. I'll fight for you. I'll fight for us. Whatever form this friendship takes."

"I know," she said.

But a second later he appeared uncomfortable.

"What is it?" she asked.

"Nothing."

"What's wrong? Tell me."

He blushed. "I have to fart."

She laughed. "So fart."

"Are you sure?"

"Of course I'm sure. If you have to fart, fart."

Jake farted. A loud roaring one, like an old-fashioned motor car. She laughed. He, blushing more deeply, laughed, too. She said, "My father always says, 'Better out than in.'"

"I think I'd like your father."

"He'd like you for sure. He already knows your work; he has one of your books." She wrapped a corner of the blanket around her, partly because of the coolness in the room, partly out of modesty. "Do you think your parents would have liked me," she asked, "if they were still alive?"

"They'd have loved you," Jake said warmly. "How could anyone not love you? I only wish you could all have met. You know, if you and I had met before I met Fran, you would have been my wife. You and I would be family now. Well, I feel like we are, in a sense, anyway."

He stopped, looking confused. Then anxious.

"What is it?" she asked.

"There's more."

And before he had time to explain, he let out another huge fart, this time followed almost instantly by a terrible stench.

"Oooh," she laughed, covering her nose with the blanket. "That's a killer!"

Jake, covering his nose, too, laughed, and then hugged her. "Now I never have to be embarrassed about anything with you," he said. "With Fran I'm always a little ashamed. I'd never fart like this with her. I always have to hold myself back. But not with you. With you I can be free."

*

Later, downstairs in the kitchen eating eggs, the telephone rang. When Jake answered it, his voice sailed with such joy at hearing whoever was on the other end, and his face turned so tender, that Eve was knifed through with jealousy. After he hung up, he said, "That was Yael. Checking something about Monday night."

Eve didn't trust herself to speak. They ate for a minute in silence and then, while she was mopping up some omelette with a piece of the soft inside of a baguette, the phone rang again. This was obviously a business call. Jake's speech was clipped and cool, his tone was brusque, and his facial expressions vacillated between disapproving and almost angry.

"Who was that?" Eve asked, wiping up the last of her egg.

"Dina," Jake said with annoyance. "Why she had to phone here is beyond me. She could have just as easily called Yael."

After all the warmth and beauty of this day, Eve froze. Her hand holding the egg-soaked bread stopped poised in the air on its way to her mouth. A black shiver, like a bone-deep warning, ran down the marrow of her arm.

21. SWINGING

EVE SITS ON BARRY AND LEAH'S LOVESEAT, and pushes the floor with her feet to see if she can get the loveseat to swing back and forth. This time, for some reason, it does. Swinging back and forth, she wonders why remembering that day with Jake just now was so different than all the times she has remembered it before. Then she realizes (back and forth, back and forth), that this time she just plain remembered what happened. She didn't re-experience it; she just remembered it. Like watching a movie, a movie replay of something in the past, such as talking on the phone two days ago to Reut. That day with Jake is in my memory now, she thinks. It's in the past. It's not in the present anymore.

This is so shocking to her that she forgets to keep rocking the swing, and just sits, staring bug-eyed in front of her. She has never before seen the movie of that day. Never heard this dialogue with any objectivity. Imagine asking Jake if he'd be her father! How totally bizarre! Sure, he was a fucked-up guy — no question about that. But she had picked him, probably, because she herself, at least in that movie, was just as infantile and symbiotic as he was. She had wanted to lose herself in him, like an infant with a parent. "Lose oneself!" she thinks with a jolt. In Hebrew that verb, *l'hitabed*, also means to commit suicide. I wanted to surrender my self, my essential Eve-ness, to Jake.

Amazing.

For a while she sits with her eyes shut, absorbing all this. Then she resumes rocking, and the swing moves back and forth in two-four rhythm. Jake was happy enough to be her father. He'd always had a thing for his daughters — a lack of boundaries with an erotic tinge — so he enjoyed playing father-daughter with her. I was his good daughter, she thinks, the one who could do no wrong. Until Fran started hating me, at which point I became the bad daughter who could do no right. I went, almost from one day to the next, from being good daughter to bad. From being Light to Darkness. From being Madonna to Whore. I became the central problem in Jake's marriage, like I'd been in Daddy and Julia's almost forty years before. The destroyer of others' happiness. The dark cloud blotting out the sun. I was a bad person. A disease that, like a tumour, had to be eliminated.

Overnight he went from loving me to hating me. From wanting me in his life to wanting me outside of it. He seemed to actually hate me.

This is the acid that's been eating away at her, at her innermost core, for all these years, but which she has never really acknowledged to herself. Jake's hatred of her. His face in front of hers, looking at her with disdain. Once the face of love, it has now become frozen in time as the face of rejection and hate. *You're no good, you're not worth loving.* Constantly, even if subliminally, she feels hated by Jake. As if some deeply wounding music is continually playing at a volume so low you can barely hear it, but you always know it's there.

It shouldn't matter so much, she knows. So what if someone doesn't like her? But she realizes now what happened: She traded her face for Jake's. His face that looks at her now with contempt and disgust was once not just the face of love for her; it was her own face looking back at her in the mirror, the face that mirrored all her love for herself. Jake's eyes had replaced her own eyes. It shouldn't have been this way, she thinks. She was an adult, not a child. You don't give your eyes away to someone else. But that's what she did.

She glances around her and notices the honeysuckle bush on her right. She tugs gently on the nearest branch, draws toward her a flower with a trembling stamen, and inhales its almost too-sweet perfume. Never mind Jake, she tells herself. This is what's real. The present. This flower. This flowered loveseat. This kibbutz. This sunny day.

People are stirring around her now. In front of her a mother and son are on the main pathway, walking hand-in-hand. Then a bickering family of five bustles past, rushing as if they're late for something, carrying between them a large metal milk jug and multiple platters, baskets, and bags. They're going somewhere — maybe to Baba and Zayda's for four o'clock tea? The pathway soon gets crowded, and it seems that all the kibbutzniks are now emerging from their houses like mice from their holes. She can hear some signs of life, some clanging, from inside Barry's house, too. He and Leah must be up now from their nap, or lovemaking, or whatever it was they were doing, and it sounds like they're putting on the kettle for tea.

Maybe Jake doesn't hate me, after all. This is the first time she has ever considered this possibility, and it is confusing, even disorienting. Her certainty that Jake hates her, and that he and Fran are her enemies, has been her bedrock for the past few years. But now, swinging on the loveseat with its rusty old hinges, it seems conceivable that maybe she's been wrong. On TV a few nights ago, the guest on an Israeli talk show was a behavioural psychologist who challenged one person after another in the audience on their most deeply-held beliefs.

"Are you one hundred percent sure," this psychologist asked one of them, a depressed widow, "can you be one hundred percent certain, that you will never remarry because, as you say, 'no man will ever want to marry a seventy-year-old widow'? One hundred percent I'm asking you for."

The un-merry widow thought for a moment and then said,

"No. I can't swear one hundred percent. Ninety-five percent yes. Perhaps even ninety-eight. But not one hundred percent."

Eve can't swear one hundred percent either that for the past five and a half years Jake has been hating her, or even that he ever hated her at all. Maybe the truth is more or less what he told her back then: that he wanted to stay friends but Fran couldn't handle it. Maybe he never hated me, she thinks, and maybe he doesn't hate me now. This thought is still so new and foreign to Eve that she laughs out loud and for the second time forgets to keep the loveseat swinging. She wonders what he really feels toward her. Assuming, that is, he feels anything at all. Which he probably doesn't because she probably never crosses his mind. He's very good at compartmentalizing. He most likely has her locked away in a little bottle in his mind.

He actually even told her about this on the phone one day, quite unabashedly, when their relationship was starting to spiral downward. He said that even if he never saw her again, he knew he would still always have her in a way, because he'd always have an image of her in his mind. She didn't like Jake shrinking her down this way to a portable image designed to replace the real her; and she told him testily that even though, phenomenologically speaking, the real and the image of the real are virtually interchangeable, she personally felt that the real had intrinsic value. Furthermore, she added, she did not agree to being distilled, boiled down into some abstract "essence of Eve," that, in her absence, he could help himself to a dab of whenever he wanted, like a dab of perfume from a blue bottle. Jake laughed. He liked the image, he said.

Already back then he was starting to make her unreal to him. She wanted to stay real, but he wouldn't allow that. Sighing and starting to swing again, she muses on what reality is. She feels the realness in her body: her bum comfortable on the soft cushions of the loveseat as she swings with pleasure back and forth, while the scent of honeysuckle fills the air around her.

She rocks back and forth, feeling so peaceful and content now that reality seems to her to be good enough — not only for this moment, but also for the future. I don't want fantasy anymore, she thinks. I want reality. In the end, despite all its limitations, it's better and safer than this imaginary world I've been living in for the past few years. This imaginary world, she recalls, started off as a happier place than her real life because Jake, who loved her, was there, and he'd remain there as long as she could keep him alive. But then it turned into hell. Trying to keep alive by sheer effort of will something that was, in fact, dead. That existed only in her mind. A type of madness. Meanwhile devaluing all the gifts that she had in her real life: her boys, her friends, her music, her job. She was never where she was, never in the present. It was like never being alive. Nothing — no reality, however frightening, shocking, or painful — can be worse than this half-life (non-life) she has been living in recent years. This liminal, unreal, in-limbo state.

Yes, she thinks, give me reality. Hard cold reality and hard cold truth. Better to look the most brutal facts right in the face than go through more of the past five and a half years, nearly losing my mind. So now she opens herself to the cold, clear truth about Jake. And what she sees is just a man. A two-legged creature like billions of others crawling the face of the Earth like ants. Nothing more, nothing less. He's just a man, she thinks with slight surprise. Like Brian or Barry, or this man in his sixties in shorts and sandals, with thin hairy legs, walking along the main kibbutz path right now, nodding curtly to her as he passes. I could call up Jake if I want, just like I call up any other person. He's just a human being. I could even call him and not hang up. I could call him and stay on the line and talk to him. And she can picture herself actually saying to him on the phone:

"Tell me, Jake: What do you think and feel about me now? And what did you feel for me back then? I'd like to know. Did you really love me? Was any of it real?"

Instantly she feels nauseated and her hands start to sweat. No. She could not call up Jake and stay on the line. She most definitely could not do that. She's a hundred percent sure. Even though she knows that in theory she could. Just as in theory she still exists for Jake somewhere in his mind, inside the little perfume bottle, or Pandora's box, that he built to contain her.

She begins to hum. She hums in the rhythm she is rocking to — two-four: Bum bum, Bum bum — and soon she has slid into a section from her love-and-hate cycle. Her *philos-aphilos* cycle. As she sings it, she is thinking, I need to find an ending for this cycle. The deadline for that competition is just ten days from now. And in less than forty-eight hours — this Monday at noon — I fly back to Toronto. I need to find an ending.

More stirrings now inside Barry and Leah's bungalow. Eve notices that at some point while she was swinging, and maybe when she was singing, they opened the window next to the front door, presumably to let in the cool late afternoon air. She can hear Barry's groggy post-nap (or post-sex) voice murmuring to Leah (though she can't hear the words), and she can imagine him shuffling around their small kitchen in his green terrycloth bathrobe with the orange diamonds on it.

What is it? she asks herself. What is the missing clue to this mystery, the hidden piece to this puzzle, that she hasn't found yet? There's something still concealed from her view. Sure, she has figured out the Daddy bit. Jake as the reincarnation of Daddy. And Fran as the reincarnation of Julia. She gets all that. But there is something more here that she doesn't yet understand. And now, for the first time, she genuinely wants to know, she is finally ready to know, what this is.

Half-closing her eyes and rocking, she can feel the answer coming toward her. It's about to emerge. It will soon break through, like a new wisdom tooth bursting through the gum. She feels the clue — the secret, the knowledge, the secret knowledge — imminently hovering like a ghost. Something is about to happen.

Now the door creaks open. Leah comes out onto the porch bearing something in her hands. "We heard you singing. Would you like some fruit?"

She holds out to Eve a plate of perfect, fresh, ripe, red strawberries.

22. SUNDAY ON THE BUS

SUNDAY MORNING AT TEN-THIRTY, Eve sits in a rickety old bus rocking slightly from side to side as it starts the two-and-a-half-hour journey to Jerusalem. Barry and Leah gave her a warm send-off beginning with an elaborate breakfast of omelettes, salads, and pastries, and ending with hugs and kisses and pleas to return again soon. Eve, as usual, pretended, while Barry was hugging her goodbye, not to notice Leah slipping a small parcel into her canvas bag. Part of the game they always play when she visits: afterwards she'll call to thank them and say how surprised she was to discover the treats Leah inserted into her bag. She smiles now thinking of Barry and Leah. What kind, caring people. Sitting alone on this bus, she feels lonely already.

The bus lurches forward. This ride, she can see, is going to be too bumpy for reading the book in her bag (a collection of Hebrew poetry in translation that Barry lent her last night). So she looks out the window at the view. Rolling green fields, industrial buildings, and signs for kibbutzim, small towns, and Arab villages. Next there are hills, then plains, and she sees grazing cattle, an airplane overhead, a greenhouse growing strawberries, and red and yellow flowers in the fields. *Do you love me?* asks a voice. That old default question popping up — typical, she knows, of times she is lonely or bored. But now, instead of answering this question automatically as usual (*No. You don't love me anymore*), she hears it as if for the first time, with the objectivity and distance with which she yesterday watched the "movie" of that day with Jake. She considers now who, in the question *Do you love me?*, is the "*you*." Of whom is she asking this question? It isn't Jake she is asking this of anymore. It can't be: he's dead. And there's no one here now except her. So she must be asking this of herself.

Yes, she answers. *I do.*

*

The bus slows to a halt at a crossroad between two major highways and picks up two more passengers. An old woman struggles up the stairs and her grandson, handsome, lean, and respectful of her, follows close behind. They sit at the front near the driver. Eve is all the way at the back, in the second to last row on the right, and the only other passenger on the bus is a young female soldier a third of the way down on the left. This young female soldier has blonde hair, which reminds Eve of a photo she saw at Jake's house of his daughter Yael in her army uniform. She wishes now she had never gone to his house. There's something about having seen Jake in his "natural habitat" that's made it harder to forget him, because at any given moment, she can picture what he is doing in his house. For example, at seven in the morning he's alone in his kitchen (while Fran still sleeps), making coffee with his special beans and grinder and espresso machine, standing there in his bathrobe, barefoot on those cold Tuscan floors. When it's lunchtime in Israel, there he is again in the kitchen, sharing a hot midday meal (as is the Israeli custom) with Fran, sitting across from her at the wooden table. Maybe smiling at her, maybe taking her hand. In between those two meals, and then again between lunch and supper, Eve pictures Jake in his den. Working at his cluttered desk, his forehead perhaps resting on his fist as he concentrates over a knotty problem. At the end of the day, at night, he's in bed under that Mennonite coverlet... But no. She doesn't like to picture that.

He's lucky. He has never had to stand in her kitchen, view photos of her kids (including their birthday parties at age three); he has never had to confront the hard realness of her life in her "natural habitat." So he hasn't been plagued constantly by the images she has. She's imagined Jake's house thousands of times since the day she visited it. Back then, despite its gloominess, she appreciated its charm and sophistication, and also its fine view, but over time she has grown to hate that house. That symbol of his domestic security and happiness, while she suffered day after day in loneliness. At one point during the second intifada, a couple of the missiles attacking Israel reached the outskirts of Tel Aviv, and she, hearing this news, eagerly hoped that the next one to strike Israel would strike Jake's house. Hit it and demolish it. Not Jake himself, or even his wife, she thought hurriedly. She wasn't *that* crazy. (Or anyway, not crazy enough to admit to desiring someone's death.) No; she just wished for the destruction of his house and property and everything he owned. The house that he and his wife had so lovingly built, carefully choosing every floor tile together, every coffee bean. This is what she wanted reduced to rubble: that house, that marriage, that life.

She looks out the bus window at the ever-changing landscape, and sighs. At this stage she couldn't care less about demolishing Jake or his house. The time for revenge fantasies is past. So is the time for hating him. It's just too tiring. It takes lots of energy to keep hatred alive.

She reaches into her canvas bag on the seat to her left, from a side pocket pulls out a pear, and bites into the soft, fleshy fruit. Sweet juice runs down her chin and onto her t-shirt, but she doesn't mind. The pear is delicious. She finishes it, disposes of the core in the paper garbage bag affixed to her seat, and huddles against the window, hoping for a nap. But the jolting of the bus makes this impossible, so she daydreams instead. This morning she was up at six, so she took a quiet stroll over to the petting zoo. For a long time she stood in front of the monkeys' cage, watching them, as if there lay the answers to all her questions. Two young monkeys were playing, chasing each other all over the ropes and swings, scampering nimbly. The grandfather monkey sat watching them. A couple, a male and female, groomed each other. One of the young monkeys stopped clambering for a moment to suck its thumb, reminding Eve of the little boy in the restaurant in Daliat. A mother monkey, as her baby sucked on her bright pink nipple, grimaced with big, sprawling lips. Eve contemplated the baby sucking and suckling: *A mother monkey suckles a baby monkey, but who does honeysuckle suckle? A baby honey?* She watched the baby monkey nursing until it was finished. Then she thought: The mouth is the place for everything. All the basics of life. Food, breath, speech, kisses, and song.

The bus halts again, this time in the small dilapidated bus station of a development town. As four passengers noisily ascend, Eve places her hand over her canvas bag and avoids eye contact with the newcomers, and she is successful: no one sits next to her or even in any of the adjacent rows. The bus lurches off again. Now very bored, she rummages around in her canvas bag to see what treasures Leah and Barry have hidden for her this time. She is hoping for some of Leah's chocolate chip *mandelbroit* or maybe a brownie. But all she finds is an envelope. *An envelope? Who can eat an envelope?* Testily she tears it open and extracts a six by four inch, black-and-white landscape photograph. The top three-quarters of the photograph is covered by a large yellow stickie with handwriting scrawled across it:

To my cuz Eve
Love, Barry

Because of this stickie, all she can see of the picture is a mouth. Again she feels annoyed with Barry: *Why is he sending her a photo of Jake?* She didn't know that Barry and Jake even knew each other. After years of cautiously avoiding all photos of Jake (in newspapers, on book jackets, anywhere), she is more than surprised — she is shocked — at being unexpectedly confronted in this way with his mouth. She turns away as quickly as she can from the photo, but still there's been time to glimpse his lips: thin, impatient, intelligent, and pursed with humour but also some superiority. In this glimpse of two or three seconds, she hasn't had time to arm herself against him — he has slipped in sideways, like a thin knife blade into a crack in her wall — and she is defenceless against the immediacy and intimacy of his mouth, suddenly so near her own that she wants to kiss it. She glances around surreptitiously. No one's watching her, or even sitting near her, but the driver has a rear-view mirror, and anyway, she wouldn't kiss Jake's photo in a public place. But for some reason her face is wet now and her nose is running. She wipes her face and blows her nose. Then her stomach turns cold with fear. Where did Barry get this picture? And even more worrying: How did he know about her and Jake? How did he know she would be interested in seeing a photo of him? She never mentioned Jake to Barry. She is sure of that (one hundred percent). So how could he know?

Her stomach does a flip-flop. Oh no, she thought. It can't be.

One day Jake said to her, smiling, "If you and I both wrote operas (disguising our identities, of course; I'd make you from Australia, and you'd make me from South Africa or somewhere) — do you think that people in New Zealand seeing both our operas would make the connection and guess they were about the same affair?"

This was somewhere toward the end of their relationship, and it was the first time he had ever used the word "affair." She replied stiffly, "Mine wouldn't be about an 'affair.' It would be about love."

But that went right past him.

He's written that opera! she thinks now. Oh God! And he's gone public in an interview somewhere, revealing that the woman in the opera is me. In order to humiliate me. To get revenge...

But a few seconds later that seems unlikely. She would have heard about it if the renowned Jacob Gladstone had, at the age of seventy, just written his first opera. Someone would certainly have mentioned it at the conference this week and it would have been big news all over the Jewish music world.

But then, back to the question: *How did Barry know?*

She glances again at Jake's mouth. Then, to get a clue as to where this picture's from, and to see the rest of it, she peels off the yellow stickie. And now she frowns — a frown of annoyance, but also confusion. There's been some mistake. This isn't Jake; it's a woman.

And then she recognizes the woman. It's Mommy.

It can't be. This is Jake's mouth. She stares at the photo, baffled. For an instant she wonders if this is one of those puzzle games Ethan used to have: those composite photos in three panels, where you can insert the nose of your friend and the eyes of a grizzly bear and the mouth of your mother. The mouth of her mother... She stares at the photo. And stares. And stares...

For all the rest of the bus ride. All the way to Jerusalem. Over and over she compares the mouth in this picture with Jake's. His mouth with her mother's mouth. Every time, to her amazement, she finds they're almost identical. If this were one of those transparent pages in an anatomy textbook, where you lay one image on top of another to compare them, and you laid these two mouths together, mouth upon mouth, they would have matched almost perfectly. It's as if someone copied her mother's mouth with a stencil and pasted it onto Jake's face. Or vice versa. That thin, sensual, sardonic, laughing mouth.

It's not just the physiological resemblance, she concludes as the bus approaches Jerusalem. It's also their expression. The impatiently pursed lips of an intelligent person who is clearly annoyed by an unintelligent world.

Maybe this is the reason, she thinks, that she was so intensely attracted to Jake, and there was always an eerie sense of familiarity with him from the moment they met. *I know you* is what she felt as soon as she looked at him. *I know everything about you.* And they hadn't yet exchanged a single word. All through their relationship she kept being drawn toward his mouth. In Daliat, she remembers, out of everything in the market, all she desired was to kiss Jake's mouth. Actually, not so much to kiss it. Rather, to be glued together with it. Glued mouth-to-mouth. Like mouth-to-mouth resuscitation. Which they gave to Mommy, but it didn't work.

The picture begins to shake. No, it's not the photo, she realizes after a second; it's her hand that's shaking.

They have the same mouth. Jake and Mommy. Mommy and Jake.

The bus is pulling into the Jerusalem station now. Unexpectedly they're in a dark tunnel, which is disorienting after the bright sunlight of the long journey. People are standing and lining up near the doors to descend. Now Eve, still in her seat, realizes that part of the conversation with Jake in yesterday's "movie," she in fact recalled incorrectly. She thought the exchange went like this:

"I could be like your mother. And you be like my father."

He looked astonished. "You'd let me be your father?"

She smiled. "As long as you're a good one."

But no. That's not what happened. She recalls now what they really said to each other:

"I could be like your mother. And you be like my father," she said to him. "But you'll have to be my mother, too, because I don't have one."

He looked astonished. "You want me to be your mother?"

"As long as you're a good one."

No wonder he looked astonished, she thinks. It's weird enough to ask your male lover to be your father. But to ask him to be your mother...!

She recalls, as well, what came a few minutes after that. Jake had been saying that whenever they had their first fight ("and we will sooner or later have a fight, because one always fights with the people one loves"), he knew that it would be okay, and that they'd kiss and make up, the same way he and Fran did, or he and the girls, after a fight.

"We'll fight, and we'll make up," he said. "Possibly many times over the years. And it doesn't matter. Because we'll always come back together again. I know this from my fights with Fran and the girls. And that's the only frame of reference I can apply with you. Because they're the only people I've ever loved the way I love you."

That was when she said, "I know. Me, too. You're not just my lover and colleague and friend. You're also my brother, and cousin, and father, and mother." She reached up and stroked his mouth, and then the area around it: perfectly smooth, hairless, and never having been shaved.

She feels dizzy now and staggers slightly getting off the bus. As though she is drunk or has heat stroke. For a minute in the bus station, she doesn't remember where or who she is. Or to whom — her mother or Jake — she is addressing the questions inside her:

Why did you leave me? Why did you go away?

23. SUNDAY NIGHT

IT'S SUNDAY NIGHT AT BEDTIME. Eve is sitting on the edge of her bed, her suitcases packed and waiting by the door. Tomorrow morning at eleven-thirty Gidi will come to take her to the airport. Gidi is the taxi driver who always drives her there and picks her up when she arrives. An enthusiastic young man, a part-time music student who used to be religious but isn't anymore, he'll pull up in front of the small, shabby, family-owned hotel where she always stays, and honk the special, unique honk that he developed himself. Her room is on the third floor facing the main street, and tomorrow morning she'll leave the window open so she can hear him honk, and then she'll go running downstairs like an eager girl skipping down the steps for a date.

Not that she is feeling eager to leave Israel. She is sad now as she usually is the night before leaving. Reut jokingly calls it her "separation anxiety" from Israel, which it is in a way. But it's also sadness over leaving Jake again. It'll be six more months till she is near him again. Not that she expects to ever again see, or talk to, Jake. It's more like the sadness of leaving a country containing the grave of someone you loved.

She turns down the bed and flicks on the fan to camouflage the street noise while she sleeps. Tonight, she knows, the noise will be much worse than usual: it's New Year's Eve, or as they call it here (after St. Sylvester) "Sylvester." There will be wild revels and tooting horns till four a.m. She sighs.

True, it is hard leaving Israel, but at the same time it has been a good trip, and she is ready to go home. She has work to do: She has that contest to enter (if only she can find an ending for her song cycle!), and the day after that deadline, she may go up north for a few days with a group of music therapists, including Darryl, to ski at the chalet of someone's friend. She is also looking forward to being back in Toronto so she can spend the last day of Chanukah with Michael and Ethan. She still buys them Chanukah presents, even though they're twenty and eighteen — she can't help spoiling them a bit, her fatherless boys — and today while out tooling around, she bought them a few small gifts. She also bought a one-ounce bottle of "holy water." Though this seemed to her like a shameless scam — she could just fill up a bottle with tap water from the hotel, she thought, instead of laying out ten bucks in a tourist shop for an ounce of the same thing. But Irma, their housekeeper and a devout Christian, had requested this.

The photo of her mother that Barry gave her this morning she originally packed in her suitcase. But then, thinking better of it, she slipped the picture into the zippered compartment of her purse along with her passport. All day today as she ran around Jerusalem doing errands and a bit of sightseeing (she dropped in to see the newly redesigned Yad Vashem), at the back of her mind she has been going *Jake Mommy. Mommy Jake. Mommy Jake. Jake Mommy*. Tonight at supper with Reut, Reut said it was amazing what had happened with that photo. "*Amazing*," she said three times with her American accent. They ate at a French restaurant, now kosher, but which wasn't when Eve and Jake ate there together. Eve, ever since university, had pretty much eaten only kosher, and hadn't realized this restaurant was *treyf* until she and Jake were already seated, scanning their menus. When she commented that most of the dishes on the menu were *treyf*, Jake laughed at her religiosity, just as her grandfather, a "free thinker," used to laugh at her grandmother's. Jake seemed to take gleeful delight in dragging her into *treyf*, saying half-jokingly that he enjoyed "corrupting" her. There was a funny misunderstanding, though, that night. He recommended the Strasbourg pâté. She said she had never eaten that before.

"It's just another name for goose liver spread," he said.

"Never had that, either."

Jake was astonished. "Really? Well then, you must try some now!" and he grew excited about this, as if he were introducing her, an innocent young girl, to the culinary equivalent of the secrets of the *Kama Sutra*. But when the goose liver spread arrived, she nearly burst out laughing. Oh! she thought, it's only *pâté de foie gras!* She had often had this as a teenager when she went out to lunch with her father. But all her experience with French cuisine had been — not surprisingly — in French. She almost told Jake just then that she had already had "Strasbourg pâté" and "goose liver spread," but restrained herself. *Let him think he's exposed me to something new.*

She slips her nightgown over her head, thinking, Yes, it's been a good trip. A "productive" trip. She has knocked off her seminar for this year (though maybe next year she should try London or New York to renew her accreditation rather than returning here). And she lucked out by attending — thanks to Miranda — that Jewish music conference. She met some interesting people, and Hector especially may be an important contact. She is feeling more hopeful now because of his generous offer to help her. *I don't need Jake anymore. Hector's just as good.*

She climbs into bed, clucking her tongue with annoyance. *Jake.* To think that she almost missed this conference because of him. She must find a way to end this thing.

Now she makes a plan — the same plan she has made on the last evening of every one of her visits here for the past five years. She no longer believes in this plan. Like a promise that's been made and broken a hundred times already, she knows she won't act on it and that it will never come to pass. But still, it's a kind of ritual to make this plan.

Tomorrow morning (The Plan goes) she will wake up early and call Jake while Fran is still sleeping. And she'll ask him all her questions:

Did you (do you) love me?

Did you (do you) hate me?

Do you ever think about me?

And maybe some other questions, too. She has assumed for years that she is hated in Jake's household, by him, Fran, and their daughters, and that she is a family joke and scapegoat. (Like Eve's one-time incompetent housekeeper, Elsie, who lost, burnt or broke everything she touched; and for years after Eve fired her, whenever anything went wrong at home — like a sock going missing in the dryer — she or Michael or Ethan would ask, "What could have happened to it?" and the other two would chime in with delight: "*Elsie!*") So this may be something she will want to ask Jake about tomorrow. She pulls the covers up to her neck. It's time to get some reality about this. Some hard facts into this story. There's nothing she could hear from him over the phone tomorrow that's worse than what she has been imagining all these years. The images and insults that swarm through her mind like devouring locusts.

I'll be a researcher, she thinks in the minute or two before she dozes off. It's always a central part of The Plan that, just like when she was conducting interviews for her Master's research, she will gather information from Jake, "collect data" from him. Because that's what she really wants from him at this point in time: data. Not love. Not apologies, excuses or explanations. But hard facts. In a sense, the questions in The Plan aren't even about her. They're impersonal. This is an impersonal exchange, a fact-finding mission. Question, answer, question, answer, as if she is following a standardized questionnaire while conducting a research interview over the phone. It's good that it's over the phone and she doesn't have to see Jake in person, face-to-face. That would be too much. It also helps that there's a natural wall between a research interviewer and her research subject, a wall that will protect her. Tomorrow morning, she thinks groggily, I'll just be gathering information. Not giving away anything of myself. I'll be safe.

24. MONDAY MORNING

THE NEXT MORNING, ON JANUARY 1ST, the start of a new year, Eve wakes up at six-twenty, a half-hour later than prescribed in The Plan. She has always been able to wake herself up without an alarm clock at any time she wants. She didn't know this was an unusual ability until she went to sleepover camp and discovered that not everyone could do this. But this morning she has overslept her inner alarm clock for only the third time in her life, and now it's very late. Jake gets up before six and Fran sometime between seven and seven-thirty, so her plan was to call Jake at six sharp so they'd have a whole hour to converse before Fran woke up. Oh well, she thinks, even forty-five minutes is better than nothing, and sitting on the edge of her bed, she dials Jake's number. In the second, though, before it starts to ring, she quickly hangs up. Immediately her hands start to sweat. She has never done this before (actually called him from her hotel room for a real conversation) and she is shocked at herself. How could she have done this? What was she thinking? Fantasy isn't reality. These two things have to be kept very clearly apart. This is all that keeps the world from spinning madly out of control and exploding into a million particles in outer space. She takes a few deep breaths and regains her composure. She still feels slightly dizzy, though.

Phew. What a narrow escape.

But the next thing she knows, her fingers, without her having given them permission, are dialling Jake's number again. The private number she knows by heart that he gave her back then — the one that rings only in his den. Now the phone, instead of ringing, screeches at her, hurting her ear, and she hangs up fast. Within a few seconds she realizes what happened. This phone number was always Jake's household's second phone line; they must have started using it, since her last pay phone call a year ago, for their fax machine. Calmly she dials Information to get his other number. The public one that's known to the outside world, not the private, secret, insiders' number he gave her. She calls Information now as if this were a perfectly normal thing to do, to request the home phone number of Jacob and Frances Gladstone in Tel Aviv, as if it were any old phone number. She waits for the voice at the other end (which she imagines belongs to a female robot) to come back with the number, and meanwhile tells herself that just because she'll soon have this number doesn't mean she ever has to use it. It's just good to have in case.

The robot lady returns and tells her the number. "For one shekel," the female robot adds, "we will automatically connect you to this number. Just press Star."

"Sure," says Eve, and presses Star. With happy expectancy and confidence (*I am a researcher, I am conducting a study...*) she listens while the phone rings once, twice, three times. Then she hears a man's voice.

"Hel-lo-o?"

That wavy way Jake always said hello: C-G-E. "Is this Jacob Gladstone?"

"Yes."

"Do you know who this is?" She is excited to be springing a surprise on him. And for the moment, because of this, to have the upper hand, like in the Six-Day War.

"No," he says impatiently.

She is faintly disappointed. He doesn't recognize her voice anymore. "It's Eve. Eve Bercovitch."

"Eve." This is said with a groan, as if he has just received a blow to the stomach. "Hold on, I'll switch phones."

There's a pause of about half a minute. It's him! It's actually him! she thinks buoyantly, as she waits a little tensely on the line. Yet this also feels surreal after all these years of imagining this moment. I'm a researcher, she reminds herself. I'm just calling to collect some information.

"Okay, I'm here," says Jake.

"Were you already working?" she asks. "I know you usually get up early."

"No. This morning I was sleeping."

She pictures him lying warm in bed next to his wife. Now he is out of bed, standing barefoot on the cold floor of their kitchen. Maybe naked (because he sleeps naked) or in a hastily-tied bathrobe. She starts to say, "Oh, you slept in," but stops herself after saying, "Oh, you." When she used the phrase "slept in" with him back then, he didn't know what it meant and she had to explain. He told her it was a Canadianism; she'd had no idea.

"What do you want?" Jake asks roughly.

She answers calmly. She feels relaxed, even light-hearted. She is so happy to be talking to him at last. "What do I *want*? I wanted to say hello. Is this disturbing to you?"

He considers this for a moment. Then says, "No. A little confusing, perhaps. But not disturbing."

The roughness, the slight hostility, is gone. He sounds warmer, closer now. He seems to be reacting as if she is being kind and considerate of his feelings, when really these are just the preliminary courtesies before beginning an interview. She notices now that Jake's voice is basically unfamiliar to her. His accent isn't as pronounced as she remembered, and she wouldn't have known it was him if she hadn't phoned him herself. She could just as well be talking to a stranger.

"I was at a Jewish music conference this week," she says, "and saw your new book there. Mazal tov." She is careful to use the Hebrew pronunciation, as she knows he would prefer, and not the Yiddish one.

"Thanks." There's a bit of a pause. "How long has it been? Three years? Four?"

You don't even know how long it's been! she thinks. And I've been counting every day... She doesn't answer him and there's a brief silence.

"Well, why now?" he asks belligerently. Then, as if hearing his harsh tone, he adds, "I don't mean that the way it sounded. But seriously, why are you calling now? Why not a year ago? Or two?"

I'm not here to answer questions; I'm here to elicit information from you. "I could ask," she says, "why you never called at all."

"Touché." She can hear him smiling. He always liked repartee, and the two of them used to spar and parry as intellectual equals. Now she has smacked the tennis ball back into his court. There's a short pause. "I suppose there are two reasons," he says. "Mainly, Fran didn't want me to."

Now there's a longer pause, as though he's finished.

"And?" she asks.

"What?"

"You said there were two reasons."

"Oh. Right." He seems a little stunned. Not the way she remembers him: quick-witted and clever. "Well," he says, "even if it weren't for Fran, I probably wouldn't have called you. It might have just seemed easier not to."

Easier! For you, but not for me. (And there's an echo at the back of her mind of that song from *West Side Story* : *For you, but not for me. For you, but not for me. But my heart, Anita, but my heart!*) You're such a coward, she thinks. At least about that I was right. You said you weren't a coward, but you are. She is filled with contempt and coldness, but she reminds herself now, Stay pleasant. Stay professional. There's information you have to collect. And she proceeds with the next question on the questionnaire.

"How have you been?" she asks in a friendly tone.

"Oh," says Jake, and it's half a groan, half a sigh. "What can I say? My marriage never recovered from what happened with you. My relationship with Fran was never a simple one, as you know, even before this happened, but now it's much less simple. And it'll never again be the way it was."

There's a catch in his voice as he says the last sentence, and there's no way not to hear the pain he feels. So he isn't happy, either, she thinks. *My marriage never recovered.* And she feels exultant.

"That's me," says Jake. "What about you?"

She doesn't want to talk about herself. "In a minute. But first, how are your daughters?"

"Yael has a son, eight months old," he replies mechanically, as if reporting insignificant information. Like telling a repairman the serial number on your washing machine.

A grandson for you. Finally another male in your all-female family. Remember when I almost gave you a son? Remember when we thought I was pregnant?

"She got married about two years ago," he adds, as if Eve were questioning the legitimacy of the baby.

"Mazal tov." Again the Hebrew pronunciation.

"Thanks. As for Dina..." Here his tone turns querulous, doubtful, almost like he himself doubts Dina's legitimacy. "She's still working at the same job."

"Is she married, too?"

He gives a snort. "She has a Vietnamese boyfriend who lives in Belgium. He comes here every once in a while; every once in a while she goes there..." He sighs. Then he asks, "What about you?"

"Well, I've finished two oratorios" (she doesn't want to go into "storatorio"; that feels too personal somehow), "and I'm now completing a song cycle."

"So you finished *Hallelujah*?"

She is pleased he recalls the title. "Yes. But I still haven't been able to get it performed. Several people said it was good, and original, and beautiful, and if I make it less about Israel, they'll be happy to consider it."

"You're joking." He sounds shocked.

"I wish I were."

"Wow! I knew things were bad out there now for Israel, and of course I've heard that it's a rough time to get any new work performed, but I didn't know things were quite this bad."

She says glumly, "You have no idea. It's life imitating art. All the anti-Israelism I described in *Hallelujah* is now being re-enacted in the responses it's getting."

They are on track now, she and Jake. They always were like-minded when it came to Israel and the phenomenon of anti-Israelism. Now this feels almost normal, like a normal conversation between two colleagues, or even friends, commiserating about the state of the music world and the world in general. Except that she knows she's acting, in fact laying it on a bit thick, and as she chatters brightly on the thin strip of stage in front of a closed curtain, she is aware that the truth behind the curtain is that all this is just pretence. She feels her own shortness of breath and tension.

"But there must be some Jewish or Israeli producers," he says, "who would be interested in a work like this."

"There are a few — not many but some. But you know how it is. That whole Jewish music scene is its own little clique. And if you're not part of it, you're out of luck." She thinks: *You're* part of it, though. You could help me if you wanted to.

There's a pause. "I thought you said that after *Hallelujah* you were never going to write another oratorio."

She laughs. She is pleased, and also surprised, that he remembers this. "It's true," she says. "I didn't mean to. But this new thing had a mind of its own."

There's another pause. Then Jake says conversationally, almost casually, "What you showed me back then from *Hallelujah* — of course it was just a small part of it — but it wasn't great."

She remembers this with painful clarity. He didn't like the first part of *Hallelujah* — all she had done of it by then — and this had come between them. Though probably he didn't know this. She'd felt she couldn't tell him he had hurt her; he had a right to be honest, after all. Yet from that point on there was a corner of their relationship, and her body, that was walled off from him.

It wasn't great. This would hurt even now if she were her, feeling what she feels, instead of a researcher conducting an interview. She pulls out the answer she prepared two or three years ago in anticipation of the comment Jake just made. (Not a total waste, those years of imaginary dialogues.)

"That was early days," she says lightly, confidently. "Now it's good. Very good, even. So is the new oratorio."

"Really!" Jake says, sounding impressed. "That's great."

"Yeah, I'm excited about it."

Another pause. Then he asks, "How are you personally, Eve?"

I'll tell him a little. I won't tell him a lot. "Well, it's been different for me than for you. The damage at this end wasn't to my marriage. It was to me."

He is silent for a bit. Then he says, "I hoped you'd be all right. I truly hoped that. And not only for selfish reasons. Not only because of guilt."

She sees and hears a woman screaming and screaming. A woman five and a half years younger than her, who has just received a goodbye email, and will continue to scream for the next twelve months. No, she thinks, I wasn't all right.

"How are Michael and Ethan?" he asks.

She is again surprised at his memory. It's a bit strange he has retained the names of her boys. He never liked them or had any interest in hearing about them. It must be Fran who remembered their names and kept them alive. In the little dollhouse play she created of Eve's life, she has made room in the script for two boy dolls. Jake would never have remembered their names himself.

"Michael's studying philosophy and doing well, and Ethan's coming to Tel Aviv in April for a year. He's in a jazz quartet and two of the guys are Israeli."

"Really!" Again he sounds impressed. "Is he thinking of moving here?"

"Maybe. He'll see." From outside her window a loud — intrusively, painfully loud — announcement comes blaring. Something is being advertised (some sort of *mivtsa*, a special deal) over a loudspeaker. One of those trucks with a loudspeaker is driving by.

"What's that?" he asks.

"Oh, some sort of *mivtsa*."

"What?" He sounds taken aback. "You're here now?"

"Yes."

"I thought you only came in the summer."

She is annoyed. *I'm not just a tourist; I too, made aliyah at one point, just like you.* But she controls her annoyance, and when she speaks, her voice is only slightly crisp, almost neutral in tone.

"I come here three times a year." You'd like to picture me six thousand miles away, she thinks, safely far from you. But I'm not.

Another silence.

"When are you here till?" he asks.

She doesn't understand why he is asking that. He is obviously not going to offer to see her. "Another couple of hours. The taxi's coming at eleven-thirty."

"I see." He sounds relieved.

She says, feeling foolish as soon as she has said it, "My email address changed. I have a new address now."

"Oh, what is it?"

She tells him. She doesn't know whether or not he is writing it down, but she doubts it. "I also have a website," she says, and feeling the need to justify this, adds, "Everyone has to nowadays."

"Do you know who goes on your website?" he asks.

"No." She actually wishes there were some way to know; all she can get from Google is the number of visitors.

"Well, *I* know," he says.

"Really?" She is surprised. He always had disdain for any kind of technology, yet now he seems to have gotten himself a website, and even figured out a way to identify one's online visitors. "How?" she asks.

"Because she told me. Fran visits your website all the time, at least once a week."

Eve sits in shocked silence on the edge of the bed, absorbing this information. For the past few years she has been posting materials on her website hoping that he would see them. Hoping he'd see that a Jewish high school in Toronto performed a section of *Hallelujah* at their annual Music Day. He'd see that Hadassah-WIZO invited her to give a talk on "Being A Jewish Composer" on *Shabbat Shira*. And so on. And all this time it's been Fran who's been following her various activities and accomplishments.

"She knows more about you than I do," he says, smiling. "She tells me all about you. She's obsessed with you."

Eve feels flattered. So she is not a complete nothing to these people. She has some place in their lives. She is important to them, in a way. Even if that way may not be the "healthiest." How did her therapist put it? "They require, and use, you psychically."

"I went out for supper last night with a friend," she says, "and we ate at Chez Maurice. You took me there my first time."

"Oh, yes," he says dreamily, "I remember." Then he adds, "We were in Jerusalem last week to see Yael and her family, and we ate there." She can feel him thinking: *We might have bumped into each other.*

"What are they doing in Jerusalem?" she asks.

"Her husband got a job at Hebrew U., so they moved there a few months ago. Not far from Chez Maurice."

"Oh! What street?"

He doesn't answer right away, which irritates her. *Why are you hesitating? Do you think I'm going to go to that street and stalk your daughter?*

"A small street," he says. "A new one. Salamone Rossi."

She laughs. "How apt."

"Yes."

There's a pause.

"How long has it been?" he asks. "Four years?"

"Five and a half," she says drily.

"That long, eh?" Then he says, "Look, Eve, the truth is Fran has never gotten over what happened with you. She just hasn't been able to come to terms with the fact that you were able to excite and interest me in a way that she couldn't. It has utterly traumatized her. I'm not saying that it's been all bad, and that there haven't been any good times, because there have. But overall it's been a very hard — what did you say?— five years. What happened with you completely shattered her self-esteem."

Shattered, thinks Eve. That's *my* word. That's how I describe what this relationship did to *me*.

"Compared to Fran," he continues easily, "I got over it quite quickly. I didn't miss you for long after it ended, once the erotic longing was gone."

Wow. This would hurt like hell if she let it. But she won't. Instead she feels clever. She had been right. By the time they split up, she was nothing to him except an erotic object. And once that faded, he didn't miss her at all.

Calmly, matter-of-factly, she continues the interview. "You once said that ageing was much harder for Fran than for you because she couldn't accept her body getting older. Maybe ageing was a part of all this."

"Maybe."

She returns to a question she asked him way back when, curious if his perspective has changed with time. "I also wondered if this whole thing happened because you were turning sixty-five."

There's a pause of a few moments. Then he says, "I don't think so. I never thought about that at all."

Which doesn't mean that it wasn't operating subconsciously.

Now his voice drops a few notes on the register, and in an intimate tone, he says intensely, "I didn't see you as a younger woman.'"

A younger woman, she thinks. *That's how Fran cast me. I can't compete with Eve's young flesh.*

"Neither did I," she says. But then recalling the whole father element, she adds, "Though there were some generational differences."

There's another silence now, and Jake asks, "What *is* the age difference between us, anyway? Ten years?"

You don't even know the age difference between us! "Fourteen."

"That's not so much," he says. Then, after a brief pause: "You know, I never imagined it would turn out this way. If I'd known then that this would cause so much harm to my marriage, I'd never have allowed it to happen."

Allowed it to happen! Like you were in control.

"I never did this before," he says, "and I never will again."

"Me, neither."

"You and I," he says, "we just wanted to get to know each other, and we wanted an adventure."

An adventure! She is amazed. She didn't want an "adventure." Such a thought never crossed her mind.

"We didn't mean to hurt anyone," he continues. "We made an agreement, right at the beginning — do you remember? — not to do anything that would hurt our families. We did say that, didn't we?"

Now she feels important and powerful. This is how it used to be — this is how he was with her. Vulnerable. Checking things out with her. Needing her to validate his thoughts and feelings.

His reality. And now his memory. For a moment she considers paying him back by denying the past. Saying: "No, that never happened." Playing with his head — what Fran called "doing evil to someone's mind." Eve first heard that expression when Jake told her that Fran, after discovering he'd been lying to her for weeks about no longer being in touch with Eve, begged him not to do evil to her mind.

"Yes," Eve says now to Jake. "We did."

"But Fran doesn't believe that. Though I guess I can see why."

There's another silence between them. Then he bursts out, in an anguished tone, "Sometimes I wish this had never happened. But how can you wish that something hadn't happened? That's like wishing that life wasn't life."

She shivers internally. He has just said, almost verbatim, something she herself has been thinking. This used to happen frequently with him, and sometimes it felt almost like he was inside her mind or her body, speaking for her. This time, the only difference between his words and hers is that he said Life where she thought God. Her formulation was that to wish something hadn't happened was like insulting God. But God, she thinks, and the essence of Life are more or less the same thing.

"Wasn't there anything good about it?" she asks Jake.

"Of course there was. But the type of good that comes from suffering. Like leaving Paradise. But one has to leave it. Not that you and I were in Paradise."

Good that comes from suffering. Paradise. She doesn't know what he's talking about. And this "not that you and I were in Paradise" sounds like he is struggling to convince himself of something. Methinks he doth protest too much. Maybe, though, what they had was, in a way, Paradise.

Softly she says, "It was deep."

"Yes. It was. If it wasn't, I couldn't have done it."

What does he mean by *it?* she wonders. Sex? If so, that's probably true. He couldn't have physically done it without believing that this relationship was true love and that they were Adam and Eve.

Another silence. All these pauses, she thinks. Like music that keeps stopping and starting again. Jerky music.

"I was innocent," he says.

Again she is confused about what he means. Does he mean "innocent" as in naive or "innocent" as in blameless?

"I couldn't see anything to do but put on the brakes."

He means blameless. She can't think of anything to say. But Eve the Researcher says, "That's because you believe a man and a woman can't be friends."

"I won't say it's absolutely impossible. But it's very, very difficult."

"You only think that because you've never had a woman friend."

"Not since I got married. I did before that."

This is news to her. She didn't know this and a part of her doubts it's true. "Well," she says, "I've always had male friends, even when I was married. So I know how to do that."

He gives a short laugh. "So we're back to where we were five years ago."

She laughs along, but her laugh is strained, almost a snicker. Not exactly, she is thinking. There's been a lot of water under the bridge.

"Maybe it will be possible, Eve, for us to be friends at some point in the future. Well, not exactly friends — something more casual…"

She doesn't answer. Why are you even saying this? she thinks impatiently. That's never going to happen and we both know it. Why are you bullshitting?

Now he says tenderly, in such a low voice it's almost a whisper, "I did try to fight for my right to have a friend."

In spite of herself, she is touched. So he *was* influenced by this argument of hers, even though at the time he seemed to not even hear it.

"Afterwards," he is saying, "I hoped you'd be okay. And not only out of guilt."

This is the second time he has said this, both times he has ended on the word "guilt," and this word resounds now with the deep resonance that follows a final note played on a kettledrum. This resonating note is asking her for something.

A moment passes. "I didn't call to guilt you," she says. Her voice lilts and swings lightly as she says this — "I *didn't call* to *guilt* you" — and she hears it in the echo left behind.

There's a long silence. Finally he says, "If it weren't for Fran... Like right now, Eve, I would love to be able to talk to you about your new oratorio. And ask you to let me see it, and help you with it, if I can. And also with *Hallelujah*. This is my impulse, this is how I feel. But I shouldn't. I *can't*."

She doesn't say anything. He continues, "Fran is still not over what happened, and she probably never will be. Here it is more than five years later, and she still brings you up at least once a month."

"She does?" Eve is astounded. "What do you mean? In what context?"

"In two situations, mainly, though sometimes other ones, too. The first is when we're getting ... romantic. A shadow will pass over her face. And that shadow is you."

And that shadow is you. She always loved the way Jake talked. So poetically, so metaphorically.

"The other time," he says, "is when she's angry at me. When Fran is in one of her rages, she flings you at me. It happened again just a few days ago."

She is silent, picturing these two scenes. "She must hate me," she says.

There's a brief pause. "I don't think she hates you now," he says. "At one point, maybe. Yes, she probably did at the beginning. But even then, she was actually more angry at me than at you."

Eve is silent, thinking about Fran. She has speculated over

the years about Fran's rages (which happened even before she came along) and her lack of boundaries. She asks Jake curiously, "I always wondered if her mother was a survivor."

"A survivor?" He sounds surprised. "No, her mother was in America during the war. She's just very narcissistic."

Like you. Fran married someone like her mother.

"Over the last few years she's lost it, though," he says. "She barely recognizes Fran anymore."

Like you and your father. She remembers him telling her, stony-faced, as they drove back from Daliat, how his father, in the months before he died, didn't recognize him.

"Fran goes to London twice a year to see her. But she's an empty shell."

An empty shell. What a way to talk about a person, she thinks with a shudder. And to say this so casually, almost cheerfully. Especially when this woman, when your second-to-last book came out, organized your only book launch in all of England, running around for weeks before to drag in all her friends and neighbours.

"Is your father still alive?" he asks.

She is surprised by the sudden catch in her throat. "No. He died shortly after you and I ended."

There's a silence now, and for the first time Jake does not rush to fill it. It feels to her like this conversation might be winding down soon. She still has a few more questions to ask, though. She'd better ask them now. She might not get another chance.

"You said that at the beginning Fran hated me. What about you? Did you hate me, too?"

"No." His answer comes quickly, firmly, warmly. "I was angry at you sometimes, but I never hated you. Anyway, I was mainly angry at myself. For letting this situation get out of hand. This whole thing shook my trust in my own judgment, in my capacity to make rational decisions. It challenged my self-confidence and my sense of certainty." He pauses and then says wryly, "But maybe that's not such a bad thing."

Not a bad thing at all. But then she recalls the time, about halfway into their relationship, when he lost touch with reality. He'd been pretending to Fran for weeks that he'd severed all contact with Eve, and one night he was unable to sleep. Fran asked why and he told her it was because he felt guilty about dumping Eve. Fran took him in her arms and comforted him, whispering that it was only because he was such a good, sensitive man that he cared so much about other people, but that she was sure that Eve was fine, and in three to five years maybe he and Eve could be casual friends. When Jake told all this to Eve the next day on the phone, he was frightened, because for a few moments there with Fran (when supposedly he was in anguish over having given up Eve, when in fact he hadn't), he didn't know anymore what was real and what wasn't.

Now she says to him, "For a while there you lost your sense of reality."

He answers sharply, testily, as if she has hit a nerve, "There's a lot I don't remember about that time. I don't recall a lot of details. I destroyed all our letters, as you know, so Fran couldn't read them on my computer. All I remember from then are general emotions and states of mind. I felt like a ship tossed at sea that didn't know if it would survive."

There's another pause. They've covered a lot of ground already, and there doesn't seem to be much left to say. But she still hasn't asked one important question. And as Daddy used to say, *Might as well be hanged for a sheep as for a lamb.*

"Other than that once a month event," she says, "do you ever think of me?"

"Yes," he answers immediately and with warmth. Then, sounding sheepish, "I'm writing an opera. Not that I know how to write an opera, but I've started one anyway about what happened with us."

"Really!"

"Yes. So far I'm only up to my relationships with girls in high school and college."

"Like Polly."

"Who?"

"Polly. You had a girlfriend Polly in college…"

"Oh, Polly. No, this part is mainly about Fran. It's true that she's stayed faithful to me since we got married, but before that, in college, she had quite a few relationships."

"That black guy she lived with," she volunteered.

"Yes, but not only. She had relationships with lots of guys."

She is disappointed, even a little hurt, that he doesn't appreciate, or even seem to notice, that she committed to memory all these details about his life.

"In my opera," he says, "you appear only briefly onstage. But you have a huge impact."

She doesn't say anything.

"But don't worry," he says, "you won't be recognizable."

"*I'm* not worried," she says calmly, coolly. Then: "What I'm writing also relates to what happened with us."

"Really!"

"Yes," she says. "At the end you said some pretty crappy things to me. But one of them was that if you wrote an opera about this, and I did too, would someone in New Zealand, watching them both, be able to tell that we were both writing about the same affair?"

He laughs. "Did I say that?"

"Yes," she says. "I didn't like that." *Mine wouldn't be about an affair,* she had answered him; *it would be about love.*

Silence on the other end of the phone.

"At that music conference I was at," she says, "Nathan Singelman was there, and I told him about *Hallelujah.*"

"I know Nathan!" says Jake.

Wow, you don't even remember we discussed him. Or that you confided in me that you thought he was second-rate.

"Now *there's* someone," Jake is saying, "who might be able to help you."

"Nah. I tried, but he blew me off."

There's another pause. Then he says, "You asked me if I ever hated you. How could I hate you, Eve? You're one of the most wonderful people I ever met."

Everything in front of her turns white. Everything goes blank and disappears. It's like she has been temporarily blinded. Sitting on the edge of the bed, her body spasming with sobs, she gropes on the night table for a tissue and presses it against her eyes the way you press hard against a wound to stop it from bleeding. Then she blows her nose. Quietly, though. Very quietly and carefully, so he won't hear her crying.

"I wanted to stay friends," she hears him saying from a great distance away.

He said I'm one of the most wonderful people he ever met. He likes me. He doesn't hate me. He thinks I'm good.

"Fran just couldn't take it," he says.

She doesn't dare to speak yet. She is sure she'll sound nasal and he'll guess she has been crying. There's been silence on the phone for quite a while now.

"I better go," he says.

She jumps in to keep him from leaving. "I was thinking..." she says, and she can hear her voice is deep and thick, as if her throat is filled with glue. She tries to sound as normal as possible as she continues. "I was thinking about Fran. And I would like her to know that I'm sorry for my part in all this. I don't know if she would ever want to talk to me — maybe she wouldn't — but if she does, I'd be happy to talk to her sometime, and tell her this myself."

"That is so lovely," he says warmly, even affectionately.

"I want her to know that," she says. "Will you tell her from me? And also ask her?"

"I will."

A moment later, he adds, "But don't call her unless I ask her first and she says she wants to."

"Obviously," she says.

There's another pause.

Then he says, sounding anxious, almost frightened, "We have to stop now."

The suddenness of this and the tone in his voice give her a start.

"Fran is going to wake up soon," he says. "In fact, she's up already. I can hear her moving around."

There's fear in his voice, and the beginning of panic, as if he is standing on the bottom rung of the panic ladder, about to ascend it. He's afraid of Fran. Like a little boy afraid of his Mommy.

Eve, on the other hand, feels totally calm. "Yes," she says. "Anyway, we're finished."

She hears the heaviness, the finality, of these words as soon as she has uttered them. But then, just before the final closing of the gate, she adds, "One thing, though. I'd like — if we're talking about what we would like — I'd like a two-line email from you, once a year, just to say *shana tova*."

There's a pause — just a beat or two on a metronome. Then he says with a warm little laugh, "And I would like much more than just two lines, Eve. But you know how it is. You understand that this isn't possible."

Smoothly, glibly he has said this. Like he had just been asked, and answered well, an easy question on a test *(What's 2+2? 4)*. What a fool I am, she thinks. Of course there was no chance he'd let me enter his real life. Even for a two-line email once a year. Oh, well. It's almost over now.

Now he is saying slightly pompously, "I no longer conceal anything from my wife. So she's not going to be happy about this, but of course I will have to tell her about this call."

"Of course," she says.

"Bye."

"Bye."

25. FINALE

FTER HANGING UP, EVE SITS for a while staring out the window at the sky. All these years she thought he hated her. She would think of him and feel *I'm nothing, I'm no good. I'm not worth loving,* just like Julia once made her feel. But now it seems that he doesn't hate her at all. In fact, she feels almost like he loves her. Neither of them used the word "love" (they were both very careful about this), but it's obvious that he still cares for her. He said that back then he'd hoped — "and not only out of guilt" — that she would be all right, and he said this twice. And he said that she was one of the most wonderful people he'd ever met. He not only doesn't hate me, she thinks with surprise; he likes me. He is even writing an opera about me. All these years she had been so hurt, believing he wasn't thinking of her at all. When every day he was writing about her in his opera! That's a form of love: to still be thinking about someone more than five years after saying goodbye. If that isn't love, what is?

With satisfaction, she finds another prooftext: the way he talked to her on the phone just now. He spoke to her, once he warmed up, exactly the way he used to: telling her everything — no walls, no barriers, no boundaries between them. He even told her, during this call, some rather personal things about Fran.

Now something flips in Eve, like that mechanical device that alternately lets in liquid from two different pipes — first one, then the other. *By what right did he share with me all those intimate details about Fran?* How could he uncover her nakedness like that? Within minutes of renewing contact with me, he once again betrayed his wife. What a creep. And what a coward, too. "Even if it weren't for Fran, I probably wouldn't have called you. It might have just seemed easier not to." *Easier! Easier?*

No, she thinks disdainfully, he doesn't love me. Maybe he doesn't love anyone, just like a psychopath. I was right in my assessment of him all these years. By the time we split up, I was nothing to him except some erotic symbol. He didn't miss me and didn't care what happened to me (to me, the real person). Even in his opera I'm probably just a symbol of something. Passion, eros, youth, forbidden fruit —- whatever it is, he is still just using me. Taking dabs of "essence of Eve" from that blue perfume bottle whenever he feels old or empty and needs to rejuvenate himself.

Ruefully she shakes her head. She is not real to him. And probably no one is truly real to Jake but himself. Hava was correct: he's a psychopath. It's good Eve presented on him at the seminar this week, and that this morning Eve the Researcher collected all this data. Between these two things, everything is now completely clear. She wanted the hard cold facts and now she's got them. This man doesn't care about her. He wouldn't even help her with *Hallelujah*. Wouldn't help her "one colleague to another" — the sort of favour that he would do for (as Daddy used to say) any *shvartz yur* in the country. Nah, she thinks. He couldn't care less if I'm alive or dead. I'm nothing to him now.

But Eve the Researcher disagrees. You're not nothing. You're something. To him and also to Fran. Whatever that something is.

I'm a weapon, answers Eve. That's all I am to them. A weapon with which to hurt each other. First Jake used me to hurt Fran, and now Fran is using me to hurt him back. I'm used in both directions. I'm part of their triangle: the third edge. A razor-sharp edge they can slash and gouge each other with. Sickies that they are.

Goodbye, you sickies. I'm done with you now. I'm too old for this.

She goes downstairs and eats breakfast. At this hotel it's not the glorious smorgasbord that it was at the King David. The buffet here is much simpler and more modest, but it's tasty just the same. She fills her plate, sits alone at a table, and through the ground-floor window watches the bustling street during morning rush hour: Jerusalemites scurrying to work or to the errands they want to get done before their workday starts. She munches on diced tomatoes and cucumbers laced with mint, sips on lukewarm cocoa, and muses on the phone call that just took place. She knows it will take time, maybe years, to fully digest what just happened. But she wishes that she had had this conversation with Jake a year ago, or two, or three. She could have saved herself years of wasted time.

But I couldn't, she answers herself, biting into a slice of warm rye bread thickly slathered with cool, smooth, white creamy cheese. I wasn't ready back then. I wasn't willing to let him go. But now I am. I'm fine with never seeing him again. He and I have nothing more to say to each other. He's just an old man who doesn't care about me.

Anyway, she thinks, contentedly munching away, he'll probably be dead soon. He already looks really old, now that he's seventy. She knows how he looks because a couple of months ago she was googling an article about a Jewish female composer from Serbia, and as soon as she opened the link to a music journal she had never heard of before, there was Jake staring right at her.

Click here, it said underneath his picture, *to hear an interview with Jacob Gladstone about his new book, "Dear Papa": The Letters of Salamone Rossi to His Father — 1586-1610.*

His face was frozen the way the faces in online videos always are: they're in suspended animation, waiting for you to press the magic button and bring them to life. Or alternately — it's up to you — leave them frozen forever in limbo-purgatory, in a state of latent life.

Eve clicked on Play, but also clicked on Mute, and played the interview in silence. She watched Jake's lips as they moved in his old, lined face. Nothing else in his face moved at all, except two or three times his eyes glanced furtively to one side. Other than this, his face was as rigid as that of a wooden doll, like Pinocchio. She kept looking at Jake's lips — she didn't know then that these were her mother's lips; she only knew that she couldn't take her eyes off them, that they hypnotized her somehow. With only his mouth moving like that, he looked not even like the "talking head" he was, but just a talking mouth. Like a ventriloquist's puppet. The whole thing was so disturbing that she turned off the video blog in less than a minute. But for the rest of the day she felt off-kilter, and there was an odd taste in her mouth, like the taste of ashes.

No, she thinks. I don't need to wish for Jake's death anymore. He's as good as dead already. As for his physical death, she has always imagined him dying at seventy-three (*just three years from now — not very long, thank God*), and she thinks this will probably come to pass, as she has often guessed right about when people will die. Brian always said she was a bit of a witch this way, same as with her uncanny instinct for time and her near-perfect inner clock. *Though I never guessed that Brian would die when he did. Or Mommy, either.*

She puts down her half-finished bread with creamy white cheese and goes back up to her room on the third floor. Gazing out the window, she pictures Jake's body, very still and stiff, being lowered into the ground. Into warm/cold sand. He's dead, she thinks. As dead as sand. And she can feel the warm/cold sand running through her fingers. The warm/cold sands of time.

"Goodbye," she says, startling the bird perched on her windowsill, which flaps its wings and flies away. "Goodbye."

*

Eve is covered in sweat. *I just lay down for a moment; I must have dozed off.* For once she has no idea what time it is. Disoriented, she looks at her watch. She has only slept about twenty minutes, but at the outer edges of her mind she can sense that she dreamt something. She tries to remember: *What did I dream?* but it eludes her. Then she knows.

She kissed death. (Death disguised as a man in a long black robe.) They were kissing mouth-to-mouth. Then pelvis to pelvis.

After that, there was another dream. Or was it a memory? There was a roundabout somewhere. Yes: Fifty-two years ago, when she was four, Daddy took her to the playground, and lifted her carefully onto the roundabout, and told her to hold on tight, and he set it spinning. It went round and round and round, and made her dizzy, and it seemed like it would never stop. She was sure it was going to go on forever. Round and round and round, and round and round and round, and round and round and round...

Now, too, she feels dizzy. Here in this hot hotel room with the sun glaring in through the windows, she can't imagine what life without Jake will be like. How will she live without him? She hears the strange quiet, the silence in this room. It is absolutely silent. She is used to there always being, whenever she is alone, some background noise in her head, some muttering: her own voice, talking either to Jake or about him. Now that's gone. Her world is silent and empty. In this loud silence, she feels a void as enormous as a chasm. She has lost her one constant companion, her primary relationship of the past five and a half years. Now it's just her, alone in the world.

She pulls the pillow over her head and presses it against her face. She can't stand this. She hates it. And what she hates isn't just about Jake; it's about everyone she has ever lost. Her parents and grandparents and aunts and uncles and cousins and friends, and Brian. It's as if up till now all of her losses and griefs have been bundled together, like into one sheaf of wheat, and now these griefs unbundle before her. And standing by himself is Brian.

Brian. For whom she barely allowed herself to grieve when he died. *I won't cry. I'll be strong. I have to be strong for the boys...* Now she sobs and sobs.

When she has finished crying and blowing her nose, she feels much lighter, like a knot inside her has been untied. It seems to her, sitting on the edge of the bed and clutching a tissue, that at the core of every life there is a knot that has to be unravelled before the person can really begin to live. A knot as daunting as the Gordian knot or any of the feats assigned to the people or gods in fairy tales and Greek myths. She feels now a loosening in the knot that's been choking her all these years. Not just recently, but for all her life.

She stands up and goes out onto the balcony. With her hands on her lower back, she arches backwards, stretching, and then straightens up again, looking out over Jerusalem. It's a beautiful, clear, sunny day. Everything is calm, silent, and still. Now she can go anywhere she wants in this country. There's nowhere she has to avoid: not Jake's neighbourhood, or concerts, or conferences, or anything. The world has returned to the way it was before she met him. It's safe again now. It doesn't matter if she bumps into him somewhere. He can't hurt her. She is free of him. She's free.

Triumphantly she surveys the view of Jerusalem. But quickly this feeling fades. She knows from past experience, from her previous attempts at exorcism, that she is not yet free of Jake. This will take a while yet. But in making this phone call, in embracing reality, she has taken a big step forward. She can now picture this freedom. She can taste it. She knows what it will feel like to be free.

Yet mixed in with this freedom is sadness. True, she'll be free of Jake at some point, and safe, but she'll also be alone. She can see ahead of her a procession of days, one following the other, spent alone and in silence. Then these days stretch into months and years. There she'll be, in five, ten, and fifteen years, taking holidays by herself: a single woman travelling alone on ships and in restaurants and hotels.

She hasn't felt single for the past five and a half years. Because she hasn't been. She has had Jake. Maybe, she thinks, it's time to start looking for another man. A real one; not just one in her head. Perhaps Darryl? No, not Darryl. But sometime soon she feels she'll be ready for someone or something.

*

Now something breaks the silence. With perfect clarity, she hears the singing of a bird. The bird that fluttered away is back on her windowsill. She recognizes this type of bird from a nature trip she once took: It's a species of pigeon called a mourning dove. Mourning dove! she thinks, as she listens to its doleful song. Are you a dove in mourning? Is the bird of peace mourning the lack of peace in this country?

The bird keeps singing its song as if answering her questions, and she, almost without thinking, picks up a pen and records the notes: E F# G A G. She hums this a few times. Then she begins to play with it, and soon she feels a tune coming. She jots down the main melody, and then she begins to compose in earnest, humming now and then lightly under her breath. This is true happiness. True freedom. Because time disappears when she composes. She feels, when she is inside her music, like she is somewhere where time never ends. She is in eternal time, Brian used to say. Where time and music go on forever.

She scribbles feverishly. Eventually she starts to wind down. As she is finishing the last page of this music, she senses dozens of mourning doves sitting invisibly on this page she is writing, and when she is done, these doves flap their wings and fly upward and away. Singing their way upward as if their singing is what's making them fly.

Now she looks at what she has composed. This could be part of the *Bird Song* she started this week, she realizes, and she considers various ways to weave this latest composition into what's already there. Suddenly it's obvious. This piece, *The Song of the Mourning Dove*, fits at the end. It's the perfect ending for *Bird Song*. It works beautifully there on every level. This is terrific, she thinks. If only it were this easy to find an ending for the love-and-hate cycle.

She begins straightening up the pages she has just written, and then stops cold. What about making *Bird Song* the final section of the love-and-hate cycle? She could do that. Of course she could! It would work well both musically and thematically. The birds that flew unbidden into her music this morning will bring her love-and-hate cycle full circle. They'll return her love-and-hate cycle (*no, it's just a love cycle now*) back to its beginning. To Jake's first letter to her, the morning after she returned to Canada:

> *By now you're back in Toronto, and I already miss you terribly. I woke up an hour ago, and I've been lying in bed listening to the birds singing outside my window. Their music is probably just as beautiful now as it was yesterday morning when you lay in my arms and we listened to them together. But now they all sound doleful. "Where is Eve?" they're singing now. "Where's my Eve gone?"*

I have my last scene now, she thinks. I've finished this at last. And with glee, and a flourish, she scrawls at the bottom of the last page the Italian word

Fine.

And then in English:

The End.

26. CODA

NOW EVE, BACK IN NORMAL TIME, realizes her taxi will be coming soon. She combines *Bird Song* and her now-completed love cycle into the same blue folder and slides it into a special compartment in her carry-on bag. Then she lines up all her suitcases near the door. When Gidi arrives, honking his special honk, she'll have to run downstairs right away to let him know she'll need help with her bags. They weigh a ton, the elevator is broken as usual, and there's no longer someone at the front desk to help with luggage, or even to answer the phone if she wants to call down and ask them to send up Gidi. For years, whenever she has come to Israel, she has stayed at this family-owned, increasingly run-down hotel. But now she thinks that the next time she's here, she'll try to stay somewhere else.

She does a final check of the room. The lone white sock that she finds under the bed she stuffs into the outer pocket of a bulging suitcase. Meanwhile thinking, In a certain way I'll probably always love him. I'll probably love him till the day I die. But still it's over now. This thing is finally over.

Or anyway insofar as anything is ever really over. She remembers again that roundabout, wooden and unpainted, spinning round and round and round. Round and round and round. And feeling slight vertigo, she thinks, It all goes round and round. In a way nothing ever ends.

Now, jolted out of her reverie, she hears Gidi honking in

the street below her window. Every time he picks her up, he honks with the same crazy honk, but she never fails to be surprised and delighted by it, and hearing it now, she laughs. Gidi is honking as if his car horn were a *shofar*, and for a tune he is tooting out the prescribed blasts of the *shofar* for Rosh Hashana. She hears him honking now:

Taaaaaaaaaaaaaaaaaaaaaa!
Taaaaa! Taaaaa! Taaaaa!
Ta ta ta ta ta ta ta ta ta!
Taaaaaaaaaaaaaaaaaaaaaaaaaaaaaaaaaaaaaaaaaaaaa!

So amazing, she thinks, as she races down the stairs. A car horn is a *shofar*. Everything is music here. Everything is music everywhere. She hurries toward Gidi as fast as she can, and he continues honking for her with the blasts of the *shofar*. As if beckoning her to enter with joy into the new year.

Abba (Hebrew) — Father, Daddy.

Aliyah (or make *aliyah*) (Hebrew) — Move permanently to Israel.

Chanukah — A Jewish holiday commemorating the Jewish struggle against the Greeks and the rededication of the Jerusalem temple to Jewish worship in 165 BCE.

Chanukiah (plural: *chanukiot*) — A nine-branched candelabra used on Chanukah.

Chazan (Hebrew) — Cantor in a synagogue.

Davening (Yiddish) — Praying/Prayers.

Dayenu (Hebrew) — A song sung at the Passover *seder* expressing gratitude for the Israelites' liberation from Egypt.

Echad Mi Yoda'at (Hebrew, in the feminine form) — "Who Knows One?" — This is a song sung at the Passover *seder*. The traditional version is written and sung in the masculine form, "*Echad Mi Yodea.*"

Gai Ben Hinnom (Hebrew) — A valley in Jerusalem. Its name

is the source of the Hebrew word *Gehinnom*, analogous to the concept of Hell.

Hadassah-WIZO — A Zionist women's organization.

Hineni (Hebrew) — "Here I am." A phrase with religious overtones.

Holy of Holies — The inner sanctum of the Temple in ancient days.

Intifada (Arabic) — Palestinian uprising.

Irgun (Hebrew) — A Zionist paramilitary organization that operated prior to the establishment of the State of Israel.

Kaddish (Hebrew) — The prayer recited by Jewish mourners.

Kibbutz (plural: *kibbutzim*) (Hebrew) — A cooperative agricultural community in Israel run primarily on socialist principles.

Kipot (Hebrew) — Skullcaps worn by Jews.

Kol Nidre (Aramaic) — An important prayer recited on the eve of Yom Kippur.

Kotel (Hebrew) — The Wailing Wall, a remnant of the western wall of the Temple in Jerusalem.

L'at l'at (Hebrew) — Slowly, slowly.

Magen David (Hebrew) — Shield of David, or Star of David. A six-pointed star made up of two triangles superimposed over each other. A symbol of Judaism.

Mandelbroit (Yiddish) — A traditional Jewish biscotti made with almonds.

Mazal tov / Mazel tov (Hebrew/Yiddish) — Congratulations.

Mayim Hayim (Hebrew) — Living Water.

Menorah (plural: *menorot*) (Hebrew) — A seven-branched candelabra used in the ancient Temple in Jerusalem.

Mezuzah (plural: *mezuzot*) (Hebrew) — A Jewish ritual object affixed to the doorposts of Jewish homes.

Miskayt (Yiddish) — An ugly person.

Naches (Yiddish) — Joy or satisfaction from the accomplishments of one's children.

Niggun (Hebrew) – A tune or melody; a form of Jewish religious song sung in a group.

Passover – see *Pesach*.

Pesach (Hebrew) — The Jewish holiday commemorating the Jewish people's deliverance from slavery in Egypt.

Rogelech (Yiddish) — Traditional Jewish crescent-shaped pastries.

Rosh Hashana (Hebrew) — The Jewish New Year.

Seder — The traditional opening of the celebration of Pesach; a festive meal with special symbolic foods.

Seder plate — A plate at the centre of every Passover *seder* table, designed to contain six symbolic foods related to this holiday.

Shabbat (Hebrew) — The Jewish Sabbath, beginning around sundown on Friday night and ending approximately one hour after sundown on Saturday night.

Shabbat Shira (Hebrew) — A special Shabbat once a year that celebrates song and music.

Shabbaton (Hebrew) — A weekend retreat focusing on study and the celebration of Shabbat.

Shana tova (Hebrew) — Have a good year. The traditional greeting for Rosh Hashanah.

Shekel (Hebrew) — A unit of Israeli currency. One shekel currently equals about twenty-five cents American.

Shir Hama'alot (Hebrew) — Song of the Steps. A traditional prayer recited by the priests on the steps of the Temple in Jerusalem.

Shofar (Hebrew) — A ram's horn blown ceremonially, primarily during Rosh Hashana and Yom Kippur.

Shul (Yiddish) — Synagogue.

Shulchan Aruch (Hebrew) — A set table. Also the title of a book by this name, a compilation of Jewish law.

Shvartz yor (Yiddish) — Literally a plague; colloquially used as an insult.

Shwaya shwaya (Arabic) — Slowly, slowly.

Tallitot (Hebrew) — Prayer shawls.

T'filat Tal (Hebrew) — The traditional prayer for dew.

Treyf (Yiddish) — Non-kosher food; food in violation of Jewish dietary laws.

Yad Vashem (Hebrew) — An institute in Jerusalem commemorating and teaching about the Holocaust.

Yartzeit (Yiddish) — The annual anniversary of a death.

Yom Kippur (Hebrew) — The Day of Atonement. A fast day devoted to individual and communal repentance, considered the holiest day of the Jewish year.

ACKNOWLEDGEMENTS

It is a pleasure to acknowledge and thank those people who have played a significant role in helping to make this book a reality.

My first thanks go to Inanna Publications, and in particular Luciana Ricciutelli, its Editor-in-Chief, for her enthusiasm about this novel, and also for the warm sense of feminist community that has characterized all our interactions. Working together on this book has been a delight.

I thank Diane Schoemperlen, as well, for helpful comments she made on an early draft of this book.

Writing a novel can be a long and isolating process. My friends contributed to this book – even if they weren't aware of it – by grounding me in the pleasures of meaningful relationships and the activities and rhythms of everyday life. For this I am grateful.

A special thank you to my remarkable, talented son, Joseph Weissgold, who brightens my days with his boundless optimism, energy, affection, and creativity, and – by connecting me to the perspectives and ideas of his generation – always keeps me learning something new.

Last but not least, I thank my extraordinary husband, Dr. David

Weiss, for supporting me in every possible way throughout the writing of this novel. His constancy, thoughtfulness, playfulness, and intelligence enrich and sustain me, and he fills my life with joy, meaning, and love.

Photo: Chris Frampton

Nora Gold is a prize-winning author and the editor of the prestigious online literary journal, *Jewish Fiction .net.* Her novel *Fields of Exile* won the 2015 Canadian Jewish Literary Award and received widespread acclaim, including from Cynthia Ozick. Gold's first book, *Marrow and Other Stories*, won a Canadian Jewish Book Award (1999), and the title story was praised by Alice Munro. Dr. Gold lives in Toronto, where she is the Writer-in-Residence and an Associate Scholar at the Centre for Women's Studies in Education, at the Ontario Institute for Studies in Education (OISE), University of Toronto.